SEEDS OF SUMMER

DEBORAH VOGTS

SEASONS *of the* TALLGRASS

SEEDS OF SUMMER

BOOK TWO

■ ZONDERVAN®

ZONDERVAN.com/
AUTHORTRACKER
follow your favorite authors

ZONDERVAN

Seeds of Summer
Copyright © 2010 by Deborah Vogts

This title is also available as a Zondervan ebook.
Visit www.zondervan.com/ebooks.

This title is also available in a Zondervan audio edition.
Visit www.zondervan.fm.

Requests for information should be addressed to:
Zondervan, *Grand Rapids, Michigan* 49530

Library of Congress Cataloging-in-Publication Data

Vogts, Deborah, 1965–
    Seeds of summer / Deborah Vogts.
        p.   cm. (Seasons of the tallgrass; bk. 2)
    Includes bibliographical references and index [if applicable].
    ISBN 978-0-310-29276-0 (pbk.)
    1. Rural families—Kansas—Fiction. I. Title.
PS3622.O363S44 2010
813'.6—dc22   2010006418

Published in association with the literary agency of WordServe Literary Group, Ltd., 10152 S. Knoll Circle, Highlands Ranch, CO 80130.

Cover design: Studio Gearbox
Cover photography: Corbis; Veer; Photos.com
Interior design: Christine Orejuela-Winkelman

Printed in the United States of America

10 11 12 13 14 15 /DCI/ 22 21 20 19 18 17 16 15 14 13 12 11 10 9 8 7 6 5 4 3 2 1

To Samantha, Maggie, and Abigail
You are my dearest treasures.

TIME SWEEPS AHEAD, NEVER BACK. IT LEAVES OLD SORROWS TO SOAK
INTO THE EARTH AND CLEARS A SPACE TO START BUILDING FOR
THE NEW YEAR ... WHETHER YOU ARE RUNNING UP A GOLDEN HILL
STRAIGHT INTO THE BLUE SKY, OR ARE ON THE STEEP DOWN GRADE WITH
THE MISTS IN SIGHT, THERE IS NO PLACE TO GO BUT AHEAD.

Quoted in *Skimming the Cream,*
Fifty Years with 'Peggy of the Flint Hills'
by Zula Bennington Green, 1983.

PROLOGUE

FEAR AND ANTICIPATION GRIPPED NATALIE ADAMS' STOMACH AS SHE waited on that Las Vegas contestant stage. But she continued to smile. *Always smile for the judges.* Her cheeks threatened to crack at any second from the building tension.

Mama's pet name for her had been Princess, but Natalie planned to take that title one step further and be queen. She'd spent most of her life preparing for this moment, the moment she could be crowned Miss Rodeo America, and she was ready. Her hard work had paid off in the horsemanship division of the competition, and despite her dad's complaints, and her penchant for a good pair of boots, her fashion budget hadn't put them in the poor house.

The competition narrowed down to two contestants — Miss Rodeo California and herself representing Kansas. Natalie could hardly breathe. Her mind spun with the possibilities of what this might mean. A year of touring, more scholarships, meeting and helping people. She'd be a national representative for the Pro Rodeo Cowboys Association for an entire year — a sport she felt most passionate about.

Oh, how she wished her mother were here to share this moment with her. She might finally break free.

With a nervous laugh, she squeezed the hand of the other contestant, willing the emcee to announce her name. The heat from the large spotlights radiated against her skin, and Natalie feared she might melt away in her red leather gown.

"And the new Miss Rodeo America is ..."

It happened so fast.

The roar from the crowd couldn't compare to the cameras flashing all around her as last year's queen crowned the woman standing beside her.

I will not cry, I will not cry, I will NOT cry. Natalie continued to smile as she hugged the new Miss Rodeo America, her own heart breaking.

She stepped back to stand with the other three ladies, while the winner walked the stage and waved at the hundreds of onlookers in the hotel showroom. When the celebration ended, the contestants and Natalie were escorted off the stage and back to the dressing room. The Miss Rodeo America song continued to boom in her ears like a bad television commercial.

Her dad grabbed her hand and enclosed her in a suffocating hug. He led her to a quiet spot and smiled down at her. "You did good out there. If your mother were alive, she'd be real proud of you."

Natalie's breath caught in her chest as a tear streaked down her father's weathered cheek. Then his expression sobered and returned to what she'd known her entire life.

"You had your chance and you did your best," he said. "Now it's time to get back to the real world ..."

ONE

FIVE MONTHS LATER

Metal scraped against metal, waking Natalie from a restless sleep. Again, the screech came from outside. With a reluctant groan, she forced herself from her cotton sheets and fumbled in the dark to find her boots.

What was out there? And why wasn't Jessie barking?

She slipped her bare feet into leather ropers, then hurried from the bedroom down the stairs, hoping she wouldn't rouse her younger siblings. An instant foreboding caused her to grab the shotgun her dad always kept behind the back door. Natalie loaded it with a couple of shells before heading to the porch—just in case. As her eyes adjusted to the outside darkness, she distinguished the faint outline of a truck backed up to the barn entrance. She crept through the barnyard.

"Who's there?" Her voice wavered as she clutched the wooden forearm of the aged Winchester, prepared to fire a warning shot at the moon if necessary.

A small beam of light darted inside the old limestone barn, then disappeared.

"Tom, is that you?" Natalie eased her finger closer to the trigger.

Silence. Then the hollow clamor of feed buckets knocked to the ground as though someone had tripped over them.

Natalie held her breath. Her heart thumped wildly against her chest as she thought about the recent thefts in the county. If only her dad were here.

But he's not, and you're in charge. Slow, mechanical breaths helped her to see this might be nothing more than their hired hand returning from a night at the bar. She knew little about Tom Walker, but the idea that he'd been out with friends on a Friday night was more probable than not.

A tall figure edged from the shadows. Natalie recognized the pale shock of curls highlighted by the luminous night.

"Hey there, don't shoot." The ranch employee rested his hands on his head. "I was only putting some stuff away in the barn."

"Working kind of late, aren't you?"

"Just got back from a rodeo." Tom's voice grew louder as he approached. "Sorry if I frightened you."

Natalie lowered the shotgun, then gazed up at the sky, relief lodged in her throat. "You could've turned on the barn lights. At least then I wouldn't have thought someone was sneaking around out here."

"Didn't want to wake the house."

In the faint moonlight, she caught the glint of an uneasy smile on the man's face. "How'd you do?"

"Tough night for steer wrestling."

Natalie knew all about rodeo and tough nights. "There'll be others."

He dropped his arms, and she noticed Jessie at his side. No wonder the faithful border collie hadn't barked. Suddenly aware of how she must look, she combed her fingers through her wayward locks. Dressed in baggy shorts, a torn T-shirt, and a pair of pink boots, she held little resemblance to her former title as Miss Rodeo Kansas, or of a rancher either.

And that's what she was now — a twenty-two-year-old ranch owner in the Flint Hills of Charris County, Kansas. She shook her head, confounded by the turn of events her life had taken in the past week. "Well, I'm sorry for interrupting your work. I'll let you get back to your business." Hoping he wouldn't sense her despair, she turned toward the house. As she did, an engine revved in the near distance. Tracing the noise, she saw a truck tear from behind the barn, its headlights aimed for the lane.

Staggering backward, she almost dropped her father's shotgun but somehow managed to bring the wooden stock to her shoulder. "Hey, you there," she called out. "Stop or I'll shoot."

The truck vaulted onto the dirt road and spun gravel as it sped away. Speechless, Natalie lowered the gun and whirled toward the hired hand, expecting him to go after the culprits sneaking around her father's barn.

Then she acknowledged the panic in the man's eyes.

"What were you and your buddies doing in there?" Her brows crinkled, and she instantly thought the worst. Dark barn, suspicious behavior. Had they been doing drugs, or were they stealing?

"It's not what you think." The hostility in the air pricked her skin as the man stepped closer. He stood a half-foot taller than her own five-foot-eight.

Natalie gripped the shotgun, her palms damp with sweat. Did she have the guts to shoot a man? She aimed the barrel at his chest. "Is this how you're going to honor my father? By stealing from him? He's not been dead a week."

"The boys and I — we were just having some fun — talking was all." His gentle voice caressed her.

Natalie recognized the seduction of his lie — the flicker of deceit in his eyes. "In the dark?"

"No law against talking in the dark." He reached in her direction, much too close for her comfort.

She shoved his lanky body back with the metal barrel and thought of all the work they needed to accomplish the next day unloading and sorting cattle. Could she and the kids get along without his help if she fired him? Could she trust him to tell the truth?

His lips pulled into a pout. "Come on, Miss Adams. I've been with your dad for nearly six months. He trusted me. We weren't doing nothing wrong ... honest."

Natalie searched the man's eyes for a hint of sincerity. "Swear on your mama's grave?" Even as the words came from her mouth, she knew she was a fool to trust him.

"Better—I'll swear on your daddy's."

Natalie's throat swelled as hot tears threatened to fall. Her good judgment now clouded with grief, she eased the barrel toward the ground and shook her head in embarrassment. "I guess the stress is getting to me. Sorry for being so jumpy."

Tom nodded in understanding. "No need to apologize. A person can't be too careful these days—especially a young woman like yourself. It's good I'm around for protection."

Natalie disregarded his remark, finding no comfort in it. Her gut twisted at the vulnerable position her father's death had placed her in as Tom drifted back to the darkness of the barn. With a weary sigh, she studied the moon above. Like a shooting star, her life had changed in an instant and no matter how much she wished it, not even the crickets or the moaning bullfrogs could set it right again.

Returning to the house, she peeked in on her twelve-year-old brother, asleep in his upstairs bedroom. His tranquil face reflected no worries, no hint of strain from their recent ordeal.

Oh, that her rest could be as peaceful.

When Natalie opened the door to her sister's bedroom, she failed to make out a form under the covers. A flick of the light revealed Chelsey's bed hadn't been slept in. She glanced about the room, and then noticed the splay of curtains caught in a warm breeze from the open dormer window.

Natalie darted back to Dillon's room.

"Where's Chelsey?" She jiggled her brother's leg and watched the young boy rouse from a deep sleep.

Dillon rubbed his eyes and sat up in bed. "What?"

"Chelsey's not in her room. Do you have any idea where she might be? Out with friends? A party somewhere?"

Her brother shook his head, then yawned. "I heard her talking on the phone to Lucas earlier. Maybe she's with him."

Natalie's mouth grew taut. Nothing good ever happened past midnight, and it was now close to two. She hoped the reckless teenagers weren't in a ditch somewhere.

A loud thump from Chelsey's room caused those thoughts to evaporate.

Natalie rounded the hallway to find her fifteen-year-old sister crumpled on the bedroom floor.

Chelsey raised her head, her eyes glazed. "Hey, sis." Her words came out slurred as she tried to stand. "Did ya miss me?"

TWO

Natalie held the dangling blonde hair from her sister's face as the girl heaved again into the toilet bowl, emptying her stomach of the alcohol in her body.

Afterwards, Chelsey clung to Natalie's side. "I don't know what I'd do without you, sis. I'm so glad you're home instead of at that stupid college."

Natalie tucked the bitter reminder to the back of her mind and fought the urge to put the girl in her place after sneaking out of the house. Instead, she helped the teenager to her room and into bed. There would be time for reprimand tomorrow.

As Chelsey slumped backward on her bed, Natalie noticed a red splotch on her sister's lower abdomen. "What is that?" Natalie stared at the design, stunned.

The heart tattoo seemed to shout back in defiance.

I-heart-Lucas.

"How could you, Chelsey?" Exasperation washed over Natalie as she considered how this might brand her sister's life forever.

"Don't worry, it's not real." The girl closed her eyes, her face peaked. "But someday it will be. I love him, and I want the world to know," she murmured.

The words rang in Natalie's ears. Love him? Chelsey hardly knew him. Her sister had been seeing the senior boy for how long ... three weeks? The child had no idea.

"YOU GONNA GROUND HER?"

Natalie sliced into an onion the next morning, and her eyes began to sting. She squeezed them tight as the first tears fell. "I know what needs done." She dumped the diced vegetables for the stew into the slow cooker and turned to Dillon, who sat slumped over his bowl of cereal. Truth was, she didn't have a clue what to do. This had been a tough week for all of them, and she wondered whether grounding Chelsey was the right choice.

Her brother stirred the cereal, not eating. "It's what Dad would have done."

"Yes, but Dad's not here." Natalie clenched her teeth as new tears formed—this time from the ache of their loss. Why did their father have to die, and die so cruelly? An image of him caught beneath the overturned tractor flashed before her, and she was again thankful she'd not been the one to find him in the ditch, though the details of his death haunted her.

How would she ever take his place as parent for this family? Granted, she'd practically raised her half brother and sister from the time she was eleven—but still ... how was she supposed to manage this ranch, raise two siblings, and finish college? The daunting tasks loomed ahead of her, out of reach.

"If you don't teach Chelsey a lesson, she'll do it again—only next time, it'll be worse. Even I know that."

Natalie smiled at the boy's wisdom. Not even a teenager, Dillon already showed a great deal of insight. More than most college students.

College ...

Her lips quivered as again her eyes brimmed with moisture.

Because of her father's death, she'd been forced to decline her marketing internship with the National Little Britches Rodeo Association in Colorado Springs. How would she ever manage to finish her last semester in the fall? And even if she did, what could her future possibly hold for her now?

She turned on the faucet and watched her dreams wash down the disposal with the vegetable peels. A few tears fell into the mix, and she quickly wiped the rest away. Shamed by the emotional display, she hoped her brother hadn't noticed. The last thing she wanted was to weigh Dillon with her problems. As the oldest in the family, this was her responsibility ... and she would be responsible.

"What time are we supposed to meet the cattle trucks?" His words were muffled as though he'd forced his breakfast down his throat.

Natalie stared out the window into the morning darkness and fought to steady her voice. Life continued, whether she wanted it to or not. "According to Dad's calendar, they should start arriving around eight. Best wake Chelsey so we can do the chores."

"No way." He came from behind and hung on Natalie's shoulders. "After last night, I'm not going in there."

Natalie whisked the dampness from her cheeks and braced herself for the next course of action. "Smart kid," she teased the boy who had not yet reached his growth spurt and still seemed considerably small for his age.

"I'm not that smart. But I'm not stupid either."

NATALIE KNOCKED ON CHELSEY'S DOOR BEFORE ENTERING THE BEDROOM. She stared at the girl stretched out on the fluffy mattress.

"Time to wake up, sleeping beauty." She noticed the slobber mark on the pillow. Not exactly a princess-like quality.

When the girl didn't stir, Natalie nudged her shoulder. "Hey, rise and shine."

Chelsey rolled over and groaned.

Tired of the gentle approach, Natalie poked her sister, none too tender. "If you're old enough to get drunk, you're old enough to take responsibility for your actions. We have cattle to unload this morning. Get up or you're grounded."

Chelsey woke with a start, her eyes puffy and red. "You don't have to be so mean." She pressed her hand to her forehead and struggled out of the bed sheets. "Besides, you can't ground me. You're not my boss."

Natalie refused to respond in anger for fear her sister might retaliate more. "I'm the oldest, and like it or not, I'm in charge." She sat on the side of the bed, hoping to mollify her sister's grumbling.

"Listen, we have to work together now. The ranch won't run itself. There are chores to do, animals and pastures to tend. We can't stop the clock just because we're mourning. And just because you're hung over, doesn't mean I'm going to cut you any slack." Natalie reached for her sister's shoulder only to have her hand shrugged away.

"Who says I want any?" Chelsey flung the covers back and stumbled to the floor to retrieve a pair of jeans.

"About last night," Natalie began. "There'll be no more sneaking out of the house after dark ... or any other time, for that matter. As for Lucas, I think it'd be best if you don't see him again."

"You're kidding." Chelsey tossed the wrinkled jeans to the floor in search of another pair. "You can't tell me who to date. He graduates today. I'm going to be with him."

"Lucas is too old for you. Too experienced. He'll only get you into trouble." Natalie thought of the fake tattoo and considered this talk might be too late. "Have you and Lucas ...?" She ducked her head, unable to finish. Oh, how she wished her father were here.

"Not yet."

Natalie looked up to see Chelsey's lips curl into a lovesick expression.

17

"Not that we don't want to — it just never seems to work out."

"It's not going to work out either." Natalie grabbed a clean pair of jeans from a nearby chair and tossed them at her sister, hitting her square in the chest. "Because you're not going out with him again."

"That's what you think."

"That's what I know. Now get dressed. We've got work to do." Natalie headed out of the room, ignoring Chelsey's protests. As soon as the door closed behind her, Natalie heard her sister's defiant scream. Then something hard crashed against the wall.

JARED LOGAN STARED AT THE BLANK PAPER UNTIL HIS EYES BLURRED. He'd never felt such pressure to come up with a sermon, yet here he was, with little more than twenty-four hours before he'd preach to his first congregation. It didn't help that this flock had been shepherded by a beloved reverend for the last eighteen years. Talk about big shoes to fill.

He glanced out the office window and caught the movement of a white-tailed rabbit behind the bushes.

Enough procrastinating.

He tore his gaze from the bright scenery, determined to move the desk away from the window when time allowed. Springtime in the Flint Hills held too many distractions — even for the most diligent student. No, not a student — a minister, serving his first parish. A minister who could be without a job if he didn't come up with a decent sermon for the devoted members of New Redeemer Church.

A soft rap pushed his office door ajar. "I'm not interrupting, am I?"

He recognized the woman's voice and leaned away from the large mahogany desk. "Not at all. Come in, Mrs. Hildebrand."

The church secretary set a plate of cinnamon rolls on his desk and smiled. "I figured you'd be working today. My daughter baked these fresh this morning." Her hands clasped in front of her wide midsection.

Jared lifted the plastic wrap and the sweet cinnamon triggered a response in his mouth he couldn't ignore. Having grown up in a small town, he relished the idea of serving the rural community of Diamond Falls where simple hospitality and charm abounded. "Thank you for thinking of me. You and your husband have been most kind, helping me move into my home and then assisting with my ordination last Sunday."

"Don't be ridiculous. We were glad to do it." She gathered a plate and napkin from a nearby supply shelf and commenced to serve him a gooey roll, thick with icing.

"There certainly was a lot of activity that day, with all your family and visitors." Her eyes remained fixed on him, watchful. "In all the commotion, I don't suppose you had a chance to meet my daughter Clarice?"

Jared noted the gleam in Mrs. Hildebrand's eyes as she mentioned her daughter's name. He remembered meeting Clarice, if only for the briefest moment. "Didn't you say she was a teacher at the elementary school?"

"She loves working with children. Hopes to have three or four once she settles down with the right fellow." The sturdy woman pushed the foam plate closer, a cheeky grin on her face.

Jared's mind sped through a list of responses that would express his regard without suggesting a romantic interest, though his mother would be delighted if it were. Nothing would please her more than for him to find a wife and have children. "I'm sure your daughter will find a suitable companion—all in God's time, I always say."

"My thoughts exactly." Mrs. Hildebrand settled into a chair by his desk, intent on conversation. "I find it extraordinary that a bright young man like yourself has agreed to serve our congregation. Who would have thought we'd snag a talented student right from seminary when we have so little to offer—and such a handsome one too."

Warmth invaded Jared's cheeks at her remark, and he shook his head in protest. Rather than comment, he busied himself in search of a fork.

The woman handed him one as though from thin air. "Since you're unmarried, I'm guessing your time here is a stepping-stone to bigger things?"

"I really couldn't say." Jared removed his wire-rimmed glasses and set them on the desk, no longer interested in the sweet roll. He'd heard tales from school about female congregants pursuing young ministers, but he'd always laughed them off. Now he sensed the gravity of such a situation through the claws of an assertive mother. "For now, I'm glad to be here and a part of your community."

"My Clarice always tells me it's better to be content with one's life than to be constantly searching for what we can't have. I believe the two of you would get along quite nicely. You never know what God might desire."

Jared cleared his throat, becoming increasingly uncomfortable with the woman's push and shove tactics. Right now, the only thing he was sure of was that God desired him to complete his sermon. He glanced at Mrs. Hildebrand whose eyes traipsed from him to the cinnamon roll. Sometimes the quickest way to a destination meant traveling a less desirable path. With a sheepish grin, he tore off a piece of the roll with his fork and lifted it to his mouth.

THREE

NATALIE LEANED OVER HER SADDLE HORN AND SWATTED A MOSQUITO. Could the day get any worse? Lined on the early morning horizon were five pot trucks waiting to unload the summer cattle, and to her left were her only cowhands, Dillon and Chelsey. Much to her displeasure, Tom took off on a ranch errand earlier that morning and had yet to return. His irresponsibility irked her to no end.

Against the silhouette of a hazy sky, the first truck backed up to the metal chute with squeaky precision. The double-decked trailer bulged from the hooves clamoring inside.

"Dillon, you watch the west gate. Hold any steers sent your way."

At his nod, Natalie turned to her sister who gave no indication of caring the least about their predicament. "Chelsey, I'll count. You sort them as they come through. I'll call out if any need doctoring and you can send them to Dillon."

With no time to consider whether her sister would carry through with her duties, Natalie dismounted her gray gelding to meet the driver. The smell of musty hide and manure seeped from the vented sides of the trailer, accompanied by the shuffle of hooves and the distressed bawl of a black-muzzled calf.

"Looks like you're short on workers this morning." The man

walked with a hitch in his stride, probably due to the many miles between here and Texas.

Natalie stared down at the rich, green bluestem. Today they would unload over five hundred cattle, the second of three shipments her dad had scheduled on the calendar this month. Just like every other year, they would double stock the pastures, then in August, fifteen hundred steers would leave, each about two hundred pounds fatter. "We'll cover our part of the grazing contract, don't worry about that."

"Makes no mind to me. I'm not the one holding the money." He turned toward the pipe cattle pens where Dillon and Chelsey waited on their horses. "You sure you've got enough experience there to handle unloading?"

The doubt in his voice made Natalie's spine bristle. Her brother and sister might be young, but they'd helped their dad every summer. The only difference was this year she was in charge of the transient grazing instead of him. "We'll manage fine. Whenever you're ready."

He tipped his straw cowboy hat and cocked a smile. "Little lady, I was born ready."

Minutes later, the end gate clanked open and the first white-faced steer bounded out, followed by three more black baldies. For every ten head, Natalie made a notch in a small notebook she carried with her, calling out when she spotted a calf that might need doctoring. As the cool morning air gave way to the heated sun, Natalie shucked her denim jacket and rolled up her long sleeves.

"Let's take a quick break," she called to her brother and sister as the third truck ambled from the chute across the flint-covered pasture.

"Figures you'd take a break as soon as I get here."

At the sound of the gravelly voice, Natalie tore her gaze from her calculations. "I think after three hundred steers, the kids deserve a break, don't you?"

"I reckon they do indeed." Willard Grover cuffed Natalie on the shoulder, then offered her a hug. "You holding up okay?"

"As good as can be expected." Natalie reached out to the man who was more like a grandfather to her than a neighbor, surprised he'd come all the way out here to check on her. "How about you?"

"You think this ol' black man's gonna wither away now that I ain't got your dad to pester no more?"

Unable to answer, Natalie stared at a nearby clump of butterfly milkweed, one of the many wildflowers adorning the pastures this spring. Willard had been the one to find her dad trapped under the overturned tractor, her father's breath all but taken from him. In Vietnam, Willard saved her grandfather's life, but he hadn't been able to rescue her father. Circumstances like that had to mess with a man's perspective.

"'My heart aches, and a drowsy numbness pains my sense, as though of hemlock I had drunk.'"

Natalie studied the old man dressed in jeans, a long sleeved shirt, and a corduroy vest. Willard's fondness for poetry never failed to amuse her. "Emerson or Longfellow?"

"'—Past the near meadows, over the still stream, up the hillside; and now 'tis buried deep in the next valley-glades: was it a vision, or a waking dream?'—Keats, my girl. Didn't I teach you anything all those years ago? Back when you were scrawny as a whip and feisty as one too."

Natalie lifted the plastic water thermos from the ground. "Back when all I could think about was how to get away from this place. Now look at me." She took a drink and welcomed the cool liquid as it relieved her parched throat.

"Nobody's forcing you to stay."

"Nobody needs to." From the corner of her eye, she noted Chelsey and Dillon's slow progress toward her. "If you two want a drink, you better hurry up. We've got two more pots waiting to unload."

"Where's Tom?" Willard's eyes searched the area. "I figured he'd be helping you today."

Natalie frowned. "He was supposed to. But I don't see him, do you?"

Willard paced the grass, his shuffling boots wearing a path in the fresh new growth. "Like I told you at the funeral, I'll help in any way I can. Money, advice, whatever you need. Might start with a good scolding to that hand of yours."

Though tempted to accept, Natalie didn't feel comfortable dumping her problems on anyone, even if he was a friend of the family. "Don't worry about us. We'll be fine."

"I promised your dad." He stopped pacing, his words terse.

Natalie's stomach turned squeamish as she handed Chelsey the water thermos. "What do you mean?"

Willard's face contorted, his words just above a whisper. "The day he died. He asked me to look out for you. Right before his heart quit him."

He swiped his dark, pooling eyes. "I gave him my word."

A brusque wind swept Natalie's ponytail into her face and threatened to steal her breath away, or maybe it was Willard's words. She didn't need the burden of a tired, old man. "The best way you can help is if you go on home. I don't mean to be disrespectful, but I have too much to do without worrying about you falling or getting run over by a young steer."

The gray-haired man waited a few seconds then poked a crooked finger at her. "I promised I'd watch out for you and the kids ... so don't tell me what to do, little missy. I served three tours as a platoon sergeant in Nam and saw men younger than you get blown to pieces by mortar and artillery fire. Most went home with missing limbs — or in a wooden box." His voice cracked with emotion. "After your grandpa sold me my land, I watched you grow up — changed your nasty little diapers, and put you to bed more times than I can count, so don't give me none of your worries — not about me. I may be old, but I can still hold my own, and I'll help who I want."

Once he'd finished, a slow smile crept onto his face.

Natalie knew when she'd been beat and secretly welcomed the support. "If you really want to help, there's a cattle prod in Dad's truck."

With a huff, he headed in that direction.

FOUR

Jared strolled down the dirt road, his fiberglass rod propped on his shoulder and a coffee can of earthworms in his hand. The late-afternoon sun ate up the blue sky while meadowlarks nested in the lush green pastures, their plaintive *see-you see-yeeer* carrying in the wind. He admired the rolling hills of Charris County, eager to try out his new stainless reel in the murky waters of the Cottonwood River and reclaim a piece of his childhood he'd been too long without. Sunday afternoon fishing—a pastime he'd enjoyed with his granddad on many occasions.

Though the man died years ago, Jared had every intention of drawing near to his memory despite the troubles they'd faced before his death. It somehow seemed fitting to do this on his granddad's birthday. Maybe he'd even cook the fish for supper—pan-fried with a cornmeal batter.

Able to imagine the salty taste on his tongue, he grinned, content with the day and pleased with his morning's sermon—a drastic change from the angst that tore at him the night before. All week he'd struggled to find the right words to say to his new congregation. Then late last night, beat down and ready to admit defeat, he finally gave his fears over to God. Once he did that, the words began to flow onto the paper.

His granddad always told him the easiest lessons were often the hardest learned. He carried that message with him as he cut through the pasture and headed for the river.

The directions Jared had been given brought him to a slope on the inside of a wide bend in the river. From here, he noted the shallow riffle over a limestone shelf where the water cut deep into the riverbed to form large swirling pools. Time and current had eaten pockets in the muddy bank beyond. That's where the flathead were, and in those pools they fed. With images of a twenty or thirty-pounder, Jared broke through the new undergrowth and scooted down the embankment, his boot heels digging into the damp earth.

When he reached the gravel bar, he prepared his line, wadding sod worms on his hook. It took a moment to remember what he once knew well ... lessons on the Republican River back home with his granddad.

Now mid-May, tufts of cottonwood seed floated from the trees and into the river. The height of spawning season, the channel was sure to be crawling with catfish. In anticipation, Jared rubbed his casting thumb, tender and no longer calloused from summers of riding and breaking the spool. His years in seminary had softened him.

Thanks to an abundance of spring rain, the water ran swift over the rocks and gushed down into the pools. Jared targeted the area of his choice — a sixty-yard throw. With timed calculation and both hands gripped around his rod, he cast his line.

Careful, ride the spool — don't bird-nest.

As he reeled the line in, he glimpsed a movement from the other side of the river. A young boy in jeans and a red ball cap headed due south in a jaunty manner.

Jared gave a nod and noted the boy's fishing pole, most attentive to the string of fish dangling at his side.

He cast again as the boy hiked past through the thick brush. An hour later, he caught sight of the sandy-haired youth, this time on Jared's side of the river, his pant legs soaked to the knees.

"Getting any bites?" the youngster asked.

Jared preferred not to acknowledge the bites he'd missed. He eyed the two big carp and three flathead on the boy's string. "Nothing to speak of."

"You new here? I don't recall seeing you around." The boy appeared too young to be crossing rivers on his own or asking so many questions.

"Yeah, I am. I'm not intruding on your fishing hole, am I? Some men at my church told me this was a good spot, so I thought I'd try it out."

"I'm done and heading back." The boy pressed the bill of his cap down and peered in the direction of what must be home.

Jared dug another worm from his can to thread onto his empty hook. "What's your name? Where's home?"

The boy squinted at him, and Jared noticed the many freckles dotting his cheeks and nose. "Name's Dillon. I live a couple miles from here."

"Do your folks know where you are?"

Dillon looked away. "It don't matter as long as I'm home before dark."

The boy's confidence reminded Jared of himself when he was young. Jared hoped that self-assurance wouldn't get the boy in trouble as it had for him. He noted the long shadows from the tree line and suspected the sun was glowing reddish pink against the rolling prairie above. "Best be moving on then, so you don't worry your mom and dad."

The slamming of a truck door carried in the wind, and Jared's eyes roamed the top of the riverbank. After a few minutes, he caught sight of a sleek-haired beauty, her long, black hair fluttering in the air, and her hands on her hips. She called Dillon's name.

"Is that your mom?"

Dillon grimaced.

Her posture noticeably relaxed when she spotted them, then almost as quickly bristled with irritation. The slender woman charged down the rocky slope, her arms pumping.

"I've been looking everywhere for you, Dillon. Do you know how worried I've been?" She glanced at Jared, and her light blue eyes offered a strained apology. "Who's your friend?"

The boy shrugged.

Jared swiped his palms on his jeans. "I recently moved here from St. Louis. My name's Jared Logan." He extended his hand, and too late, noticed his fingers marred with mud.

She ignored his greeting. Dressed in slim-fitting jeans and a button-up shirt tied snug at the waist, she came across as one who wouldn't care to get her hands dirty.

"I was visiting with your son." Jared lowered his hand with as much nonchalance as he could muster. "From the looks of his stringer, he appears to have good fishing sense."

Her eyes narrowed. "My brother might know about fishing, but I question his good sense."

She turned to Dillon and thumped him on the head. "The next time you get an urge to leave home, you better tell someone where you're going. Chelsey's got supper on the stove, and your chores need done."

Dillon frowned down at his catch, then offered the stringer to Jared. "Guess I won't have time to clean these. You want them?"

Jared glanced between the boy and his sister and wondered at the considerable age difference. "Are you sure?"

"Help yourself. We have plenty in the freezer," the young woman answered for her brother. As though she had no time for indecision, she grabbed the fish from Dillon's hand and shoved them at Jared, the stench of the muddy river clinging to their scales. "Enjoy your supper."

She turned and prodded the boy up the riverbank. Jared stumbled after them. "Wait, I didn't catch your name."

Her blue eyes flickered back at him. "I'm sure we'll see each other again." She smiled, and her white teeth gleamed against her perfect olive complexion.

Jared couldn't remember when he'd seen such a vision. He watched as she ascended the rocky bank, but her countenance stayed with him. He couldn't decide which was more impressive — her eyes, her smile, or the black crown of hair that floated about her face. All had stirred his senses.

FIVE

NATALIE PEERED AT HER BROTHER AS SHE DROVE UP THE DIRT ROAD TO their ranch. "You'll catch more," she said at the crushed expression on her brother's face.

Dillon stared at his lap, his sullenness intensifying her guilt. "Like you said, we have lots in the freezer."

She nodded. "Just tell me next time, so I don't have to worry. Okay?" Natalie had searched in every barn and outbuilding on the ranch and called his name so much her throat still felt raw from the effort. If Willard hadn't spotted Dillon walking toward the river with his pole, she wasn't sure what she would have done.

It had to be a guy thing—fishing on the river. She considered the dark-haired man, a city boy from St. Louis, probably hoping to commune with nature or some such nonsense. Judging from his pale complexion, the man didn't get out much.

"You think Dad was in a lot of pain when he died?"

Dillon's question jerked Natalie out of her thoughts and back to the real world—right where her father had always instructed her to live. She debated lying to the boy. As intuitive as he was, he'd probably see right through her.

"I don't know, Dillon. It's better not to think about it." At least, that's what she tried to do. She smiled and reached across the seat to squeeze his shoulder. "Concentrate on the good times you had — all those overnight trips you took to the river, and helping him at roundup. I know how much you liked herding steers."

His brown eyes brightened. "Especially hunting strays. Or drinking from the windmills."

"More like swimming in the water tanks." She pinched his ear, and he pulled away.

"Do you miss him?"

The tires hit a chuckhole as Natalie turned into their lane, and the two of them jostled inside the cab of the truck. "What kind of question is that?"

Dillon cracked his knuckles, a habit she loathed almost as much as her sister's nail biting. "You haven't been around much lately. I thought maybe you and Dad ... that maybe you didn't get along so well anymore."

Natalie pulled up to the house and shut off the Ford's diesel engine. Sometimes her brother saw things through a magnifying glass, things she'd rather not acknowledge. But it was true. Life hadn't been the same since Vegas.

"It's not that we didn't get along." She opened the truck door and the hinges groaned. "I've been busy ... trying to figure out what to do with my life. Sometimes we grownups don't always see eye-to-eye."

Dillon frowned. "Are you sad about the contest?"

She fought back the emotion, allowed it to deaden her senses. "Not so much."

"What about that guy ... Ryan. You still dating him?"

"No, I'm not." Natalie scowled. Ryan was the last person she cared to think about. Unwilling to say more, she headed for the house.

Chelsey met her on the back porch, a dishtowel slung over her shoulder. "A guy's waiting for you in Dad's office — says his name's Mr. Thompson."

A curse slipped from Natalie's tongue as she checked her watch. She'd forgotten about her appointment with Dad's attorney. One glance in the hall mirror confirmed her hair was a mess, and she quickly raked her fingers through the black strands before entering her father's office.

The man sat with his back to her, his balding crown framed by dark tufts of hair on each side.

"I'm sorry for keeping you." She reached out her hand and offered him a warm smile.

"No problem." He started to stand. "Since I've been out of the office all week, I figured you'd want to get this over with as soon as possible, but if today isn't convenient we can reschedule for another time."

"You said on the phone that my father had a will?" Natalie noted his briefcase and cleared a space on the oak desk.

"Yes, albeit a short one." Mr. Thompson laid half a dozen papers on the desk, spreading them out for her to view. He then withdrew two scrolls of paper each tied with a string and handed them to her. "Before we begin, here are a couple of items your father gave me to go along with the will. They're addressed to your brother and sister. I believe he mentioned they were poems."

Natalie lifted an eyebrow, never knowing her father to write an ounce of poetry. Willard, yes, but not her dad. She stared at the scribbled names, wondering why he'd given them to his lawyer and why there wasn't one for her.

"Your father was a unique man."

She glanced up from the scrolls. "That's putting it mildly, wouldn't you say?"

"What I mean is that while he wanted his legal matters in order, he failed to do the same with his finances."

Natalie eased into the wooden desk chair. "What do you mean, exactly?"

"Trust me, your father planned for your futures, but his plan had a few ... kinks." The attorney rushed on. "As his only heirs, he left you and your brother and sister the entire estate, to be divided equally among you when they reach the age of twenty-one. Until then, he appointed you guardian of the children and conservator of the ranch. You're also the executor of the estate."

She skimmed the papers on the desk. "Then I don't understand."

"The problem isn't the real estate … he owned his land free and clear." The man twisted in his seat as a bead of sweat formed on his upper lip. "The dilemma comes in determining your father's cash assets. He once told me he had a great dislike for financial institutions. Said he could protect his money better than a bank. I guess he wasn't kidding."

"I'm afraid I'm not following …"

"Well …" The attorney drew out the word before he continued. "I've spoken to your father's accountant. We have his tax records, and his quarterly ledgers. Your father had an account at the bank for his business transactions, but we're quite certain there was more. We just don't know where."

Natalie stared at the man in disbelief. "What about investments?"

Mr. Thompson frowned and shook his head. "We have no records of any such business. Maybe he gambled the money or gave it away. We have no way of knowing."

Natalie scrunched her brow. Her father didn't gamble. "But there's money in the ranch account?"

"You have enough to cover operating expenses—for a few months, anyway."

As Natalie digested what this meant, her hand began to tremble.

The attorney offered her a consoling shrug. "I'm sorry. I know how much he loved all of you. I'm certain it wasn't his intention to make your lives difficult. That's really all I can offer."

"There's no savings? Nothing I can draw upon?"

"You have the ranch, all fifty-six hundred acres. And who knows, maybe you'll get lucky and find the money hidden in a shoe somewhere." He rose and gave her a weak smile. "Stranger things have happened."

SIX

JARED STRETCHED HIS NECK AND SHOULDERS, TENSE FROM AN AFTERNOON of preparing his second sermon. Nearly a week had passed since he'd first met Dillon and his sister on the Cottonwood River, and still, he remembered the color of her eyes — the color of a Kansas summer sky. He shook the image from his mind, and another thought struck him. He still had the boy's stringer.

That evening after work, Jared climbed into his Toyota Tercel and drove to the bend in the river where he'd fished on Sunday. A mile and a half further, he came upon a small house. An old black man in overalls sat on the front steps with a book in his hands. Soon after, Jared spotted a larger property with a one-and-a-half-story home and a wrap-around porch flanked by several sheds and a substantial limestone barn.

He noted the name on the mailbox and turned into the lane of the Double-A-Ranch. As he pulled up to the house, a border collie barked at the car and sniffed the tires. A young teen stepped out and called to the dog.

"Good afternoon. I'm looking for a boy named Dillon." Jared crawled from his car, banging his knee on the steering wheel.

The girl bounded down the porch steps with bare feet, her

blonde hair floating in the breeze. He tried to determine whether she was related to the woman he'd met on Sunday, but their features were too dissimilar.

"This is Dillon's home. Who are you?"

"Forgive me." Jared reached out his hand and introduced himself. "I met Dillon fishing the other day. He gave me his catch, and I wanted to return his stringer."

She shrugged. "He should be back in a bit if you want to wait on him."

Jared surveyed the property for signs of Dillon or his other sister. "Are your parents home?"

Already on her way back to the house, she glanced over her shoulder with an odd look and frowned. "They're dead. My dad died two weeks ago."

Jared balked at this information, caught even more off guard by the callousness in her voice. "I'm sorry . . . I didn't know. Do you need anything? Any help or assistance?"

"A crystal ball would be good," the girl called out, then disappeared inside the house.

Having no clue what she meant, Jared followed her to the porch and waited outside the open door. The teen stood at the kitchen stove, scraping scorched potatoes from the bottom of a cast iron skillet. Dressed in a pair of cutoff shorts and a pink tank top, the girl swayed to a song on the radio while she cooked.

Jared studied the broken hinge on the screen door. Instead of slamming shut, the door creaked back and forth with the shifting breeze. "What would you do with a crystal ball?"

She sent him a scornful look. "Tell the future, duh."

"Yes, well . . ." He noted the pile of dirty laundry near the entryway and the muddy footprints on the linoleum. "Do you have other brothers and sisters? Someone to take care of you?"

"My older sister's in charge." She shut the burner off and shoved the skillet to the back of the stove. "It's just the three of us—unless you count Tom—when you can find him."

"Who's Tom?"

"What's with the questions?" Her voice grated.

Jared braced one hand on the door frame. "I only wondered how you were getting along without your ..." He pressed his lips together and shook his head at his lack of sensitivity. "I'm sorry. It's none of my business."

"That's right, it's not," a crisp voice said from behind.

Jared turned to see the sister he'd met before, this time with a ball cap on her head, her black hair pulled into a ponytail that swished over her shoulder. Light blue eyes glared at him, ever cynical. He countered with a smile and offered his hand. "We meet again ... from the other day ... at the river. Jared Logan."

She shook his hand, her grip firm and warm. "I remember—big city boy from the East." Shoving the rickety screen door out of her way, the woman stepped through the kitchen maze to the refrigerator and pulled out a bottle of water.

Jared splayed his fingers, ignoring the tingling sensation there. "Actually, I'm not a city boy at all. I grew up in the small town of Concordia, Kansas. My father served as a pastor there."

"The son of a preacher man, huh?" She took a long drink, then wiped her mouth with the back of her fingers. "The preacher kids I knew in school got away with murder, right under their parents' noses."

Jared offered an unsettled grin, having known a few kids like that as well. "I didn't catch your name?"

The woman's thin brows arched higher.

"She's Natalie Adams, and I'm Chelsey." The girl at the stove answered for her. "Want to stay for supper?"

Natalie's gaze snapped to her sister, unable to believe Chelsey would ask such a thing. "I'm sure Mr. Logan has more important plans this evening than to share a meal with strangers."

The man loosened his tie and leaned against the door frame. "Actually, I'm free this evening. Nowhere to go, no one to see. I was a stranger and you invited me in."

She caught the glint of amusement in his eyes. Hers drifted to his dimpled grin and the dark shadow of a new beard against his pale skin. He looked to be some sort of businessman, dressed in navy pants and a short-sleeved dress shirt.

"No wife to go home to?" Her attention settled on his left hand, which boasted the absence of a ring, though that didn't necessarily mean anything these days.

He shook his head. "The only thing waiting for me at home is an empty refrigerator."

Her eyes narrowed. "Well, no sense standing there letting in flies." She pulled out a chair and motioned for him to sit. "Where's Dillon?" she asked Chelsey as she placed another plate on the table.

"I thought he was doing chores with you."

Natalie groaned. How many times this past week had Dillon snuck out on his own, not telling anyone where he was going, his chores abandoned? She headed for the porch and called his name, tired of the responsibility.

"If you'd like, I'll look for him while you finish up in here." The man stepped out of the way, his elbow brushing against hers.

She glanced down and caught the contrast of his fair skin next to her tanned arm. Who was this man, and why was he here? She tilted her head to study his face and a trace of musky aftershave stirred her senses. "I have a better idea. You can help me look, and while we look, you can tell me why you're so interested in our family."

Without another word, Natalie took off toward the barnyard and heard the rapid footfall of his steps behind her.

"I wanted to thank you for your generosity the other day," he said as he caught up to her. "Since I'm new in Diamond Falls, I thought it might be nice for us to visit and get to know one another."

Now even more on guard, Natalie hollered for Dillon as she

peeked into the tool shed. "A neighborly visit, huh?" As a former rodeo queen, she'd had more than her share of men who wanted to be neighborly—most of their motives suspect.

"Well, yes, and to return the stringer I borrowed."

"And that's why you're staying for supper?"

Two red splotches colored his cheeks. "I have to confess—your sister's cooking smelled delicious, much better than anything I could stir up at home."

Natalie smirked at the man's sincerity. Judging from his tall but slight build, he probably didn't get home cooked meals too often. Unable to think of a clever response, she headed for the next outbuilding.

"Chelsey told me about your dad." He trailed behind. "I'm sorry for your loss. Perhaps I might be able to help?"

Natalie stared at the ground, growing accustomed to such condolences, though the harsh reality of her dad's death still left her cold and numb. "I appreciate you wanting to help, but quite honestly, I don't see how that's possible."

"Oh, but that's the easy part." He grinned, his eyes trained on something in the distance. "I'll start by helping you find your brother."

SEVEN

JARED LED NATALIE TO THE ENTRANCE OF THE LIMESTONE BARN WHERE he'd seen Dillon sneak past. It took a moment for his eyes to adjust to the cool darkness, but he soon distinguished the thick rock walls of the structure built more than a century ago. A movement behind a wooden cattle stanchion caught his attention, and he quietly motioned Natalie to follow.

Together they watched unnoticed while the freckled-nosed boy pinned a wiry kitten to his chest. The scene caused Jared's chest to squeeze, reminded of his own youth and fondness for little creatures. He smiled at Natalie, but recognized the exasperation on her face.

"We've been looking all over for you, Dillon, and here you are playing with a cat. Have you even started your chores?" She shook her head and cursed.

Jared inwardly cringed, perplexed by Natalie's attitude. Dillon was just a kid, after all.

The boy dropped the kitten and stood before his sister, his eyes downcast. "I'll do them now. Go ahead and eat without me." He peeked up at Jared, his mouth a straight line. The sadness there made Jared want to take the kid fishing, play catch, anything but stand here and witness his dejection.

"Maybe I could help with those chores." Jared eased into the conversation. "Then we could have dinner together."

Dillon's brown eyes filled with guarded curiosity. "You're gonna eat with us?"

"That's right. Maybe afterward, you could share a few of your fishing secrets. Those flathead you caught made for some mighty fine eating." Jared knew this suggestion overstepped his boundaries but deemed the risk worth taking. He'd fend off big sister later. In fact, he felt her gaze blazing a hole through him this very second.

NATALIE PICKED UP AN OVERTURNED BUCKET AND HANDED IT TO DILLON. The man had a lot of nerve intruding on their life this way. "Let's get through supper, shall we, before we go sharing any secrets." She shot a warning glance at Mr. Logan and then her brother.

Dillon's smile faded, his disappointment designating her as the bad guy, always the bad guy.

Despite her annoyance, she watched as Jared and her brother headed out of the barn with buckets of grain to feed the horses and goats. Plagued by guilt, she peered up at the wooden rafters and breathed in the scent of aged cedar. A tear trickled down her cheek as she thought of days long past, when she'd skipped beside her father as he carried buckets of grain too heavy for her to manage. She could almost hear his hearty laughter as he lifted her onto his shoulders to pet the horses on the other side of the pen. Those moments became particularly special after her mother passed away, their bond growing even stronger.

Would Dillon look back with such remembrances of their father? She could only hope. But what about now? How was she to manage getting the kids through this ordeal?

"Oh, Dad, why did you have to go?" she whispered, the ache so fierce in her chest it threatened to steal her breath. Biting back fresh tears, she spun on her boot heels to return to the house. This was not the time to wimp out—not with Chelsey needing help with supper, and a stranger joining them at their table.

NATALIE PURPOSELY SAT ACROSS FROM JARED LOGAN, WANTING TO KEEP an eye on him throughout the meal. Despite his helpful sentiments, she didn't trust the man. Strangers weren't that thoughtful and caring—and if they were, it was normally because they wanted something.

She passed Dillon the bowl of fried potatoes, then stabbed a pork chop with her fork. "What brings you to Diamond Falls, Mr. Logan? I mean, let's face it, unless you own land or have family here, it's not the most happening place to live."

Dillon passed him the bowl of potatoes, and Jared scooped out a meager portion. "It's where God wanted me to be."

Natalie sipped her iced tea and studied the clean-cut man, having already determined he didn't hold a blue-collar job or one in ranching. "What makes you so sure?"

"I'm here, aren't I?" He grinned and accepted the next dish handed to him.

"If I were you, I think I'd ask for a transfer." She allowed her lips to curve upward, so as not to appear inhospitable.

"I don't know why you'd say that." His eyes, the color of dark coffee, seemed to look directly through her, as though he could see her inmost thoughts. "Here you are, living on this beautiful ranch, rich with cattle, grass, and I'm sure a treasure of memories. Most of the people I've talked to consider themselves fortunate to live in the Flint Hills. Why not you?"

Natalie broke eye contact as she cut into the golden-crusted meat on her plate. "We weren't talking about me, Mr. Logan. Do you own land?"

"No, but that doesn't keep me from enjoying it." He winked at Chelsey, who in turn giggled.

"Okay, you enjoy fishing." She tried a different approach. "What else? Hunting? Horseback riding?"

"Some of my best memories include fishing on my granddad's farm. I spent my summers there, helping him in the fields and driving a tractor."

"Is that why you're here, then? To relive your childhood?"

"No, those days are over." The gleam in Jared's eyes dimmed. "I put away childish ways long ago."

Natalie considered his strange words throughout the rest of dinner, and afterward peered out the window at Jared and Dillon sifting through her brother's tackle box on the front porch. Jared's enthusiasm matched that of the boy's as her brother gave a detailed explanation for each of the lures and its use.

Did God truly look after people? She lifted the curtain to study the man on the porch. If so, why had God allowed such doom to fall on her family? It made no sense. She'd always believed that if you went after something with enough determination you would succeed. Her life testified to this. She'd succeeded at everything she pursued, whether it was barrel racing, a college scholarship, or being crowned Miss Rodeo Kansas.

Her theory stumbled in Las Vegas when her hard work failed to pay off ... and that downward spiral continued to this day. What was the answer? Who was in charge of her future? God ... or herself?

Jared glanced up at the window then, his hand batting at the night insects that drifted from the porch light. She let the curtain fall and stepped away, hoping he hadn't seen her. To her dismay, the man rose from his position and moved to the front door.

Rather than be caught peeping, Natalie fell into a nearby chair and grabbed the closest book. When Jared and her brother entered the room, she realized she held a telephone directory.

"I wondered if we might talk before I go?" Jared aimed his question at Natalie.

She slid the volume to a wooden stand. "Dillon, isn't it your bedtime?"

Her brother's happy disposition plummeted. "But it's early."

"Yes, and it's a school night too." She waited for him to explode into a tantrum as he'd done every night this week since returning to school. Perhaps it had been a mistake to send him back after their father's funeral.

"You'd better do as your sister says," Jared interceded. "We'll have lots of time this summer to talk about fishing—with your sister's permission, of course."

To Natalie's surprise, Dillon said good night and bounded up the flight of stairs without another word of argument.

"I wish he minded me that well." Natalie rose from her chair, feeling foolish for not having better control of the situation.

Jared went to the door and held it open. "It's a beautiful evening. Walk with me to my car?"

Natalie wondered what he had in mind. She'd handled all sorts of situations as Miss Rodeo Kansas, she could surely handle Jared Logan.

"Okay, you have my undivided attention," she said once they were on the front steps. "What did you want to talk to me about?"

He held her elbow as she went down the concrete steps, his fingers cool against her skin. "Thank you for allowing me to stay for dinner—for opening your home when you made it quite clear you didn't want me here."

She hugged her arms to her chest, moving away from his touch. "You have a way with kids, or at least with Dillon. He really likes you."

"He's a sharp boy, which is one of the reasons I wanted to speak to you. I have experience with grief counseling. Have you considered that for your family?"

Natalie swallowed the automatic refusal on her tongue. "I appreciate your concern, but we're fine, or at least we will be. It's only been a couple of weeks. We're surely allowed some time to come to terms with . . . his death." Her throat tightened at having to say the word aloud.

He stopped at his car and leaned against the dusty frame. "All I meant was it's an option, should you find yourselves unable to cope. From what I can tell, Dillon and Chelsey seem to be doing well."

Yes, but if you only knew . . . She wrestled down the anxious reply. He didn't know about Chelsey's reckless behavior, or Dillon's silent retreats from the family. Or how difficult it was to be an older sister —a confidant—and then suddenly be the one who makes all the rules, in charge of everything and everyone, and not having the slightest clue what her future held.

"What about you?" he asked. "Dillon told me you came home from college to take care of him and Chelsey. That's quite a sacrifice."

Natalie's eyes filled with tears. She spun away to swipe the dampness from her cheeks, but it was useless. One concerned comment from a complete stranger had caused the floodgate to burst. Tears gushed from her like a fountain. Then a gentle grip on her forearm urged her to turn and be comforted.

EIGHT

JARED TOOK THE YOUNG WOMAN AWKWARDLY IN HIS ARMS, UNABLE TO resist consoling her tears. "I know it's hard, but I can tell you're a strong person. You'll get through this. God can help you."

She cried into his shoulder. Most people, he'd learned from seminary, kept their grief bound until it burst from inside, usually at the least expected moment. His heart ached for this girl and her family, and he timidly patted her back.

"Sometimes it's easier to speak to a stranger than it is to confide in someone you know."

Her sobs eased, and she pulled away, her embarrassment palpable. "It's been so hard." Her words came out choked, and Jared strained to hear.

"I'm listening." He closed his eyes and had to concentrate to absorb her words and not the light flowery scent of her hair.

"He died so unexpectedly. Trapped beneath a tractor. A horrid death—but I can't tell Dillon that. The kids and I weren't here when it happened, but still the images come to me in my sleep. They won't go away." Another sob escaped her lips.

Jared nodded and gazed at her, the porch light illuminating her face in the dark night. "I know it doesn't seem like it now, but once you're over the shock, the nightmares will fade."

"I planned to graduate from college next fall, but that's not going to happen now." She wiped her cheeks and sniffed. "Not with the ranch, the kids, the summer hay crop and cattle ... So much for my queen scholarships. They'll all be for nothing."

Jared straightened, wondering if he'd heard correctly. "Queen scholarships?" He conjured a picture of her in one of those long sequined gowns. Somehow, the image didn't fit her personality.

"Go ahead, laugh. Everyone does." She leaned against the side of the car, and her teary eyes glistened beneath the stars. "You're looking at the former Miss Rodeo Kansas, first runner up in the Miss Rodeo America pageant held last December."

Jared tried not to gawk. Not only was this woman beautiful, she was accomplished—and exposed. "Obviously, the judges didn't know what they were doing when they gave the prize to someone else," he said under his breath. "Forgive my ignorance, but what does a rodeo queen do besides look pretty?"

She shook her head as though she'd been asked that question before. "Why do people always assume it's all about being pretty?"

"Probably because the participants are gorgeous." He grinned, present company included. "Okay, you've piqued my interest. What does it take to be a rodeo queen?"

Natalie sniffed and wiped the remaining tears from her eyes. "I like to think of the pageant as a scholarship program—based on appearance, personality, and horsemanship. It's so much more than a beauty pageant—at least it is for me."

Jared imagined Natalie on a galloping horse with a white hat and western garb. It suited her better than a sequined gown on a lighted runway. "A beauty pageant on a horse," he said, unable to keep the teasing note from his voice.

"It's harder than you think." Her eyes narrowed. "We're expected to know everything about the sport of rodeo and its profession, from who won last year's world championships to horse-related injuries or diseases. And that's just the interview portion."

"Yet, it probably seems easy compared to what you're up against today." Jared shifted to see her better and considered her trials. Raising a family was hard enough when circumstances were good, but having to raise two siblings, run a ranch, and deal with her father's death might prove too much for a young woman to bear. He knew then that God had called him to help this family. "I want you to know that if you need anything, you can call me. Even if it's to help around the ranch or to spend time with Dillon."

Natalie stared at her boots. "Why would you do that? You hardly know us."

"I know your circumstances." When the moment turned too quiet, he nudged her elbow. "Come on, let me see your smile ... that competition smile you save for judges."

Her mouth angled into a slight grin and soon widened into a dazzling smile he'd seen once before when they'd first met. Though he figured she'd trained for such moments, his heart thumped against his chest just as it had done at the river. If he'd been one of the judges in December, he'd have given her the title—no question.

NATALIE DASHED TO THE BATHROOM AND SPLASHED HER PUFFY EYES WITH cold water. She pressed a wet washcloth to her hot cheeks. What was she thinking? To confide in their dinner guest, a man she hardly knew, and to lose control so thoroughly? Her father would be ashamed of her weakness. She turned off the faucet and heard the grandfather clock ticking in the next room joined by the muffled bass from Chelsey's stereo upstairs. At least the kids hadn't witnessed the breakdown.

In no mood to deal with her father's unorganized finances, Natalie ignored the office as she passed by and spotted instead her mother's buffet cabinet where family pictures and other items were stored. Feeling nostalgic, she opened one of the pine doors and a stack of boxes greeted her, friends from her childhood. She pulled out one of the puzzles with a picture of galloping horses against a stormy sky. Captivated, she was about to lift the lid when a knock sounded from the kitchen screen. Natalie looked up to see Willard's head peek in through the door.

"I saw your light on. Thought you might like some company."

The familiar voice comforted her. "Like old times?" She set the puzzle aside.

Willard joined her in the dining room, his tall frame beginning to slump at the neck and shoulders. His gaze wandered to the open door of the buffet cabinet. "Going through your dad's things?"

Natalie shrugged. "Not if I can talk you into a game of checkers."

He flashed a smile, his white dentures gleaming. "If I'm not mistaken, I think your dad kept a set in the top drawer over there." A long crooked finger pointed to the coffee table in the living room.

"It's been a while since you and I played checkers." Natalie followed him to the table and noticed his limp, which had grown worse this past year. "I was never very good, but Dad loved the game."

The man chuckled. "He probably got that from his daddy. He and I used to play in Nam. That's how we knew each other so well. Your grandpa insisted we play every evening after chow. Said it reminded him of home. Even though I was his sergeant, I enjoyed listening to his tales, like the night he and his friends roped a young cow in the middle of a pasture, only his mount spooked and dragged the pesky heifer a couple miles before they shut the horse down." His eyes glistened at the memory as he eased himself onto the worn couch.

Natalie didn't remember much about her grandpa, but she always enjoyed Willard's narratives about the past. His calm, soothing voice comforted her soul, especially now. "Dad told that story a hundred times while I was growing up." She knelt beside the coffee table and began lining up the black pieces on the checkerboard. "Want some popcorn or something to drink?"

Willard leaned against the sofa and rested his hands on his stomach. "I don't suppose you have any soda pop in your refrigerator?"

"Orange Crush, right?" At his nod, Natalie held back her amusement and eased herself from the floor. As she walked past, she patted his spongy gray hair, glad for his company. "I'll see what I can find."

Minutes later, she returned with two bottles of root beer. "Sorry, we didn't have any orange soda, but hopefully, this will do." She handed Willard the cold drink, deciding to broach the discussion she'd had with her father's attorney. "Did Dad ever mention his dislike for banks?"

Willard latched onto the bottle and scooted to the edge of his seat. "I remember him cussing when a bank teller charged him for a box of checks. He was right mad about that. Guess you could say he had a genuine dislike for them."

"What about his money? He never gambled, did he?" Natalie practically choked out the words.

His bushy eyebrows arched. "What kind of nonsense are you talking, girl?"

Natalie forced a smile. How much could she reveal without casting an unpleasant light on their situation? She'd rather eat dirt than confess they barely had enough money to make it through the summer. "I visited with Dad's lawyer the other day. He told me there were no savings accounts in Dad's records."

"Your dad never lacked for money. He inherited this ranch debt-free when your grandfather died."

"Mr. Thompson suggested Dad might have gambled the money or given it away—like to a charity. I'd hoped he might have mentioned something to you."

Willard ducked his chin and frowned. "You know your dad. He

wasn't one to throw away money. I can't imagine him doing such a fool thing."

Natalie couldn't imagine it either. But then she hadn't been aware of his dabbling in poetry. "Did you know he wrote poems for Chelsey and Dillon?"

"Is that so?"

"According to Mr. Thompson, he wrote one for each of them," she said, hiding the resentment that he'd given them such a personal gift of love. Natalie had set the poems aside, thinking it best to show the kids after they'd had time to accept their father's death. Then again, maybe it was more a matter of putting them out of sight, out of mind.

Willard scratched his bristly chin. "He once gave me a poem called 'Boots.' I thought it odd at the time, but you know my fondness for verse."

Natalie's stomach twisted. It seemed her dad had written poetry for everyone but her. Had he been mad or upset with her? Or had he sensed the same disconnection she'd felt since Las Vegas? "Do you still have it?"

"I don't even know." He twisted the bottle cap, and a puff of mist sprayed out the neck. His gaze bore into her as though reading one of his favorite books. "You ready to play checkers or is there something else on your mind?"

Natalie rolled her bottle of root beer between her hands, the condensation cool and moist against her palms. "Actually, there was something I wanted to ask you." She pressed her lips together, willing her mouth to form the words.

"The other day when we were unloading cattle, you said Dad made you promise to take care of us. That you were with him when he died. You'll probably think I'm crazy . . ." She stared up at the yellow water ring that stained the ceiling and took a deep breath. "Was he in a lot of pain? Was he scared — to die?"

Willard set his soda on the coffee table and reached for her hand.

"The Lord giveth and the Lord taketh away. As far as I could tell, your daddy was ready."

Natalie clung to his warm fingers, her own as cold as a December day. She searched Willard's eyes and tried to see what he'd seen the day he'd found her father trapped beneath the fallen tractor. His straw hat lying beside him, his wrinkled forehead drenched with a clammy sweat. A tear trickled down her cheek.

"Did he say anything else?" She hated to ask. It seemed like such a selfish question, but she didn't think she could stand another day not knowing. "About me, I mean?"

Willard nodded and his gaze reached deep into her own. "Your daddy's exact words to me were ... 'Take care of my little girl. Take care of my Natalie.'"

NINE

THE FOLLOWING WEDNESDAY, JARED CLUTCHED THE THICK HYMNAL AND waited for a response from the three elders in his office. Carl Ellis sat with his arms bolted across his chest, his back plastered to the chair. Bob Douglas rested his elbows on his knees, massaging his temple as though he had a headache.

"Come on, fellas, all I ask is that you take a look at this hymnal and see what you think. The publisher went to great lengths to mix the traditional songs with the new. I think you'll be pleasantly surprised at the result."

George Hobart, a tall gruff man, leaned against the wall and rubbed his chin. "I don't know. Too much change stirs up folks and makes 'em mad."

"I've already talked to our organist, and she loves it." Jared wished the others would share Mrs. Sanders' enthusiasm. If he could win the elders' approval, he'd take it to the women's study group this afternoon and get their reaction.

Bob stopped rubbing his temple and looked up, his eyes glazed. "You're already asking for a men's Bible study breakfast. Maybe we should see how that goes before we add anything else."

"If you want my vote, I say no," Carl grumbled. "There's nothing wrong with the hymnal we have. No reason to spend money on things we don't need."

Jared laid the new hymnal on his desk, knowing better than to push the case further. At least they'd approved his Bible study, albeit grudgingly. Maybe he'd try again another day. "All right, so we'll schedule our first men's breakfast next Friday. Shall we meet here or at Clara's Café? She has a room in the back we can use if we want."

Carl's frown deepened.

"Most of us are at Clara's every morning, anyways," George said. "Sitting at a Bible study is a far cry better than listening to the local scuttlebutt."

"That's the spirit." Jared smiled, careful to avoid Carl's face. "Are we in agreement to meet at Clara's then?"

George and Bob nodded. They turned to Carl.

The seconds ticked by.

"Don't let me stand in your way." Carl finally gave in. "I'll have to check with my wife and see if we have anything going on that morning."

George snorted. "We all know Ina Mae ain't got nothing to say about you being at the café. You'll be there, and you know it."

Jared checked his watch and considered the matter closed. With just enough time to prepare for the women's luncheon, he stood and opened his office door. "Gentlemen, thanks for coming in. I appreciate your help." He shook hands with each as they passed by, then twenty minutes later he greeted the women as they filed in through the hallway with covered dishes. One meeting down, two to go.

NATALIE SMOOTHED HER HAND OVER HER DAD'S LEATHER SADDLE, recalling their many trips to the pasture to check cattle and fence. Worn to a shine, the saddle reflected her father's diligent work ethic, which he'd handed down to her. Given a choice between mucking a stall or going to a movie, Natalie would reach for a pitchfork every time, which accounted for her entire afternoon spent in the barn. She'd rather clean stalls and tack than sort through her father's paperwork in the house.

A good portion of the leather needed to be cleaned, so she searched the tack room for a tub of saddle soap and spotted some on her father's workbench. When she removed the container from its cubbyhole, she noticed a thick envelope crushed behind. Curious, she pulled it out and examined the crinkled paper, yellowed with age.

Unmarked but sealed, the bulky envelope practically begged to be opened.

Wondering what might be enclosed, she lifted the seal with the tip of her fingernail and stared at the contents, too stunned to let out a gasp.

She reached inside and pulled out a wad of twenty-dollar bills bound by a thick rubber band. Her fingers shuffled through them.

One hundred bills to be exact.

Shaking with excitement, Natalie counted them again, the sweet scent of cash and good fortune floating to her nose.

"Five-hundred, six-hundred, seven-hundred . . ."

Natalie heard the school bus shift gears and roar into their driveway. Unable to keep from grinning, she stepped into the light of the barn entrance and called to Dillon after the bus pulled away. "Take your books to the house, then come here. I have something to show you."

She returned to the stack of twenties, feeling as though she'd won the lottery. Could Mr. Thompson's offhand remark about finding money in a shoe be correct? A giggle escaped her mouth as she considered whether her father might have stashed more money on the ranch.

Natalie had actually read newspaper accounts where family members found money from their deceased tucked between the pages of a book, stuffed under a mattress, or stashed in a flowerpot in the basement. The possibilities were endless. And this scenario went right along with the attorney's statement about her father not trusting banks.

Dillon shuffled through the barn door, munching on a cookie. "How come Chelsey didn't ride the bus tonight?"

Her fingers paused their counting. "She's going to a youth meeting with Sarah."

"I thought you grounded her?"

"Not entirely." Natalie tore her gaze from the aged bills. "Don't worry, Sarah's a good kid."

"Whatever you say." Her brother finished the rest of his chocolate-chip cookie. "What did you want to show me?"

"This." Natalie clasped the bills and fanned them in front of her. "Have you ever seen so much money?"

His eyes widened. "Where did you get that?"

She sank onto a nearby stool. When he came to her side, she brushed back his long bangs, only to have him comb them forward with his fingers. "Did Dad ever mention hiding money on the ranch?"

A shadow creased Dillon's face, and she realized before he answered that he knew nothing. "Why?"

"Mr. Thompson suggested that he might have." She showed her brother the empty envelope. "I found this hidden in the cubby over there, so I guess it's a possibility. Do you know what that means?"

Dillon shrugged. "That we're rich?"

"Not quite." She chuckled. "But there might be more. I think we should go on a treasure hunt. We can each take a portion of the ranch — we'll dig through everything. Starting with this room."

Dillon's eyes transformed into animated twinkles. "This is cool — just like those reality shows on television." He rushed over to the workbench and began shoveling through their father's tools.

Natalie walked up behind her brother and turned him to face her. "It's okay to have fun. Make it a game if you want. But it's important that you don't tell anyone what we're doing. Not even Tom, do you understand?"

Dillon's chin bobbed up and down. "How come we can't tell anyone?"

Natalie took a moment before responding. "Let's just say we wouldn't want anyone to get any ideas."

Her brother's eyes lit with understanding. "Don't worry. I won't tell a soul."

"Good. Trust no one."

TEN

That afternoon, Jared stopped by Clara's Café to set up the arrangements for the men's Bible study. He filed through the on-slaught of school-aged children with their candy bars and drinks and grabbed the only stool available at the counter. The proprietor and another waitress were busy taking orders. He'd noticed that about Clara Lambert the first time he'd eaten here. She enjoyed serving her customers.

The auburn-haired woman greeted him with a smile. "What can I get for you, Pastor Logan?"

Still unaccustomed to the title, Jared studied the list of specials on the whiteboard. "I believe I'll try your coconut cream pie today. That used to be my favorite, so we'll see if my tastes have changed through the years."

She chuckled and went directly to the display that held the homemade pies—all baked by Clara herself. "How do you like Diamond Falls? Are you getting situated?"

"I'm holding my first youth meeting tonight."

"A word of advice—don't let them know you're nervous." She set the pie in front of him, its fluffy meringue sprinkled with toasted coconut. "Are you serving snacks?"

Jared hadn't given food a thought. "Should I?"

The woman nodded with certainty. "Al serves pizza out on the highway at the gas station. If you want to make a good impression..."

Needing all the help he could get, Jared needed Clara's instruction. That evening, he picked up his order of pizzas and took them to the church. The sharp tang of pepperoni and mozzarella cheese hung in the air in anticipation. Of his three Wednesday meetings, this one scared him the most. Adults and children didn't usually intimidate him, but teenagers were a whole different ballgame.

Five minutes to six, the youth began drifting inside. Once everyone arrived, Jared offered prayer, then greeted the teens as they filed through the pizza line. Two girls giggled at the end. One he recognized from church. The other was Chelsey Adams.

As they neared, he handed them each a plate. "It's nice to see you, Chelsey."

She nudged her friend and snickered. "You never told us you were a preacher."

Jared shook his head and grinned. "No, I guess I didn't. Forgive me, and welcome to New Redeemer." He noted her casual attire, worn jeans tucked into lime green cowboy boots and a matching tank top. Tinted glasses perched on the top of her head. And she seemed almost giddy—unlike the frustrated girl he'd met before.

When the two passed by to get their pizza, Jared caught the distinct odor of beer on their breath.

He looked up at the ceiling and murmured a quick prayer for help. Why tonight? His first meeting with the teens? Jared ran through a list of options. He could drag the two girls to his office and call their guardians. Just thinking about adding to Natalie's troubles made him cringe, but if he waited until the meeting was over, the girls would likely skip out. Either alternative made a mockery of his youth meeting.

He handed the remaining plates to a nearby youth leader and asked the name of Chelsey's friend.

"Sarah Sanders," the woman responded. "As in the daughter of Mrs. Sanders, the chairwoman of the women's study group."

Jared groaned.

"I need to make a few phone calls. Could you start the meeting without me?" he asked, glad that tonight's program included a film.

"No problem. Is everything okay?" The woman's brow dipped in concern.

He considered the two girls, and how their actions would affect those around them. "Everything's under control. But I might borrow your husband for a while, if that's okay."

"Sure, whatever you need to do."

Back at his desk, Jared set the receiver in its cradle and frowned at Dan Trevor, having informed him of what had happened. "I managed to contact your parents, Sarah, but no one answered at your house," he told Chelsey as he studied both girls on the couch. "What were you thinking? Where did you get the beer?"

Sarah looked close to tears, but Chelsey's gaze didn't waver. She stared right through him, as though used to interrogation. Neither answered.

"I'm sure your folks will want to know the answer to that as well. It might be better if you tell us now," Dan added.

Sarah's face cracked, and the tears began to fall as she doubled over onto her knees. "My mom's going to kill me. I can't believe I let you talk me into this, Chelsey."

Chelsey shot arrows at the girl's head, and her lips pressed even tighter. "It was your dad's beer, and you were the one who insisted we go to this stupid meeting. If you hadn't acted so dopey, we wouldn't have gotten caught."

"Mom would have found out if we'd skipped. She knows everything that happens in this church."

"Yeah, well, she knows about this now." Chelsey shook her head, contempt oozing from her expression.

"Okay, so the two of you thought you'd have a little fun." Jared stepped in to mediate. "You stole some beer and now you have to pay the price. How are you going to make this right?"

Blank faces stared back at him.

"What do you mean?" Sarah's voice quivered as she rose from her stooped position.

"You're both minors. Unless you walked here, which I highly doubt, you were driving under the influence, which is a Class C misdemeanor. The law didn't catch you, but you did get caught. Now what are we going to do about it?"

Sarah shook her head vehemently. "We didn't drive. Honest. Chelsey's boyfriend dropped us off."

"You gonna turn us in?" Chelsey chewed her thumbnail.

Jared exchanged looks with Dan. "That's up to Natalie and your parents." He decided to let the girls stew for a few minutes and waited at the entrance for the Sanders' arrival. When he spotted their car, he took a deep breath and prepared himself for the next round.

Mr. Sanders went directly to his daughter and pulled Sarah up by the arm. "Pastor Logan said you've been drinking. Is that true?"

Tears gushed down Sarah's cheeks as she nodded.

The man's abashed face turned to Jared. "I apologize for my daughter's behavior and for my wife not joining us. I'm afraid she's not accepting this news very well."

"I understand." Jared imagined Mrs. Sanders would have a difficult time facing the members of the congregation once word got out about the situation.

"Where do we go from here?" Mr. Sanders asked.

"I have a suggestion." Dan spoke from the other side of the room. "My wife and I could use some help with a project we're working on. The girls could assist us with that, under Pastor's supervision, of course."

Jared nodded, wishing he'd thought of the idea. "They could help with Vacation Bible School as well. Does twenty hours of church service sound fair?"

"I don't go to church," Chelsey boldly stated.

Jared looked the girl square in the face, up for the challenge. "Well, maybe it's time you start. Either that, or we can turn you over to the authorities."

To this, she had no response.

"They have two more days before summer break begins. Shall we have them meet here after school tomorrow?" he asked Dan, and the man agreed.

Jared jotted a few notes onto a sheet of paper and handed it to Mr. Sanders. "See that Sarah's here on time."

NATALIE PEEKED OUT THE KITCHEN WINDOW WHEN SHE SAW THE headlights shine into their drive. She pulled the plug to the dirty dishwater in the sink, hoping Chelsey had eaten. They had just finished supper, and Natalie didn't want another mess to clean up. It had been a long night already—thanks to Tom, who was once again missing in action.

The man had impeccable timing. Some of the new steers had gotten out, and with Tom nowhere to be found, she and Dillon were left to get them back in the pasture. Why was their hired hand never available when needed?

She draped the wet dishtowel over the back of a chair and waited for Chelsey to come in, hoping her sister's evening had gone better than her own. When Chelsey appeared at the door, Natalie was surprised to see Jared Logan right behind—and wearing a black shirt and clerical collar.

"What's going on?" She directed the question to the man who continued to confound her. "You're a preacher?"

Jared fingered his white collar. "I'm the new pastor at New Redeemer Church. Chelsey joined us for our youth meeting tonight. I tried to call, but couldn't get any answer here at the house."

"Dillon and I were out chasing steers." She wondered why they needed to reach her. And why had Jared driven Chelsey home? Sensing they were about to drop a bomb, Natalie sank into the nearest chair. "I'll ask again—what's going on?"

Jared and Chelsey towered over her. "Your sister and her friend had a little party after school today," Jared said. "Apparently, they found some beer at Sarah's house and came to church tipsy. Sarah's dad picked her up, and when we couldn't reach you, I decided to drive Chelsey home myself."

Natalie studied the man before her and noticed, of all things, how his dark shirt seemed to make his teeth gleam. Probably from the stark contrast of his white collar. She should have guessed that Jared was a preacher from all his talk about God. Embarrassment seeped from within that she'd poured out her heart to this man.

"Mind if I go to my room while you two plan my punishment?" Chelsey cocked her hip, her expression stoic.

"Yes, I mind." Natalie reached across the table and shoved back a chair. What had happened to her little sister? The sweet girl who'd followed her around with childish zeal, singing songs and making up games of pretend for them to play, who never seemed bothered by anything the world threw at her? Who, in fact, had always been able to shut out the world. "And Jared, I'd appreciate it if I could have a word with you too, please."

ELEVEN

Natalie contemplated the two at the table. Jared had deceived her into thinking he was a normal person ... a friend even. For Pete's sake, he'd allowed her to cry on his shoulder. It grieved her to think how she'd bared her soul to this man — the things she'd said. She could only imagine what he must think of her.

Her gaze shifted to her sister, angered that she had to deal with this problem on top of everything else weighing on her, and do it in front of the mighty minister who seemed to consider her family his personal mission project.

"Why are you doing this?" she asked Chelsey who attacked her fingernails like a beaver. Natalie understood teens were curious about drugs and alcohol. Although she'd never fallen for such temptation, she'd seen plenty who had, especially on the rodeo circuit. But why her little sister? "Is it because of Dad? Are you trying to lash out at him for leaving us?"

"Why do you care? Miss higher-than-everyone-else Rodeo Queen. When you didn't get what you wanted in Vegas, you left us. Don't try to pretend we matter to you now. Where were you the last five months?" Chelsey shot up from her chair and stormed from the room.

Her words stung Natalie's cheek ... and her heart. Ignoring her guest, Natalie rushed after Chelsey and caught her by the arm at the staircase. "I'm sorry I didn't come home. Can't you see that? I missed that time with him. If I'd been here, maybe I could have helped. Prevented it somehow."

"Don't think you're special," her sister spit back, but some of the anger fizzled. "We all have those thoughts. The difference is, Dillon and I were here, and you weren't. Now you're home, and you want to run our lives."

Natalie balked. "Is that how you see it? That I want to control your life?"

"That's how it's always been. You were the honor student, the beauty queen, the devoted sister who took precious care of her family—Daddy's favorite. I'm sick of trying to follow in your footsteps." She pulled herself from Natalie's grasp and thundered up the stairs.

Natalie watched her go. Her vision blurred with tears as condemnation tightened her stomach. Were Chelsey's words true? Had she abandoned them, and was she a control freak? A firm grip tugged on her shoulder, and she turned to see the gentle eyes of the man in black.

"I couldn't help overhearing." He patted her back, the charge in his fingertips tentative and wary.

"My life is such a mess." Natalie pressed her hands against her forehead, ready to overlook her annoyance with Jared if he could offer any suggestions.

"I know you don't like my interference," he said. "But for whatever reason, God has put me in your path, first with Dillon and now Chelsey."

She closed her eyes, preparing herself for another lecture. "Go ahead. Tell me what I'm doing wrong."

"I'm not here to criticize, Natalie. Your family is suffering. It's only natural for there to be some whiplash."

"Is that what you call it?" Natalie stepped away from him. She'd be more inclined to say her life was out of control with her on a runaway horse about to jump off a cliff. "So, what happens now?"

She listened while Jared outlined their plan for community service. "You think this will help?" Natalie studied the man's confident expression and took comfort in the determined set of his jaw although she couldn't help but wonder if a swift kick in the behind was all her sister needed.

"It might help her to think of other people instead of wallowing in self-pity, maybe learn to manage her anger in a healthier way. No more shutting doors on the people she loves."

Natalie lingered at the empty staircase, the bass vibrations from Chelsey's stereo traveling through her like small currents of electricity. "'Men shut their doors against a setting sun.'"

The broken screen door creaked in the kitchen, and Natalie's heart skipped a beat. She stepped back to see who had entered their house unannounced.

"Those are pretty bleak words, even for you." Willard's gravelly voice carried to her from the kitchen.

Natalie signaled her neighbor to come in. She had no idea where her words had come from, only that they had fallen from her tongue with ease, as though hidden in her soul, waiting for such a moment to make their exit.

"If I'm not mistaken, it's Shakespeare," Jared said.

Natalie's gaze traveled to Jared's, and their eyes locked.

"Timon of Athens to be exact." Willard joined them in the living room, breaking the connection. The two men shook hands as though they'd been friends forever. "You read poetry?"

"I read everything." Jared smiled back.

"You're the new pastor in town."

"That's correct." Jared's grin expanded at the observation.

Natalie watched their interaction with interest. Willard had obviously been sitting in on the early morning coffee sessions at Clara's Café. How else would he know what even she failed to recognize?

"My wife babysat Natalie and the kids when they were young. Natalie used to sit on my knee while I read poetry to her. I guess she must have retained more than I realized." Willard winked at her, and she smiled at the remembrance.

"I admire a man who enjoys poetry," Jared said.

"And I admire a man of God." Willard shifted his focus to Jared. "How do you know each other, anyway? Are you old friends? From college perhaps?"

Jared shook his head and extended his hands in her direction. "I'll let Natalie fill you in on the details."

All this jolly interaction made Natalie uneasy, like her arms and body were bound in a lariat and she couldn't get loose. She needed space. A quiet place to clear her mind and think through her decisions — from the past and for the future. These two men with their talk and laughter seemed to lap up all the available air in the room. "Would you mind doing the honors? I need to step out to the barn and see if Tom made it back. If not, then I should finish unsaddling the horses."

Willard's brow furrowed. "We can do that for you," he offered.

"No need. The fresh air will do me good." Natalie managed a smile, then escaped before they could protest further.

JARED CLEARED HIS THROAT AND SCANNED THE UNFAMILIAR ROOM. HIS attention returned to the man who liked poetry. "I failed to introduce myself. I'm Jared Logan."

The black man's large hand reached out once more and encompassed Jared's, his grip firm and strong. "Forgive my poor manners. Natalie's family and I go way back. I live down the road. Willard Grover."

Jared remembered seeing Willard on his porch the day he'd first visited Natalie's home. He caught the hint of peppermint on the man's breath. "You're probably wondering why I'm here. About my connection to Natalie."

"I am at that." Willard's expression remained intent. His dark eyes offered friendship but also warned not to get too close.

A nervous chuckle issued from Jared's throat. "I met Dillon awhile back fishing."

"Natalie told me about Dillon's disappearance to the river. I saw the boy head off in that direction, but never thought nothing about it. Should have known it'd rattle Natalie's cage. I reckon it would have put my wife in a tizzy too."

"How long have you been married?"

"Cancer took Martha after our fortieth anniversary. She was the best thing that ever happened to me." The man slumped onto a stair step and leaned back on his elbows. "She and this family, that is."

"You're close to Natalie and the kids?" That would explain the man's unannounced entrance into the kitchen. Jared pulled up a chair, hoping to learn more.

"About as close as a bird is to its nest. Their grandfather sold me a piece of his land, when we came home from Vietnam. Not a huge acreage but enough to call my own."

Jared studied the man seated before him with increasing admiration. "Retired?"

"Ought to, but I enjoy work too much. I have me a leather shop at home, and it keeps me busy. Mostly repair work."

Jared noted the man's thick fingers, gnarled from arthritis. "You watched the kids grow up then? I understand their father passed away recently."

The man stared down at his hands and frowned. "Adrian was a good man, as good as his father."

Intrigued by Willard's connections to Natalie's family, Jared's interest grew. "What about their mother?"

"Which one?" Willard seemed to travel back in time. "Natalie's mama didn't have a selfish bone in her body. She was a pretty girl—

like Natalie. When Natalie entered grade school, her mama died. Adrian was mighty tore up after that. The man was always quiet, but after her death there were days when he wouldn't speak to no one."

"That must have been hard on Natalie." Jared rested his arms on his knees and clasped his hands together, hoping the man would go on.

"It wasn't long before Adrian married again—whether from loneliness or to give Natalie a mama, I couldn't say. She was a real doozy, and that marriage only lasted long enough to bring Chelsey and Dillon into the world. Guess you could say Natalie raised those kids, with a little help from friends and family."

Jared's chest clenched at the thought. "Did they attend church?"

Willard rubbed his gray whiskers, considering. "Natalie used to go with her mama before she died. After that, not so much, though my wife took the kids on occasion."

"What about you? Are you a religious man?"

The man grinned as though he'd been caught. "I've been known to enter the doors of a church, but mostly my sanctuary is under the shade of a great big oak tree."

Deciding not to press further, Jared went to the kitchen window and stared out at the glowing yard lights, the night insects haloed around the bright globes. "Think we should go help her?"

"I think if she wanted our help, she would have asked for it."

TWELVE

NATALIE SEARCHED THE DIMLY LIT BARN FOR TOM, WONDERING WHERE he'd slipped off to and why he hadn't returned. She took a deep breath and inhaled the fresh night air, thankful for its calming effect. Peace and quiet. No words, no uncertainty, just wood, dirt, and the sweet smell of hay and horses.

The frogs croaked from a nearby pond, reminding her of the many times her dad had taken them frog hunting. Had she really neglected her family like her sister said?

The repulsive thought had flitted through her mind more than once since her father's death, but she'd been afraid to linger on it too long for fear of the truth.

Yes, she'd stayed away, but not because she didn't love them. Not because she didn't care, but because she yearned to start a new life for herself. Natalie had needed to move on with her dreams, especially now that her rodeo queen days were over. Prove that she could make it on her own — without the ties to her family, without being responsible for anyone but herself.

She shrugged the traitorous feelings away. What was so wrong with not wanting to be responsible for a change?

Her horse nickered from the open stall where he'd been feeding. He probably fancied more grain. Natalie grinned, familiar with how his mind operated. She strode over to Jackson and removed his saddle and blanket, welcoming the familiar scent that floated to her nose. She pressed her forehead to his warm skin, willing the sensation to override the war inside.

Closing her eyes, Natalie allowed her mind to drift to the night six months ago in Vegas when her dad had clapped her on the back and told her to stop dreaming. "It's time to get back to the real world." His words echoed in her mind.

Well, Dad, my life certainly doesn't have room for dreams now, does it?

Though his lecture had been cold, his eyes shone with warmth, and perhaps even a flicker of sorrow. In that remembrance, Natalie realized something that hadn't occurred to her before, and her eyes filled with tears.

That night—that awful night—when she'd been too distraught to appreciate it, had been the last time she'd hugged her father—the last time she'd ever be able to hug him again.

The tightness in Natalie's chest swelled until it felt like it might explode from keeping the anguish inside. She raked her fingers through Jackson's coarse dark mane, yearning relief. Though it was night, she debated climbing onto her faithful gelding and riding bareback through the pastures. She'd give him the rein, with only a crescent moon and stars to guide them over the rocks and hills. He could carry her away with his strong legs and sure feet. With the wind on her face and in her hair, maybe the hurt would stop hurting.

Her plan evaporated as Tom's noisy diesel roared up to the barn. Natalie swiped the moisture from her face and tucked her grief to a safer place for when she had more time and energy. Right now, she needed to be strong, present herself like the rancher her father would want her to be. She straightened to her full height, prepared to give her hired hand a piece of her mind.

"Hey Nat," Tom called from the other side of the barn.

She cringed at the nickname, reserved only for her closest

friends. "Where have you been, Tom? I've been trying to call you for hours."

"Really? Well, you know how it is out here. I must have been in a dead zone." He lifted the straw hat from his head and tossed it in the cab of his truck, his yellow curls matted. "I went into town to get some supper. I told you that before I left."

Natalie picked up a currycomb and commenced to brush her horse's back. "I don't remember any such thing, just like I didn't recall your similar excuse when you were supposed to help us unload the second shipment of summer cattle."

He shut the truck door and shuffled forward. "I explained about that too. You can't blame me for an emergency."

Natalie shifted so that Jackson stood between her and the hired hand. "I can and I will. I've given this lots of thought, Tom, and I've made a decision. Your position on the Double-A is over, effective immediately. You're never around when I need you, so it makes no sense to waste hard-earned money on a hand who doesn't work. You can stop at the house to get your final pay. I'll have it ready before you leave."

Tom's eyes narrowed into disbelieving slants. "You're making a big mistake, firing the only manpower you've got on this ranch."

Natalie stifled a laugh and slid the comb over Jackson's rump. "Men are a dime a dozen in this county. If I need one, I know where to find one." She hardened her gaze, hoping Tom would see she meant every word. When he stepped backward, she allowed herself freedom to breathe naturally. No way did she want to get in a tussle with this guy, though she was confident she could hold her own.

"Okay, I'll go. If you're sure that's what you want." He jammed his hands in his front jean pockets. "But since you're not giving me any advance notice, you better make that last paycheck twice the usual amount. For my trouble."

She clenched the currycomb and debated throwing it at him. Or better yet, she could hop on Jackson and chase the yellow-bellied cowboy off their land with a switch. "I have a better idea. You leave without a fuss, or I'll make sure every rancher in Charris County knows what a loser you are, and you won't work in this part of Kansas for years. Then we'll see how far your excuses get you."

The man scowled but didn't offer any more resistance. Once he'd disappeared into the darkness, Natalie put Jackson to pasture, then headed for the house, glad to see Willard and Jared's vehicles parked in front. Should Tom get a wild hair and decide to cause trouble, there would be strength in numbers—even if those numbers included a broken-down war veteran and a pale-faced preacher.

The two sat at the kitchen table, coffee mugs in hand. They perked up at her entrance, but Natalie kept walking.

"What's your hurry?' Willard called to her from behind.

"I fired Tom."

And now she had to pay him.

Minutes later Tom knocked on their front door. Natalie tore the freshly signed check from her father's ranch account and hurried to the living room, hoping Willard and Jared would stay in the kitchen while she handled this awkward task. She'd never fired anyone before, and a part of her felt guilty for putting this man out of a job.

Before she turned the metal handle of the front door, Tom barged in. His syrupy expression appeared borderline volatile. "You sure you won't change your mind about firing me?"

Natalie held the check out for him. "Here's the last of your pay—and don't worry, I'm being generous." She managed to keep her voice from wavering.

The hired hand cursed and banged the door against the wall, jarring the house with its vibration. "Why can't you be reasonable? All I did was take a few hours for myself, and you're calling it a crime. Don't you know a man has to have time off?"

She didn't want to argue and had no reason to do so. "Time off, yes, but occasionally, you do have to show up for work."

"Your daddy would have known better than to fire me." With every word, his voice escalated. He moved closer and raised his finger so that it almost touched her cheek. He stood so close she could smell onion on his breath. "You're making a big mistake. And you'll regret it, watch and see."

THIRTEEN

Jared tuned in to the escalating words from the next room, though muffled from the walls. Getting fired was never good, but for a man like Tom, being fired by a woman would sting even worse. "Think we should help her?"

Willard growled. "I don't suppose Natalie would cry for help if she had a knife to her throat." He scooted from the kitchen chair, and as he rounded the corner to the living room, his voice thundered from within. "Her only mistake was not firing you sooner." Willard spat the words out hard and powerful while Jared watched from behind.

"Stay out of this, old timer." Tom's arrogant gaze darted to Natalie. "Are these the men you're gonna hire to take my place?"

The ranch hand cackled, and Willard took a step forward. Jared clutched Williard's arm to hold him back.

A natural protective instinct kicked in, and Jared stepped forward to position himself between Natalie and the cowboy. His pulse thumped with adrenaline, but he forced himself to remain calm.

"Come on now, no one wants trouble," he said, hoping to defuse the situation.

"What is this? A church service?"

Ignoring the taunt, Jared inched closer, now eye-level with the irate man. "Let's not make this worse than it is. I'm sure you had your reasons for not showing up for work, and Natalie has hers for letting you go. Getting riled won't change things."

"Maybe not, but it'll make me feel better," Tom rasped back, his chin cocked like a banty rooster.

"I'm sure that'll happen when you cash your check." Jared attempted to guide the cowboy out the door, praying he wouldn't resist. If Tom turned violent, Jared would have no choice but to fight the man—and he'd lose.

"Back off." Tom shoved Jared's hand away and made a fist. "I don't need no preacher telling me what to do. I've had to listen to this here woman, and that's bad enough."

The cowboy was in Jared's face now, his nostrils flaring. Jared swallowed his fear. Though the two were the same height, Tom had more strength and inclination. Not good odds.

"I'm not a fighting man, Tom. But I'm not going to stand here and let you talk bad about Miss Adams. You'd better leave quietly before someone says or does something he'll regret. Then if you want to talk about it later, you can visit me in church on Sunday."

Tom's lips curled in disgust. "You're kidding. You think I'm going to hang out at your church." He flung his hands in the air and backed down the porch steps into the darkness. "I don't need this. No job's worth putting up with this crap."

When he got halfway down the front path, he turned and pointed his finger at them, his gesture lit by a yard light. "Don't talk to any ranchers about me, either. 'Cause if I hear you've been telling lies, I'll take you to court faster than a hound after a rabbit."

Prepared to chase the man off the property, Jared clenched his fist as though he carried Moses' staff in his hand. "Do what you have to do, but don't come back here again."

NATALIE MANAGED A SMILE FOR JARED WHEN HE RETURNED TO THE PORCH. He'd surprised her. Not only had he taken an explosive situation and turned it on its heel, but he'd done so without the use of violence or force. For that, she had to give him credit. "You handled that like a pro. Are you okay?"

"Did you see him take off? Like the devil was after him." Jared peered over his shoulder, and Natalie noted the bobbing headlights of Tom's truck as it roared down the dirt road.

"Good riddance." Natalie scowled. "Only now I don't have a hired hand."

Willard shook his head. "You're better off. Tom was a disgrace to anyone who calls himself a cowboy. I have no idea why your daddy hired him unless he felt sorry for the boy."

That might be true, but it didn't solve Natalie's situation. The haying season would start in a month. Pastures and cattle to tend. Plus a queen clinic she'd promised to help with. "I planned to brand cattle Saturday. How am I going to vaccinate three hundred calves with only Dillon and Chelsey for help?"

"You can count me in," Willard said. "I'm not a young buck, but I can wield a branding iron just fine. I'll check around and see if we can scrounge up a few more hands."

Natalie smiled at the man, once again hating her dependence on others. "I'm much obliged for your help, Willard. And for yours too." Her eyes darted to Jared's. "I appreciate how you handled Tom. It takes courage to stand up to men like that without getting into a fight."

"Thanks, but the courage wasn't mine."

Natalie heard the humility in Jared's voice but didn't understand what he meant.

He cleared his throat. "I should go so you can get to bed. I'm sure you've had a long day."

"I need to get home too." Willard held out his hand to Jared. "It was nice to make your acquaintance."

"Yours too. Stop by my office sometime, and we'll discuss the deep meanings of prose and poetry." Jared chuckled and turned to Natalie. "I'll plan on seeing Chelsey after school tomorrow?"

Natalie frowned at the reminder. One more item to put on her list, as though she didn't have enough to think about.

THE NEXT MORNING, NATALIE SET OUT A BOX OF CEREAL AND FRESH strawberries for the kids to eat before the bus arrived. Chelsey shuffled into the kitchen wearing cowboy boots and a jean skirt so short it probably violated the school dress code. "Glad you're up. I was afraid I might have to haul you out of bed."

Chelsey scowled. "Why wouldn't I be?" She picked up a strawberry and examined it before taking a bite.

"You haven't forgotten about your arrangement with Jared, have you?"

"*Pastor* Jared, you mean?"

Natalie's eyes narrowed. "He wants to meet you at the church after school. No dawdling or cruising with friends, understand? You'll work two hours, and then I'll pick you up."

"What? You mean I can't drive?"

"Your driving is suspended until I say otherwise."

"What about Sarah?"

"I'm not in charge of Sarah. It'll be a wonder if her folks let her have anything to do with you after the stunt you pulled last night."

"It was only a few beers."

Natalie faced the kitchen sink and drew a deep breath. Did she have the willpower or knowledge to raise a teenager? Tattoos, alcohol, sex, obvious disdain. What might Chelsey try next, drugs? She wanted to strangle the stupid kid and knock some sense into her head. Instead, she forced herself to be calm. *Think good thoughts, Think like a parent.* She returned to the table and sat down, willing herself to step into her father's boots. "You want to drink beer? Fine, you can buy as many six-packs as you want when you're twenty-one."

Chelsey rolled her eyes and chewed her fingernail, polished an iridescent green.

Dillon trudged into the kitchen. "You two aren't fighting again, are you?" He laid his backpack on the table, then poured rice cereal into one of the bowls. "That's all you do anymore. How would that make Dad feel?"

As usual, Dillon's insight astounded Natalie. It also gave her a new perspective on the situation.

"Dillon's right. We're family. Now that Dad's gone, the three of us need to get along." She reached for Chelsey's fingers and inspected her nubbed-off nails. Though tempted, she refrained from admonishing her sister about taking better care of her hands. The truce had to start somewhere and it may as well start with her.

Once the kids left for school, Natalie saddled Jackson to ride through the pastures and check the summer steers and fences. It would be quicker to use her father's four-wheeler or even the pickup, but this morning she longed for the squeak of leather beneath her and the weight of the reins on her fingertips.

Other than supplying salt blocks and water, her contracted grazing duties included keeping count of the cattle, maintaining the fences and windmills, and caring for sick animals. With over three thousand acres to cover, it was a full-time job, and that didn't include their personal herd of three hundred cow-calf pairs, which they would brand this weekend. She had no idea how she would do the work on her own. Thankfully, her brother and sister only had two more days of school, but she still might need to hire help. That meant spending more money from an already dwindling account — something she wanted to avoid if at all possible.

Hours later after riding fence on two of the pastures, she stopped on top of Flat Ridge, which overlooked the bordering north and east sections of their property. From here, she could see for miles. It was one of her favorite places, especially this time of year when purple beardtongue, larkspur, and wild indigo dotted the prairie in profusion. Below her, the draws and gullies extended into Sage Creek, now full from the wet season they'd had.

She sat atop Jackson and counted the cattle. Clicking him forward, she moved to get a better view of the steers as they grazed below. When finished recording the numbers, she returned her notepad to her shirt pocket and watched a hawk circle the blue sky above.

Its loud screech filled her with a loneliness that settled in her soul. Although she loved ranching and the Flint Hills, it was a solitary life, and so unlike the one she'd imagined for herself.

She closed her eyes and saw Ryan Frazier's handsome face. He'd reminded her of a movie star, with his gorgeous blue eyes, dimpled smile, and straight blonde hair swept to one side. Young and ready for adventure, Natalie had allowed the professional commentator to smooth talk his way into her life and capture her heart. As the wind whistled in her ear, she remembered his words of hope and a future ...

Bright lights shone down on Natalie at the Dodge City Rodeo as she waited at the arena gate, ready to make her final appearance before they announced the new Miss Rodeo Kansas.

"Don't be sad, Nat. This is the beginning of great things for us," Ryan said, his hand reaching up to the saddle for hers. "You finish off your year as Miss Rodeo Kansas and then if all goes well, you'll hold the national title. After that, we'll go places, you and I—Montana, Australia, Hawaii."

"The first place I'll go is back to school," she said, trying to quell the hope stirring in her heart. She couldn't imagine anything better than spending the rest of her life with the man who'd followed her to practically every rodeo on her tour this past year—who'd whispered words of love she would never forget.

"Sure, but you'll have breaks, and we'll have the summer rodeo cir-

cuits." He kissed her hand, and the soft touch of his lips sent a tremor of tingles up her arm.

"Right now I need to concentrate on this last run in the arena and give my attention to this new horse I'm on. I don't want a repeat of that bucking bronc I rode a few weeks ago."

"I won't let him hurt you, Nat, I promise." Ryan's eyes twinkled up at her, and the weight of that promise floated in the air as light as a feather.

Then a few months later, the man's promise dropped dead at her feet and crushed her heart into a thousand pieces. Yet another painful memory of Las Vegas . . .

Natalie opened her eyes to the bright green pasture below, still grieved by the broken promises. Pressing her spurs into Jackson's side, she nudged him down the steep ridge. What would Ryan think of her life now?

FOURTEEN

Jared peered through the office window as a red Corvette pulled under the church awning, its back bumper plastered with colorful rodeo slogans and advertisements. Chelsey stepped out of the passenger side, and he noted the driver, a scruffy looking boy wearing a ball cap.

"We're still waiting for Sarah, so come on in and have a seat," he said when she entered through the front doors. "I see you found a ride."

Her brown eyes darted to his, and he read the guilt there. "A friend dropped me off."

He continued to clear his desk of the papers he'd been working on, wishing his secretary would return soon. "Does your sister know about him?"

"Yeah, she's cool with it. We've been dating for a while now." Chelsey propped herself against the corner of the couch and crossed her ankles.

Jared recognized her green boots from the night before. He wondered what Natalie thought about the boy. "An upperclassman?"

The girl studied the tips of her fingers, avoiding eye contact. "He graduated this month. So, what do you have planned for Sarah and me? We gonna scrub floors?"

Jared chuckled. "I don't think that's the sort of mission work Mr. Trevor has in mind."

"How old are you anyway?" Chelsey rose from the couch and scooted across the room to lean against his desk. "You don't look much older than my sister. What should I call you? Jared? Mr. Jared? Pastor J?" She grinned.

"Pastor Jared will be fine." He rolled his chair from the desk to create space between him and the short-skirted teen. At that moment, Mrs. Hildebrand walked in, her gaze taking in the girl's position on his desk. She sniffed in disapproval but didn't say a word.

Jared stood and moved to the hallway. "To answer your question, I'm probably several years older than your sister. What is she, around twenty-two or three?" Quite young to be harnessed with such responsibility, yet he knew from the few times they'd spoken that she was more than up to the challenge.

Chelsey shrugged. "Something like that."

A car pulled up to the church, and the other teen traipsed in. "Sorry I'm late. I had to stay after school to finish a test."

Jared waited for Sarah at his office door. "Well, you're here now, so I guess we can get started."

He led the girls to a small storage room packed with boxes and grocery sacks of nonperishable items donated to the church's food pantry. "Mr. Trevor wants you to go through all of this and stack the cans and boxes on the shelves according to the labels, just like in a grocery store."

The two girls groaned.

"This is going to take forever," Chelsey said.

Jared checked his watch. "You have two hours. I'll have Mrs. Hildebrand get you started, and if you need anything else, I'll be in my office."

Forty minutes crept by while Jared outlined his next sermon. In that time, Carol Trevor came in with two more boxes of food. He waved hello and pointed the youth leader down the hall. "They're in the storage room, working like Egyptian slaves," he teased.

Indeed, each instance he'd checked on the girls, they'd been hard at work organizing the room, despite the giggles that drifted to his office. Once his outline was finished, he went to evaluate the storage room and carried a set of empty cardboard boxes with him. Rows of neatly stacked food greeted him.

Chelsey stood with her hands on her hips, looking proud of her accomplishment. "How'd we do, Pastor J?"

"Not bad for two juvenile delinquents." He grinned and set one of the boxes on a table. "I understand a member of your community had a house burn down a few days ago. His family could probably use some assistance, so I thought we could pack them some food."

"That's a great idea, and then I can deliver it to them on my way home." Carol smiled, and Sarah's face brightened. The two immediately selected several items from the shelves to put in the box.

"Don't you want to help?" Jared asked Chelsey, noting how she hung back in the corner.

The girl shrugged. "I'd just get in the way."

Jared wondered at her change in mood. "How many children do the Sheldon's have?"

"Three," Sarah said. "Two in grade school and one in ..."

"Sixth grade," Chelsey finished for her. "She's in the same class as Dillon."

"They'd probably appreciate some macaroni and cheese?" He gathered three containers of the pasta mix and placed them in the box. "What else?"

Before long, both boxes were full. Jared checked his watch, and seeing that they still had time, he had the girls carry the boxes to Mrs. Trevor's Suburban.

"We chose this activity because we think there's a lesson to be learned from it," Carol said as she opened the back doors to her vehicle.

"That's right," Jared continued. "We don't know why you got into that beer last night, or why you decided to come to the youth meeting intoxicated, but we do know this—everything we do in life has consequences, whether good or not. No matter how bad we think things are, there is always someone else worse off. Take the Sheldons for example." He lifted one of the heavy boxes into the back of the Suburban.

"One night they woke up to a house full of flames," Carol said. "The mom had left a candle burning, and it tipped over while they were sleeping. A simple mistake, but look at the consequences. All of them got out except one—their four-year-old daughter."

Jared watched as Chelsey swiped her eyes with the back of her hand. He knew it was a hard lesson for the girl to hear, but this was exactly the reaction he'd hoped for.

NATALIE RETURNED TO THE HOUSE, HER LEGS AND BACK STIFF AFTER EIGHT hours of riding fence and counting cattle.

"Where have you been?" Dillon sat at the kitchen table, eating a sandwich.

She set her cowboy hat on the counter, drawn to the smell of peanut butter. "Out in the pasture. Have you done your homework?" She reached for a slice of bread to make her own sandwich. The apple and crackers she'd eaten for lunch had long worn off, and her stomach roiled with hunger.

"Did you forget you were supposed to pick up Chelsey at church?"

Natalie checked the clock above the refrigerator and cursed. Slathering peanut butter on the piece of bread, she quickly folded it into a sandwich. "Come on, Chelsey's going to kill me for making her wait."

Twenty minutes later, she and Dillon pulled into the church

parking lot and met Jared as he was getting into his car. Natalie rolled down her window. "I'm sorry I'm late. I got caught up with pasture work and lost track of time." No way would she admit she'd forgotten about Chelsey's service commitment. Not with her sister glaring at her from the back seat of Jared's car.

Jared offered a courteous smile. "Do you have a few minutes to talk?"

Natalie nodded and parked her truck.

"Did you see the look on Chelsey's face?" Dillon bounced on the bench seat, making the wire springs squeak beneath him. "You are so dead."

Natalie shot her brother a warning glance. She could imagine Dillon teasing Chelsey, causing the situation to go from bad to worse. "You'd best keep your mouth quiet. I don't need any extra trouble, understand?"

His bouncing stopped as he set his arms in front of his chest and slouched in his seat. Natalie eased from behind the steering wheel and met her sister as she transferred her backpack from Jared's car to the truck. Chelsey brushed past with a sneer.

"How'd it go today?" Natalie walked up to Jared, fully aware of the man's black attire. "I mean, other than my failure to pick up my sister?"

He held a water bottle in one hand and twisted the cap with the other. "You're here now, so don't worry about it."

Natalie chided herself for putting the preacher in such an awkward position, fully aware of the scrutiny he might suffer for offering a young girl a ride home. "It won't happen again, I assure you."

His brows furrowed. "I'm more concerned about you. You seem stressed."

She leaned against his car. Stress didn't come close to describing what she felt inside. But how could she unload on this man again?

"Need a friend to talk to?" His voice balm to her ears, Natalie didn't require further inducement.

"I'm in over my head. It took all day to cover a quarter of the pastures. At this rate, I'll spend sixty hours a week on ranch work alone, only to come home to dirty laundry and a mailbox full of bills. Then I have to deal with the kids." She touched her fingers to her throat, desperation threatening to choke her. "I can't do it. I feel like I'm going to suffocate."

"Take a deep breath, Natalie. It's going to be all right." With his free hand Jared took hold of her elbow and captured her with his dark eyes, assuring her everything would be okay. "You don't have to carry this yoke alone. You have friends, and you have God."

Natalie's gaze broke from his embrace and traveled to the church in front of her. Made of limestone like her father's barn, its foundation was sure to be strong. And though bright and beautiful, the stained glass windows depicted signs of hope and peace, but they also blocked a person from viewing inside. "I hardly see how God is going to take care of the ranch for me. Or handle Chelsey's problems either, for that matter."

He released her elbow. "You don't like talking about God, do you? And it offends you that I'm a pastor."

She stepped away from his car and paced the length of the vehicle. "You could have mentioned your occupation the day we met."

"You're right, I should have told you. I have to wonder though, if you would have given me the time of day if I'd admitted I was a pastor. What happened in your life to turn you so against religion?"

Natalie gritted her teeth. "Nothing happened. Maybe that's my problem."

Unable to face Jared, she concentrated on a pair of bluebirds fluttering in and out of a nearby birdhouse. The man's eyes bore into her, all sympathetic and kind, as though she needed his help and wouldn't survive without it.

"I've been to church." The words flew from her mouth. "I've watched people at altar calls who gave their lives to Jesus, who swore it made a difference … but honestly, I don't get it."

"You mean you don't want to get it." Jared swallowed the last of his water, then squeezed the empty bottle until it crackled between his fingers. "God calls on those who listen. I'd love to help you, Natalie, but you have to want the help. It's like those bluebirds over there. Sometimes you have to completely stop what you're doing in order to hear their song."

She watched him saunter back to the church with his head down and his hands in his pockets. Who did he think he was to speak to her that way? And what did he expect? For her to break out in song and admit all her faults and weaknesses, concede everything she'd ever done wrong and beg for God's help and forgiveness? Well, Jared Logan could wait for hell to freeze over as far as she was concerned. She'd made it this far in life without anyone's help, she'd manage her current troubles too—and would be all the wiser for it.

FIFTEEN

"I HEARD YOU HAD SOME EXCITEMENT HERE WEDNESDAY NIGHT." GEORGE Hobart's thick frame hovered over Jared's desk early Saturday morning.

Jared glanced at the three grim-faced elders, prepared to give account for the recent problems with the youth, though he could think of a hundred things he'd rather be doing this weekend.

Bob Douglas cleared his throat and took a seat on the couch. "We hated to call a meeting, but after talking to Mr. Sanders, we thought it best to get your version."

"I assure you I handled the problem with discretion." Jared loathed his need for explanation. "As soon as I learned of the alcohol, I took the girls to my office—away from the other kids."

"Were the others aware the girls had been drinking?"

Jared rubbed his chin. "According to Mrs. Trevor there was a lot of whispering."

"What about this other girl with Sarah Sanders?" George asked, inches from Jared's face. "What do you know about her?"

"Sarah brought a friend to the meeting—Chelsey Adams. I'm sure you've heard how Chelsey recently lost her father in a tractor accident. I met Chelsey's family two weeks ago."

"Adams? That's the rodeo queen gal, isn't it?" Carl spoke up from the other side of the room.

Jared leaned back in his chair. "Chelsey's sister. The three of them have no family, no church home. Considering their troubles, I thought it best to handle the matter quietly."

"You were trying to protect the family." George crossed his arms and nodded his approval to the other men.

"I've visited them a couple of times," Jared continued. "I believe it's our responsibility to help them if we can."

"Mrs. Sanders is none too happy about your form of discipline." Bob shifted on the couch. "She thinks Sarah got pulled into this mess and believes you're trying to make an example of her daughter by punishing her the same as the Adams' girl."

Jared exhaled slowly. "Sarah and Chelsey were guilty of the same act, no matter whose idea it was to take that first drink. The Trevors thought a little mission work might help them focus on things more meaningful."

"You're not being too hard on Sarah, considering her good reputation?" Carl frowned.

"She should have thought about her reputation before she came to a youth meeting half-tanked." Jared went on to explain his plans for involving the girls in Vacation Bible School. After ten more minutes of questions and answers, the three men left, seemingly satisfied.

Jared drummed his fingers on the desk and stared out the window at the blue sky. The spring air called to him, a perfect morning for fishing. He'd already gone over his sermon notes, and now that his elders' meeting was finished, he had a mind to gather his tackle and head for the river. Then he remembered Natalie's plan to brand cattle today. Guilt settled in. He recalled their last conversation here at the church.

Heated.

Though he couldn't deny the woman's beauty, it took a backseat to her hard-headedness—her desire to conquer the world with her own two hands. He probably shouldn't have been so hard on her, but the woman seemed to have a negative effect on his logic.

Should he go fishing or help Natalie and her family vaccinate cattle? Jared glanced at his brown loafers and flexed his fingers, growling at the lingering doubt. He might not remember everything about working cattle and might very well make a fool of himself, but he was still a man in the prime of his life. Despite whatever differences Natalie and he had, she needed the help. Nothing but pride stood in his way.

NATALIE LIFTED HER HAT TO WIPE HER BROW WITH HER SHIRTSLEEVE, STILL amazed at how many friends and neighbors had shown up to help with the branding. With just enough notice the night before, she and Chelsey prepared breakfast for a crew of twelve who arrived on their doorstep around four that morning. Together they'd served hot biscuits and gravy, scrambled eggs, sausage, and bacon to the hungry workers. Afterward, they gathered their horses in the dark corral behind her father's towering limestone barn.

Now late morning, Natalie gazed at the many helpers of all ages and size. Bruce and Ray Bennett, a father and son team, had driven over thirty miles to heel and drag calves to the ground crews, as did the Edwards brothers and Charles Knight, a good friend of her father's. Gene and Lori Carpenter helped Dillon and Chelsey with the branding and vaccinating along with their two kids, who sometimes climbed on the corral fence and watched.

Others included Willard at the sorting gates, and country veterinarian Mattie McCray, along with her husband, Gil, a former NFL quarterback. John McCray came too, although because of his health, he mostly stood behind and handed people things. Natalie first met the McCrays when training for the Miss Rodeo Kansas competition and remembered well the day Gil proposed to Mattie in the rodeo arena. His declaration of love had caused many hearts to flutter that day, including hers.

Although overcome with gratitude that these people cared enough to be here, her heart ached from memories of past brandings with her dad. Blue sky above, dust fogging the ground, the sound of calves bawling, and the occasional curse from one who'd missed his roping target. So much the same, yet so many changes. She waited for Gil to flank the next calf to the dirt, then pressed her knee into its shoulder while Dillon stretched out its back leg to keep it immobile.

With two ground crews working at the same time, they had fallen into a pattern so efficient and skilled it took less than a minute for them to perform the tasks on each calf. In tandem precision, Mattie plunged the hypodermic needle into the calf's flesh as the others did their part. The new steer let out a haunting bellow as the stench of burnt hair and hide hung in the air after the branding.

"How many of our calves have we done?" Dillon asked, his face streaked with dust and sweat.

"Over half. Why don't you trade off with Brody and rope for awhile?" Natalie eased from her position and looked up to see another neighbor approach from the far side of the barn. As he neared, she realized it was Jared. Dressed in faded jeans, work boots and a gray T-shirt, he stopped at the corral and waved.

"What brings you here?" She met him at the gate and studied the shadow of his face beneath the long-rimmed ball cap.

"You seem surprised." His brown eyes crinkled into a smile.

She caught the hint of his musky cologne as it wrestled with the strong odor of cattle, horses and dirt. "After our last visit, I didn't figure you'd come around again."

Amusement stole through the side of his mouth. "What can I say? My conscience wouldn't allow me to enjoy a peaceful day at the river while you were out here toiling in the sun. What can I do to help?"

She glanced at his hands and remembered their soft touch. "Have you ever worked cattle?"

"I helped my granddad every summer."

"That's right . . . I forgot you were on a quest to relive your childhood." She opened the green aluminum gate, wondering where to station the man so he'd have the least chance of getting hurt. "Can you rope, or would you feel safer on the ground?"

"I can ride, although I haven't done so —"

"— since you were a boy?" She couldn't keep the lilt from pervading her voice. "You can ride my horse. Jackson's used to strangers and will tolerate most anything."

She watched Jared study the other cowboys who were roping and dragging calves to the butane branding fire. A hint of panic pulled on his jaw.

"If you'd rather, you can help with the inoculations." She indicated the second ground crew beside her own — all working together when necessary.

"No, this will be fine. Just point me in the right direction, and Jackson and I will start roping us some doggies."

Unsure whether he made fun or was serious, Natalie led him to her gray gelding tied outside the holding pen. She watched as he struggled with the reins and stirrups and debated helping him but decided to see if he could hold his own. Minutes later, he rode past Willard at the gate, jerking Jackson's reins unnecessarily as he fumbled with his coiled lariat. Once he got the rope situated, he swung a loop and it twisted over his head. Tossing it anyway, he missed the calf by a good stretch of the imagination. *No surprise, but at least he isn't tugging on Jackson's bit any longer.*

When she looked up from her work the next time, Jared was joking with Bruce Bennett, who was showing him how to swing a rope. She shook her head then tackled her next steer to the ground. After two more, she heard cheers from the riders and peered up to see Jared had caught a calf by its hind legs and was dragging it to the branding fire.

"Looks like he's getting the hang of it." Willard came to her side, all smiles.

"More like beginner's luck." She caught the dark strands of hair fluttering in her face and pinned them under her straw cowboy hat.

"You don't like the young pastor much, do you?"

Her eyes darted to Willard's, her own guarded. "Do you?"

Willard scrunched his mouth and nodded. "He's a likeable guy, and he came to help. Hard to fault a man willing to give up his free time, especially when it's painfully obvious he hasn't got a clue what he's doing." He chuckled and mopped his face with a blue bandana.

It figured that Willard would like Jared. They both shared a fondness for poetry. Natalie couldn't help but be wary around the man, with all of his meddling, first with Dillon and now Chelsey. Like he was some kind of lifesaver or something. "Kinda makes you wonder what he wants though, doesn't it?"

"He's here to help, so let him help." Willard turned his attention back to Jared, and together they assessed the man's attempt to recoil his rope after his last throw. It hung in a tangled mess at Jackson's feet. "Then again, in the words of Emerson, 'the only way to have a friend is to be one.'"

As the morning wore on, Natalie kept track of Jared's progress. By the time they'd finished, they'd worked over three hundred calves. Out of those, the young pastor might have roped twelve or thirteen, but every little bit helped, she supposed. She dusted the dirt from her jeans and went to meet him as he dismounted her horse.

"Guess you got along okay with Jackson." She watched as Jared's feet hit the ground, his legs a bit unsteady.

"I hope I didn't abuse him too much." He offered a meek smile and clutched Jackson's reins.

Unable to ignore his humble remark, she motioned toward the house where Willard was already grilling hamburgers. "You're welcome to join us for a late lunch. It's not much, but it's our way of saying thanks."

Jared straightened to his full height and stretched his arms and shoulders. "Sounds good, I'm starving."

She took the reins from his hands, noticing the red sunburn on his neck and forearms where his T-shirt left his skin exposed.

"I forgot my sun lotion." He studied his arms and hands, as though guessing her thoughts. "Next time I'll know to dress like a cowboy."

Natalie led Jackson outside the pen and hitched him to a post, all the while fighting back the image of Jared in a long-sleeved western shirt and black felt hat—a color that would suit him quite well as long as it wasn't part of a clergy outfit.

SIXTEEN

Jared followed Natalie to the house and extended his elbows over his head. He couldn't believe how much his arms ached from throwing a rope the past two hours, not to mention the stiffness that had settled in his lower body. Hovering over a desk all day couldn't compare to sitting in a saddle. He'd never again mistake cowboying as a passive sport that didn't require athletic ability.

After washing in the utility room with the rest of the crew, he joined Willard at the charcoal grill, the afternoon sun beating down on their heads.

"You did pretty well out there." Willard flipped a burger, the blazing fire licking up the grease as it hit the coals.

A trail of mesquite smoke pursued Jared, and his stomach rumbled. "Not bad for a greenhorn, you mean?" He glanced at his raw calloused hands, and his embarrassment seeped through as he noted the real cowboys visiting beneath the shade trees. No way could he compare to the Edwards' brothers or to Bruce and Ray Bennett — men who made their living from the Flint Hills. They probably considered him a fool for trying, which shamed him even more. He swallowed the inadequacy that rose from his gut and tried instead to make light of the experience. "It's a day I'll not soon forget, that's for sure."

"At least not until your backside stops hurting." Willard grinned, and his white teeth stood out against his dark, leathery skin. "Sleep is sweet for the man who labors long." He shot Jared a knowing look and chuckled.

Dillon rushed up to the two men with a platter in his hand. "Chelsey wants to know when the burgers will be ready." He eyed the sizzling patties on the grill, looking nearly as famished as Jared felt.

"Tell her to give me another ten minutes." Willard jabbed a charcoaled bratwurst with a long handled fork and laid it on the boy's plate. "Taste this and let me know if it's cooked enough."

"Gee thanks." Dillon let it cool for a few seconds then picked it up and bit off half, causing his cheeks to bulge. He held out the empty plate. "Got any more?"

Willard smiled great big. "Guess it passed inspection?"

Dillon nodded. "Are you guys going to the rodeo tonight?" he asked as soon as he'd swallowed enough to speak.

Jared shrugged, having heard lots of talk about the event at the café. "I don't know. I have church in the morning. Are you?" He stared down at the boy's freckled cheeks, remembering the fun he'd had when his granddad drove him to the local rodeo back home.

"If I can talk Nat into taking me. I heard Chelsey and her arguing about it earlier, but I don't think she's going to let Chelsey go 'cause of all the trouble she's gotten into lately." He said this as though it were old news. "What about you, Willard? You going?"

Willard shook his head. "I don't suppose I'll have a mind to do anything this evening besides sit in my recliner and maybe read a book. I haven't gone to a rodeo in years—but that ain't no reason you young folks can't go and enjoy it."

The hopeful spark in the boy's eyes dwindled, and his dejection tugged at Jared's heart. Dillon had been through more than most adults these past few weeks, and the poor kid needed to get out and have some fun. Chelsey and Natalie too. An idea began to form, and Jared scratched his chin as he considered the possibilities. "Let me talk to your sister and see what her plans are. Maybe we can work out a way for you to go."

Willard's eyebrows puckered. Then he seized the platter from the boy's hands. "Best tell Chelsey to be setting out her food. These here burgers are just about ready to serve." Once he shooed Dillon to the house, he peered over at Jared, his eyes narrow slits.

"Natalie won't like you interfering, if that's what you have a mind to do."

"The boy misses his dad." Jared challenged the old man.

Willard thrust the platter toward Jared without a word.

"I'm not condemning Natalie." Jared held the plate steady while Willard piled the cooked meat onto it. "I know she has a lot on her mind. I just want to give the boy a chance to have some fun. She doesn't realize how much he needs it."

Willard smiled then, and Jared caught a glimpse of understanding. "If you get her to see what we see, you'll be accomplishing a mighty task, indeed."

NATALIE LIFTED THE BOWL OF POTATO SALAD FROM THE KITCHEN COUNTER and grabbed a bag of chips on her way outside. Mattie and Lori followed with more food in tow. Now the end of May, the temperature outside had turned hot and humid. "Thank goodness for air conditioners," Natalie said as she made her way to the porch.

"We've had ours on for a month already," Mattie admitted with a chuckle. "When Gil comes inside after work, he wants to cool off fast—unlike John, who prefers the attic fan. It's caused more than one argument since we've been married."

"Dad was like that too." Natalie's father believed fresh air, even if it was ninety degrees outside, was better for a person than air condi-tioning. Now that he was gone, she guessed it wouldn't be an issue.

When Natalie reached the bottom of the porch steps, a hand pressed against her shoulder. She turned to see Mattie's green eyes, soft and thoughtful.

"We're real sorry about your dad. If you kids need anything, be sure and let us know. Gil and I don't live that far away, and we'd be happy to help."

"That goes for us too," Lori said. "If there's anything we can do to make your life easier, all you have to do is call."

Natalie smiled at the women who were both nearing the age of thirty. She considered Willard's words from earlier that if you wanted a friend you had to be one. "Your being here means a lot. We would have struggled to get done today without the extra help."

"That's what friends are for." Mattie grinned and Natalie took an instant liking to the red-haired veterinarian.

They made their way across the yard to the picnic table where Chelsey arranged the items with care beneath the shade tree. Last night Natalie and her sister had stayed up late preparing this lunch, making baked beans, potato salad, and coleslaw. Though Natalie knew how to cook, it wasn't something she enjoyed like Chelsey, who had baked two apple pies and a chocolate cake to go with ev-erything else.

"You did good, sis." Natalie hugged her sister, pleased with the results and proud of the teen's efforts. It felt nice to get along after all the bad incidents this past month. Maybe everything would work out okay, after all.

While the others went to get more food, Chelsey stepped away from the table, chewing on a fingernail. "You think it'll be enough?"

Natalie took in the large spread before them and noted the flies now swarming around the food. "We should be more worried about the insects eating it." She tried to shoo the flies away, but they seemed to multiply by twos.

Willard and Jared arrived with the hamburgers and sausages, and the others soon joined them. "Would you like me to ask the blessing?" Jared eyed Natalie, and she reluctantly nodded, not sure why this man annoyed her so. When he finished the prayer, she retreated further into the shade, allowing the guests to fill their plates.

She inwardly groaned when Jared followed. Could he not see that she wanted a little privacy? A little time to relax?

"Chelsey makes a good hostess." He stood next to her, his gray T-shirt spotted with sweat.

Natalie nodded. Perhaps if she remained quiet, he would get the message and go away.

He kicked the ground with the heel of his work boot and rubbed the dark growth already shadowing his jaw. "Dillon mentioned going to a rodeo tonight. It sounds like fun. Are you and the kids planning to attend?"

Withering under his scrutiny, Natalie fanned her face with her hand. As a former Miss Rodeo Kansas, a major supporter of all things rodeo, she couldn't ignore his question though she wanted to. Nor could she refrain from attending the rodeo. She would be expected to go, but more than that, she wanted to be there.

"Maybe," she said in a voice so low she hoped he wouldn't hear.

He leaned closer, as though straining to catch the words in his ear. "Maybe yes or maybe no?" he asked.

She shrugged, not willing to admit her plans.

"Well then, maybe I could take you and the kids," he suggested. "Or if that doesn't work, perhaps you'd let me take Dillon. I haven't been to a rodeo in years. It'd do your brother good to get out and forget some of his troubles."

Appalled at where his trail of questions had led, Natalie cleared her throat and readjusted her ponytail. "I hardly think so. Dillon doesn't need you for a babysitter. If he goes anywhere, he'll go with me."

"You'll take him, then?"

She folded her arms across her chest, feeling backed against a barn door. "Why is it any of your business if we go or not? Just because you have Chelsey under your thumb doesn't mean the rest of us have to report in every day."

"Maybe if you did report in, you wouldn't feel so overwhelmed." He looked down his nose at her with a condescending air. "It's sometimes referred to as sharing one's load."

His tone raked across her nerves, and her mouth gaped.

"Relax." He latched on to her elbow and steered her toward the picnic table. "I know you're hungry."

A south breeze gusted toward them, carrying with it the man's sweet musky scent muddled with sweat. That she found the smell not the least bit distasteful irritated her even more. She yanked her elbow from his grasp and distanced herself on the opposite side of the table.

"I am relaxed." She spoke beneath her breath, hoping the others were too involved in their own conversations to notice. "Who do you think you are, talking to me this way?"

"I'd like to think I'm your friend." He heaped a large spoonful of potato salad onto his plate then slopped some baked beans right beside it. "Not a mortal enemy. A friend."

Natalie followed, dishing up small portions for herself. "Some friend. We hardly know each other."

With every scoop of food, the man's agitation appeared to rise until they met at the end of the table, face-to-face, plate-to-plate.

"From the moment we met, you've treated me with disdain." His hushed voice vibrated the lump in his throat. "And what did I do to deserve it? I tried to befriend your brother, that's what. To befriend you. Your sister. I even gave up fishing to help you with your cattle today. But can you say thanks? No ..." He flung a handful of potato chips to his plate, half of them falling to the ground.

"This picnic is our thanks," Natalie said through tight lips, tempted to argue that she hadn't asked for, nor did they need his help. She had to wonder at his motives for doing so, anyway. Was he offering the help out of kindness, or were his motives more self-serving, like Ryan's had been?

"You're too busy dissecting everything I say to appreciate that I'm only trying to help." He set his plate on the table. "Do you even realize how much Dillon is hurting? How much he misses his father?"

Natalie's eyes darted to her brother on the porch steps, tossing bits of food to Jessie, their border collie. "Of course, he does. We all do."

"Then what are you doing about it?"

She shook her head, feeling trapped. "What do you mean? We're working. We're keeping busy."

Jared brought a chip to his mouth and crunched into it slowly. "Take him to the rodeo. Relax for a change."

"Okay already." Natalie raised her chin to the hot sun now hiding behind a puffy white cloud. "I planned to take him all along. If you hadn't been so intent on questioning me, I might've told you before."

"It's about time you come to your senses." He smiled and winked at her. "What do you think? Can we call a truce?"

She shook her head, frazzled at trying to keep up with his wordplay.

Willard joined them at the table, a wooden toothpick poking from his mouth. "Are you two done trading punches?"

Natalie sobered at the scene they'd caused. She knew better than to be controlled by her emotions, had spent the last year guarding her words, practicing diplomacy on every count. Yet her year of royalty hadn't made one bit of difference when it came to this man. He still had a way of getting under her skin.

"I believe we're quite finished." She eyed Jared, who'd stuffed his mouth with a bite of hamburger.

"That's good." Willard slid a grin between the two of them and nodded toward the yellow sedan that had pulled into the driveway. "I'd hate for your company to be caught in the thick of battle."

SEVENTEEN

THE WOMAN APPROACHED THEM, HER BLEACHED-BLONDE HAIR FLOATING out from under a white cowboy hat. As she neared, Natalie had the oddest sensation come over her—as though she knew the lady.

Willard stepped in front of Natalie and blocked the middle-aged woman from view, his arms crossed over his chest. "What are you doing here?" Condemnation filled his voice.

Natalie eased to his side to get a better look.

"Still the watchdog, I see." The woman's brown eyes sparked with fire against a dark tan and ruddy cheeks. "It's good to see you, Willard. It's been a long time."

"Not nearly enough."

She laughed, then fixed her gaze on Natalie. "This must be my little Nat. My, but you've grown. And a beauty queen too, I hear." She reached out for a hug, smelling of coconut tanning oil.

Natalie wasn't sure how to respond, thinking the stranger must be one of her father's relatives, a long-lost aunt or cousin, perhaps.

"You don't recognize me, do you?"

The woman's face seemed vaguely familiar, but Natalie shook her head.

"Well, I suppose the last time you saw me you were pretty young."

Her smile cracked as she searched the yard, as though looking for something or someone. "I'm sorry to hear about your dad. That's why I came. I thought I might be able to help."

Willard's hands moved to his hips. "She don't need your help, Libby, so you might as well go back to whatever hole you climbed out of."

When Natalie heard the name, her mind snapped to a time long ago—a time long forgotten.

With the reaction of a bulldog, the woman gave Willard a nasty snarl and shoved past him to take Natalie by the arm. "Where are my babies? I'm dying to see them."

Natalie choked back a response. Could this be her father's second wife, Libby? But how could that be? She'd left them years ago, had been killed in a car accident. At least that's what Dad told them. "I thought you were dead."

The woman's chin dropped in a deep-throated chuckle. "Oh sweetheart, I'm very much alive, I assure you."

Dressed in peach colored jeans and a matching tank top that emphasized her plump bosom and thick waist, she strode with purpose toward the porch where Dillon sat with their dog. Natalie followed in a daze, not sure whether to believe the woman or ask to see proof of her identity.

Willard came up beside Natalie, his eyes peeled on the woman in question.

"What do you make of this?" Natalie asked. "You recognized her, didn't you? You knew Libby was alive?"

Her friend's teeth clamped down on the wooden toothpick he'd been chewing. "Mark my words, that woman ain't nothing but trouble."

"But why would Dad tell us Libby had died, and why would she come back after all these years?"

"Maybe he was protecting you. Didn't want you to feel abandoned. As to why she's back, I have no idea … but I aim to find out."

They caught up to Libby before she'd reached the porch, and Natalie lurched in front, blocking the woman from her brother's curious stare. "Libby, wait."

The woman stopped, a trace of urgency and irritation on her face. "What? I just wanted to say hello to my boy. That is my boy there, isn't it? He looks just like his dad."

"I don't think that's a good idea."

"You've become quite the mother hen, haven't you? Guess that's to be expected. You always were protective of them."

Jessie got up to sniff the woman's boots, as unsure of her identity as Natalie.

Could this really be her brother and sister's mom? The woman who abandoned them when Dillon was only a few months old? She remembered the day Libby left. Natalie had clung to her, screamed at the top of her lungs. Her dad had been gone when her stepmother dragged her suitcase out the door, leaving Natalie to care for her half brother and sister all by herself.

Disgust replaced confusion. Natalie looked around at the neighbors who visited under the shade tree, unaware of her turmoil. She turned in a circle and everything blurred together—the vehicles and buildings, the home she'd grown up in, the ranch that spread out before her—all she knew and loved—her haven of safety. Chelsey arranged food on the picnic table, and Dillon lingered on the porch steps, as though sensing something amiss.

"Dillon and Chelsey believe you're dead," she managed to say. "They have no idea their mother's alive. I think it would be best for me to talk to them—prepare them for the shock."

The woman huffed like a teenager. "I don't want to hurt them, I want to hug them." She shuffled to move past Natalie, apparently set on doing just that.

"Libby, you'll do no such thing." Willard gripped her arm and stopped her progress.

From the corner of her eye, Natalie noticed Jared ambling toward them. Her stomach knotted at the thought of the preacher getting involved with yet another complication in their lives.

"Everything okay over here?" He handed Natalie her plate, his mood unhampered and jovial, completely oblivious to the tension in the air. "You left your food on the table. I hope our little discussion didn't spoil your appetite."

Natalie took her plate and attempted to steer him in another direction. She had no desire for Jared to know the gritty details of their life, especially when she didn't understand them herself. "How would you like to tell Dillon that we're going to the rodeo tonight? I thought he might enjoy hearing it from you, since you're such good buddies and all."

Jared's brow crinkled, and he stared back at Willard and Libby. "I can stick around if you need me." His gaze didn't waver, and she wondered if he might be more in tune to the situation than she thought.

"Take Dillon away from here. She leaned in closer. Please? I can't get into it now, but I'll fill—"

"And who is this?" Too late, Libby joined their conversation. She came and stood inches from Jared, eyeing him from head to foot. "Is this your fellow, Nat? Not bad, not bad at all."

Embarrassment coursed through Natalie's veins. "No ... I don't have a—"

Jared reached out to greet her. "I'm one of the extra cowhands today. I'm also the pastor at New Redeemer Church, Jared Logan. Pleased to meet you."

Libby accepted his hand, her eyes contemplating him like a piece of sterling silver. "A pastor, huh? If all pastors are as handsome as you, I might start hanging out at church."

Jared chuckled. "I can't think of a better place for you to hang out."

Libby grasped his left hand and boldly turned it over. "Are you single?"

"I am."

"Even better." Her stepmom grinned.

Natalie found the entire conversation distasteful and couldn't believe Jared was encouraging the woman's interest.

"I was just about to browse the desserts if you'd care to join me." He took the woman's arm, and she switched gears faster than a racecar driver, apparently no longer interested in visiting Dillon.

Jared stole a peak at Natalie before strolling off. "Do you still want me to talk to Dillon about the rodeo?"

Natalie shook her head, wishing he hadn't mentioned their plans aloud. "No, that's okay. I'll take care of it."

The woman stopped and crooned. "Are you going to the rodeo tonight?"

Jared waited for Natalie's response.

"Yes, I guess we are," she managed.

"That's perfect." Libby smiled up at Jared. "Now I'll have someone to sit with."

Natalie thought she might throw up. How would she explain this woman's presence to Chelsey and Dillon? Not only that, but now she'd have to figure out a way to do it before the rodeo.

Willard came to her side and offered a meager smile. "Come to think of it, a little night air might do me good too. I think I'll join you folks if you don't mind the extra company. What time shall I pick you up, Natalie?"

EIGHTEEN

J̲ared spotted N̲atalie and D̲illon on the bleachers, amazed at how she stood out in the crowd. Her black hair gleamed beneath the white felt hat, and her countenance exuded a quiet dignity and an almost queenly grace. Ignoring the music that blared from the speakers, he weaved in and out of the crowd. Halfway to his destination, he ran into Willard leaving the concession stand, loaded with hotdogs and drinks.

"Here, let me help you with that." Jared relieved the man of the tray of sodas.

"Thanks, I would have asked Dillon but didn't want him missing any of the grand entry."

Jared checked the rodeo arena where horses and riders circled in a throng. "I thought you were going to stay home and read a book tonight?"

Willard cocked an eyebrow. "That was before Miss Libby entered the equation."

Jared knew by their initial reaction that the woman made Willard and Natalie uncomfortable. What he didn't know was why. "What's her story?"

"You don't know?"

Jared had heard enough of their earlier conversation to realize there was a family connection. "I know Natalie seemed distressed—and protective."

"That's because Libby threw her for a loop. She thought the kids' mother was dead."

Jared's eyes grew wide, unable to hide his astonishment. "Dillon and Chelsey's mom?"

"You got it."

No wonder Natalie behaved so oddly this afternoon. She'd been in shock. He followed beside Willard, careful not to bump anyone with his drinks. "You mean Libby just showed up without a warning?"

"You saw it with your own eyes the same as me. The question is why?"

Two boys darted in front of them, and Jared's drinks teetered on the tray. He managed to balance them but had difficulty balancing his thoughts. In seminary, he'd been taught not to judge others, to try to understand why people behaved the way they did and then find ways to reach out to them. To prayerfully consider all angles. Why would Libby leave her kids, only to return after all these years? Because she'd heard of their father's death and wanted to help? Because she realized she'd made a horrible mistake in leaving them?

"Did you know she was alive?" Jared asked.

The old man blew out a long breath and continued toward the bleachers. "Would you want your kids to know their mother deserted them? Didn't love them enough to try to stick it out?"

"But you don't know that. She might have had other reasons for leaving."

Willard's brow creased with agitation. "Tell that to Natalie. Or better yet, to Dillon. He was only a few months old when Libby left him ... and she never looked back. No mother walks away from her kids like that if she loves them."

Obviously, Willard was in no mood for charity. "Okay, so Mr.

Adams told his kids their mother died. How did they take the news when Natalie revealed Libby was alive?"

"She hasn't told them yet." Now only a few yards from where Natalie and Dillon sat, Willard's pace slowed. "If Natalie thought she had problems before, it weren't nothing to the trouble ahead. Which means you and I are going to have our hands full keeping Libby away from the kids tonight. The last thing they need is to hear that she's their mama rose up from the grave."

NINETEEN

NATALIE WATCHED AS WILLARD AND JARED APPROACHED WITH THEIR food and couldn't help admiring the younger man's attire. Dressed in a pair of new Wranglers, cowboy boots, and a navy western shirt, he almost looked in his element. She considered the various times she'd seen him—as a fisherman, a casually clad businessman, a wannabe cowboy, and a preacher. For sure, the man was an odd duck.

Willard handed her the hotdogs wrapped in tissue, and she offered one to Dillon. She scooted over to allow space for the two men and was surprised when they sandwiched her and Dillon, with Jared seated on her left and Willard on Dillon's right. Before she could protest that she'd been saving a spot for Chelsey, the announcer requested everyone stand for the national anthem.

The music swelled from the speakers and a young rider entered the arena, carrying the American flag stretched out and waving in full glory. Goosebumps covered Natalie's arm as she removed her felt hat, honored to have had the privilege of carrying that flag many times herself. It gave her chills to know that she was witness to one of America's oldest pastimes, a tradition that began out on an empty prairie with men and women on horseback, looking to pass a few lonely hours doing something they loved. And while the sport had changed some through the years, it comforted her to know that the cowboys rarely did.

Upon the song's conclusion, Natalie strained to spot her sister in the crowd and debated whether to go look for the teen. After all, Chelsey could have run into Lucas, or worse, Libby. Both were off-limits.

Jared nudged her arm and pointed to her sister, traipsing toward them and laughing with two friends. "You're going to give yourself gray hair if you don't stop worrying so much."

Yeah, right. Natalie wished all she had to worry about were gray hairs. Instead, she had a growing list of things, which now included a stepmother she thought was dead. How would she make the introduction to her brother and sister? She'd been trying to figure it out all afternoon, but could think of no good way to tell them.

Natalie attempted to make room for Chelsey on the bleacher, but the girl declined and took a seat below her.

"Where have you been?" Natalie poked her with the toe of her boot.

Chelsey turned and frowned. "I ran into Marcy. I suppose now you're going to ground me from talking to my friends?"

Natalie placed her hat back on and forced a grin in case anyone might be listening to their conversation. "I'm not trying to be mean, Chelsey. I'm only doing what's good for you."

A movement from the arena caught Natalie's eye. A clown on the other side of the fence motioned for her to stand.

Natalie touched her hand to her chest. "Me?"

"Looks like it's going to take more than a whistle to get her attention," the announcer blurted over the speakers. "Folks, put your hands together to welcome our honored guest, Miss Natalie Adams, last year's Miss Rodeo Kansas and first runner-up Miss Rodeo America."

Though caught off guard, Natalie shifted into performance

mode. With the biggest smile she could muster, she stood and waved to her fans, then tipped her hat to the announcer.

"You're a real celebrity," Jared said when she returned to her seat.

"Just call her Miss Congeniality." Chelsey groaned. "Everybody loves a rodeo queen."

Natalie leaned over the girl's shoulder. "You could have entered competitions. There's still time to sign up for the queen clinic we're having in a couple of weeks."

"I'd rather go to Pastor J's church than stand around with a bunch of beauty queens."

Natalie bristled at her sister's remark. "I'll have you know that most rodeo queens go on to be doctors, teachers, or whatever profession they desire—and most continue to represent the cowboy way of life. Don't judge them for that."

Jared pressed closer and cleared his throat. "What made you want to be a rodeo queen?"

She stared into the arena and watched as a contestant darted after a calf let out of the chute. "I remember sitting by my mama when I saw my first rodeo queen on a magnificent black horse prancing along in a parade and wearing a white hat and fancy leather chaps. I thought she was the most beautiful woman I'd ever seen. And I knew then that's what I wanted to be one day. Or at least try. Silly, huh?"

"Not silly at all. Your dad must have been very proud of you for going after your dream."

Natalie wrinkled her nose, recalling the occasions she'd asked her dad for help. He always answered the same. *There's work to do and better ways to spend your time than chasing after such foolishness.* "My grandma took me to my first competition when I was twelve. When she died, I went with friends or by myself. Dad drove me to a few." *Despite his better judgment.*

Jared remained quiet for a moment. "But you never gave up. Not many girls can claim to be first runner up to Miss Rodeo America. I'd say all of your work paid off well."

Natalie shrugged. Right now, it didn't seem like much of an accomplishment.

Out in the arena, the calf-roping event continued as a cowboy threw his lariat and the loop bounced off the steer's back.

Natalie peered into the crowd, wondering if Libby had changed her mind. Surely, if she planned to attend, she'd be here by now. When three more events concluded with no sign of her stepmom, Natalie allowed herself to relax and enjoy the program. They were in the clear. Now she had time to break the news to the kids gently.

Her joy was short lived, however, as Libby appeared right before the barrel races began. The woman waved from the foot of the stands. Dressed in turquoise pants and a fitted western shirt loaded with bling, she climbed up to them and plopped beside Chelsey.

"Looks like I made it just in time," she told Chelsey. "I was a barrel racer once. Competed with the best of 'em—and not that long ago, either. Bet you didn't know that about me, did you?" She patted Chelsey's leg like they'd been friends forever.

Chelsey glanced back at Natalie and screwed her face as though a crazy woman had sat beside her. She scooted away, and Natalie held her breath, wondering what Libby might do or say next. The entire situation was a ticking time bomb.

"Come on, kids." Natalie tugged on her brother's shirt. "I'm still hungry. Let's get some popcorn or nachos."

Libby looked up and frowned. "But I just got here."

"You go," Chelsey said. "I want to watch the barrel races."

Natalie refused to take no for an answer. "Come on, Chels, you can help carry the snacks. We won't be long." She practically had to drag the girl away, but finally her sister gave in.

As soon as Natalie left her seat, she felt the weight shift on the bleachers. Glancing back, she saw Willard sit next to Libby.

WHEN THE OLD MAN SCOOTED DOWN BESIDE LIBBY, JARED MODIFIED HIS position. Out in the arena, another contestant ran a pattern around the barrels and gunned it on the home stretch. The crowd cheered the girl's time of fourteen point two.

"Now that's a good run," Libby said. "Reminds me of the old days. Remember how we used to follow the home circuit from Nebraska to Oklahoma?"

Jared trained his ears to the conversation below.

"What are you doing here, Libby?" Willard asked.

Libby chuckled. "I like rodeos. You know that."

"Yes, but why did you come back to Diamond Falls? Why are you bothering these people?"

Her voice turned cold. "These people happen to be my family."

"You gave up that right a long time ago."

"I made a mistake. Everyone deserves a second chance."

Willard leaned back and groaned, then passed a worried frown to Jared.

"What? I was young. I shouldn't have left like I did, but I can't undo the past." She adjusted her turquoise blouse, the material stretched tight across the back of her shoulders.

Not knowing the woman or her history, Jared was inclined to believe her. She could have changed. Maybe her ex-husband's death provided the perfect opportunity for her to make things right. Willard and Natalie should at least give her the benefit of the doubt.

"Excuse me, I couldn't help but overhear." Jared clutched both their shoulders to interrupt the heated debate. "From what I can tell everyone's a little anxious about your return and understandably so. Maybe it would help ease our minds if you could answer a few questions?"

Libby glanced at him with uncertainty. "I never figured this would be easy   stepping back into my kids' lives."

Jared silently begged Willard's permission to go forward. At the man's nod, Jared cleared his throat. "What are your plans, Libby? Are you here on a short visit, or do you intend to move back?"

"Yeah, and where have you been all this time?" Willard jumped in before she could answer Jared's questions. "Let's not forget about money, either. As in, do you have any?"

Libby rubbed her hands on her jeans. "I figured I'd wait and see how things went with the kids. As for my whereabouts, I've been a little bit of everywhere—Georgia, Texas, New Mexico, California. You name it, I've probably been there."

"You're here for a brief stay then?" Jared tried to draw out as much information as possible. "You must have a lot of vacation built up at your current job."

The woman squirmed. "I told you, I don't know."

Willard scowled at Jared, clear he didn't trust her. "Which translates, she don't have a job."

"Listen, boys." Libby turned to stare them both hard in the face. "Where I go and what I do is my own business. You two are just going to have to sit back and let Natalie take it from here. If she wants me to stay, I'll stay. If she wants me to go, I'll go. Easy as that."

TWENTY

Natalie paid for the nachos and popcorn and handed them to Dillon and Chelsey. "Before we head back, I need to talk to you about something." She ushered them to a deserted picnic table behind the concession stand.

"We're missing the barrel races." Chelsey craned to see the arena from where they stood.

"I know, but this is important." Natalie hated adding more chaos to her siblings' lives but what option did she have? She couldn't allow Libby to announce that she was their mom without any fore-warning. "It's about that woman sitting on the bleachers."

"I saw her at our house today." Dillon crunched into a cheesy nacho. "Seems kinda weird. Who is she?"

Natalie caught her brother's hand and pulled him to sit with her at the table. "Listen, what I have to tell you is going to sound really crazy, but you need to trust me on this." She locked gazes with Chelsey, hoping this news about her mother wouldn't cause the teen to spiral even more out of control. Swallowing the fear in her throat, Natalie decided not to mince words. "That woman out there—Libby, she's your mom."

Chelsey's brow puckered into a frown. "That's not possible. Mom died a long time ago."

"Yeah, in a car wreck." Dillon's comment echoed his sister's apprehension. "Dad told us. She was killed in an accident."

Natalie squeezed her brother's hand. "That's what I thought too. But apparently, it wasn't true. Willard recognized her. He said Dad didn't want to hurt us, so he lied about what happened. I don't know why she left all those years ago, but she didn't die. She's alive, and she's here."

Chelsey dropped to the other side of the table as though in shock.

Natalie gripped her sister's hand, and the three of them formed an intimate circle. "I understand this is a lot to take in. Especially now that Dad's gone. But she seems eager to meet you—to reconnect with us."

"I don't even remember her." Chelsey's words were drawn out, as though in a daze. "And Dillon was just a baby."

The day Libby left had been ingrained in Natalie's mind, but she knew better than to discuss those nightmares with the kids. It gave her pause that the woman wanted back in their lives, and she secretly vowed to keep a close eye on her stepmother should she decide to break their hearts again.

"We don't have to go back to the bleachers," Natalie said. "We can go home right now if you want. Give this news some time to sink in."

"Does she want to be our mom? Will she live with us?" Dillon's brown eyes searched Natalie's for an answer—an answer Natalie didn't have. She recognized the sadness and longing on his face. The boy had never had a mother to call his own.

"I don't know, Dillon. I don't know where she's been or what she wants. I'm as shocked about this as you are—but she's your mama. You tell me what to do."

Chelsey rubbed her forehead as though it might be too much.

After a few minutes, she looked up. "I'm willing to talk to her if you are, Dillon."

Natalie waited for her brother's response. Like a pup that follows his owner without question or fear, he quietly nodded in solemn resolve.

"All right then, let's do it." Natalie rose from the table and held out her hands in a three-musketeer handshake. "All for one and one for all?"

Chelsey rolled her eyes, but Dillon added his hand to the stack. Pretty soon, Chelsey joined them. Her protective instincts stronger than ever, Natalie hooked her arms around her brother and sister. "It's going to be okay. We have each other, and nobody can take that from us."

Natalie rounded the corner to the bleachers, leading Chelsey and Dillon as though to battle. She exchanged looks with Willard and gave a slight nod to where the kids waited behind the bleachers. He caught her unspoken message and climbed down to join them. Libby's face brightened at Natalie's approach.

"Okay, Libby. I've told the kids. They'd like to speak to you, if you don't mind."

Her stepmother gazed out at the rodeo arena where men in a sponsored Dodge pickup loaded barrels, and a clown dressed in over-sized pants and a bright striped shirt set up for a performance.

"Sure, we can do that." Libby eased from her seat. "I'd hate to miss the bull riding, though. We can make this quick, right?"

Natalie didn't bother answering. Instead, she led the woman to the kids, and Willard ushered them behind the bleachers where he stood guard to give them as much privacy as possible. Dillon and Chelsey stared at Libby as though she were an alien creature and not their mother.

"Kids, I'd like you to meet your mom." Natalie placed her hands on their shoulders to offer a bit of comfort. "Libby, this is Chelsey and Dillon."

Unable to contain her emotions, the woman rushed at the two with open arms. "Oh my goodness, you don't know how I've missed you." She pinched Chelsey's cheek and tried to give Dillon a kiss, but he backed out of her reach before she made contact.

"When I heard about your dad, I just had to come see you, to make sure you were okay. I can't believe how much you've grown." She shook her head in disbelief and then gazed at Natalie.

"And you, Nat. You always were a little mommy, looking out for your brother and sister. I knew I could count on you to care for my babies."

A chill raced down Natalie's spine. Ten-year-olds weren't supposed to be mommies. She slipped her hands in her jean pockets and held her tongue.

Libby returned her attention to the kids. "But that doesn't matter now, because I'm back. I'm here for you—all of you." Her long eyelashes fluttered.

Dillon eased a step forward. "Are you really our mom?"

The woman's head dipped back as laughter roared from her mouth. "You bet I am. And boy, do I have plans for you. See this rodeo?" She stretched her arm toward the arena. "This is the life I know, and it's the life I can teach you."

Natalie found her voice. "You're planning to stay in Diamond Falls, then?"

Libby's excitement stalled. "Well, yes. I think that's a wonderful idea." She cast a persuasive glance between the two kids. "Would you like me to stay?"

As though hypnotized, Chelsey and Dillon each gave a slow nod.

Libby turned to Natalie. "I ... don't suppose you have an extra room at your house? It would save time and money if I could stay with you. I've been gone so long, I hate to miss even one minute now that I'm back. We have so much catching up to do, I can hardly stand it."

A strong hand gripped Natalie's arm, and she acknowledged Willard's presence as well as his warning. She also noted the yearning on her brother and sister's faces. Wouldn't she give anything to have her mama come back? Did she really have the right to deny them that privilege no matter how disinclined she might feel toward the idea?

"If you'll give me a day, I suppose you could stay in Dad's room."

Natalie heard Willard's groan and clenched her teeth, wondering if she'd made too rash a decision. "Unless you'd prefer to sleep downstairs on the couch."

"She could sleep on my bed," Dillon offered. "I don't mind sleeping on the couch."

"I wouldn't dream of making a mess of your living quarters, or of throwing you out of your bed." The woman winked at Dillon, then drew back her shoulders. "Your dad's room will be more than comfortable. I appreciate the offer."

"It's settled then." Natalie forced a smile. "I'll work on it tomorrow, and we'll expect you for supper around seven?"

Libby's eyes danced. "I couldn't ask for more."

TWENTY-ONE

THE NEXT MORNING, NATALIE SORTED THROUGH THE CLOTHES IN HER father's closet. Cleaning out his room took longer than she expected, as every now and then she found an item that touched on a particular memory, and she fast-forwarded the event like a scene in a movie.

Had it not been for her promise to allow her stepmom to stay with them, she'd be tempted to leave his bedroom untouched and not pack up his clothes and personal items. What had she been thinking to ask Libby to stay with them—and in her father's room of all places?

Questions churned in Natalie's mind. Why did Libby leave, and was she still married to her dad or had they divorced? It boggled her mind to think of all she didn't know.

She removed one of her dad's favorite western shirts from a hanger and smoothed the material against her cheek. It still smelled of him, and she laid it on her keepsake pile. Again, the craziness of the situation hit her.

Her dad was gone and her stepmom, whom she thought dead, was alive.

Natalie made her way through the rest of her dad's clothes, then moved on to his shoes, among them his worn work boots and the pair of Tony Lama's she'd given him after the Miss Rodeo Kansas competition. It had taken a good chunk of her savings to buy the exotic elephant hide, but she'd wanted to thank him for his support, and a good pair of boots was the best thanks she could imagine at the time. She hugged the tan leather to her chest and debated whether to add them to the packed boxes. Though she knew they would give some man great pleasure, the rich leather scent embraced her like a hug and reminded her of the precious moments she and her dad had shared. With a pang of guilt, she set them aside for her own keeping then spotted a metal box in the corner of the near-empty closet.

Drawn to the rectangular container, she lifted it up and found it locked. She recalled seeing keys on her father's bureau, and upon returning to the dresser she noted other items that had gone untouched since his death. Left as though he'd deposited them from his jean pockets before going to bed were a pile of quarters, two pieces of peppermint candy, and a wadded up piece of paper. On the silver keychain were two keys tiny enough to open the box. She tried one and when that didn't work, she fumbled for the second.

Her heart drummed like hooves running across the prairie. Could the box hold more money? Possibly even more than the two thousand she'd already found?

When she turned the key, the lock clicked and the metal lid opened to reveal a pile of papers. She thumbed through them and found items normally housed in a safe. Birth certificates, vehicle titles, a marriage license to Natalie's mom as well as her death certificate. Another marriage license, this one to Libby.

Natalie half expected to come across a death certificate for her as well, but instead discovered a certificate of divorce.

It was true. Her father and Libby were divorced.

Her mouth went dry as she considered what her dad would think of his ex-wife staying in his room. He'd probably roll in his grave if he knew Libby intended to once again sleep in his bed. When she finished going through every slip of paper, disappointment seeped from her lips.

No money.

Her gaze drifted to the wadded paper on the dresser. Probably one of her father's many lists. Prepared to toss the note in the wastebasket, she took a quick peek to make sure it wasn't an important document.

There on the crumpled paper and written in black ink were words not of a list, but of a poem entitled "Poetry."

Prose and Poetry
Men who had a love for words
Shakespeare, Hawthorne, Keats

Natalie read the words again. Odd words that seemed to be in the pattern of haiku, a form of poetry she'd once learned in high school. While the writing was far from literary genius, her eyes filled with tears. Her dad obviously had a love for words as well — a secret he'd kept from all of them. She wiped the moisture from her eyes and took a deep breath. The job of cleaning out her father's room had turned into an emotional ordeal, and although Natalie had expected it to be so, she hadn't counted on its intensity.

She did her best to straighten the piece of paper and laid it on top of her keepsake pile. Crumpled or not, it was something her father had written, and she would treasure it forever. The poem reminded her of the scrolls he'd left for her brother and sister. Perhaps it was time to let them read his last words to them.

JARED GREETED THE CONGREGATION MEMBERS AS THEY FILED OUT OF THE sanctuary, praying they'd take with them a portion of his Sunday sermon, if only a crumb. His arms and legs were stiff and sore from the previous days' ranch work, but he tried to hide his discomfort.

"Nice sermon, Pastor. A little long, but not too bad," one parishioner said.

Another grumbled from behind. "A forty minute sermon is more than long—it's agony. The only thing worse is a long line to the coffee pot or to the bathroom."

"Thank you. I'm glad you enjoyed it," he told the first and tried to mask that he'd heard the other. He never understood how some people could speak in front of another as though they didn't have ears.

The complainer shook his hand and fled, not willing to stick around for small talk.

"Don't worry about him." John McCray stood before him, followed by Gil and Mattie. "Some folks don't know how blessed they are to have a young minister full of energy and eager to spread God's Word. Believe me, I know, because I used to be one of them on the sidelines."

Jared shook the old man's hand, having met all three of the McCray's yesterday at Natalie's house. "I'm glad you're no longer a bystander—and I'm thankful for your support."

"I watched you rope those calves yesterday." John McCray looked up at him with bright blue eyes. "It's not easy to step out of your comfort zone—but you made an effort to help out. That's worth something in my book."

Jared chuckled. "I'm afraid I wasn't much help, but you're right, I did try." Eager to know this family better, he made a mental note to visit the McCrays in the future, then moved on to greet those next in line, an elderly couple with a young woman he'd never seen before.

"Good morning, Pastor," the older woman said. "You haven't met our granddaughter, Jane, have you? She's staying with us for a few weeks this summer."

He noted the girl's short blonde hair and shook her hand. "I'm sure you'll have a delightful time with your grandparents. And I'll look forward to seeing you at our services while you're here."

"Oh yes, Jane never misses a church service. She's on her summer break from Bethany College and plans to go into mission work." The woman's voice gurgled like a brook. "We'd love to have you for dinner one Sunday to visit. Today even?"

Jared rubbed his chin, aware of the woman's intention. It seemed Mrs. Hildebrand wasn't the only one who enjoyed sharpening her matchmaking skills. "Thank you for the invitation, but I already have plans this afternoon."

And in fact, he did have plans—he wanted to check on a gentleman in his congregation who was in the county hospital, and then he planned to drive out to see how Natalie and the kids fared after their visit with Libby the night before.

"Perhaps another time then," the woman suggested.

The line had stalled with their ongoing conversation, and Jared smiled with unease. "Of course, I'll look forward to it."

Back in his office, he hung his stole in the closet and changed out of his linen garments. Glad to have his third sermon over, he hummed the refrain of the closing hymn, "Nearer, My God, to Thee."

A knock sounded on his door, and Mr. Sanders slipped his head inside. "Pastor, I wondered if I might have a word with you."

Jared stopped humming, and in stepped Mr. Sanders with his wife prodding him from behind. He loosened his clerical collar and stared at the couple as they stationed themselves like wardens in his office. "How may I help you?"

Mrs. Sanders poked her husband as though her hand was an electric cattle prod. He grimaced back at her. "My wife and I wanted to talk to you about what happened with Sarah." His gaze fell to his black shoes.

Jared pulled out two folding chairs and invited the couple to sit. "I understand your concern. From what I can tell, though, your daughter shows sincere remorse for her actions."

Mr. Sanders scratched his thinning hair and took a seat.

"Of course Sarah's sorry." Mrs. Sanders remained standing. "It's this friend of hers that talked her into trouble. Sarah's never been able to say no, and you see where that got her."

Jared leaned against his desk and nodded. "Peer pressure can be hard to overcome, especially for a freshman like Sarah." He didn't doubt for one second that stealing the beer had been Chelsey's idea, but he didn't want to let the Sanders girl off the hook too easily.

"I'm hoping Vacation Bible School will show the girls a more worthy way to spend their time — get them involved in helping others, like the mission work they did last week. I think it might go a long way in teaching them to make good decisions for their future."

"Maybe for Sarah, but I question how much it's going to help Chelsey." The woman sat down with a huff and repositioned her suit jacket, clearly dissatisfied, and clearly used to getting her way.

Mr. Sanders shot his wife another warning. "Don't get us wrong, Pastor. The two girls have been friends since grade school. But this past year, we've seen a lot of changes in Chelsey. We're concerned, that's all. Maybe splitting up the two would be better than having them work together."

Jared couldn't believe the Sanders would be so uncharitable. He sent up a silent prayer for immediate wisdom. "As you said, the girls have been friends for a long time. What good will it do to separate them? Wouldn't it be better to demonstrate a forgiving heart and a helping hand? Let Sarah show her repentance and pray that it has an effect on Chelsey. I'm of the opinion that it will, with God's help, of course."

Mr. Sanders stretched his arm behind his wife's back. "See, I told you. He knows what he's doing."

"I'm not convinced. What if Chelsey gets our daughter into trouble again?" The woman's voice bordered hysteria.

Jared tried to understand her fear but wished she would have more faith. "The Bible doesn't promise that we won't be hurt in this life, but it does tell us that if we don't run the race, we'll never taste victory."

Mrs. Sanders frowned. "You're determined to do this, no matter our concerns?"

Jared pressed his lips together and nodded. "You can hold me completely responsible for the outcome. If Sarah turns into a delinquent, I'll accept the blame one hundred percent."

Her frown deepened. "Pastor, this is no joking matter. Your plan better not fail."

TWENTY-TWO

NATALIE SAT WITH DILLON AND CHELSEY IN THE LIVING ROOM AFTER they'd read their poems. It seemed their father had a fondness for haiku and had written one for each of his younger children.

"Why didn't Dad give you one?" Dillon scrunched his freckled nose, having already read his aloud, a poem about horses and puzzles.

"Yeah, I don't get it," Chelsey said. "And what is mine supposed to mean — 'Find comfort in food, Cook's cupboard is her treasure, Contentment in life'?"

"I don't know, and it really doesn't matter." Natalie shook her head in bewilderment. "I found the same kind of poem in his room about Shakespeare and some other poets. Dad must have had a secret desire to be a poet — and considering his talent, I guess it's best he kept it a secret." She chuckled, then got up from her chair and ruffled her brother's hair. "Come on, we should get the chores done before Libby arrives."

Chelsey chewed her fingernail. "What will it be like having her here? How long do you think she'll stay?"

Natalie shrugged. "I have no idea."

Dillon sat up from his reclined position on the couch. "What should we call her? Mom or Libby?"

Natalie's throat tightened at what he and Chelsey must be feeling—at what she felt herself. What did you call the mother you didn't know, who'd been absent most of your life? "Call her whatever you feel comfortable with," she said.

Before they could discuss it further, a knock sounded on the front door. Natalie's heart skipped as she stared at the entrance. "Do you suppose she's here already?"

With reluctance, Natalie made her way through the living room and braced herself for yet another change in their lives. Her relief poured out when she saw Jared on the porch wearing khaki pants and a polo shirt. "Oh, it's you."

JARED SMILED WHEN NATALIE GREETED HIM WITH BARE FEET. DRESSED IN cut off shorts and a sleeveless top, she wore her hair in a ponytail, tied with a red ribbon.

"I'm sorry, were you expecting someone?" He rested his hands on the door frame. "If you'd like, I can come back another time."

The warm afternoon breeze whisked a few stray hairs into Natalie's face as she stepped outside. She caught them with her slender fingers and tucked them behind her ear. "What brings you here?"

"I wanted to see how you were. After last night, I mean. With Libby and all." He followed her to the porch railing and shook his head at his incoherence. More often than not, the woman left him tongue-tied. "Willard told me about Libby's identity." He tried again. "I wanted to make sure the kids were okay after meeting their mother."

Natalie gripped one of the porch columns and hugged it close. "She's coming over tonight—to stay with us for awhile."

Jared tucked his hands in his pockets. "I'm glad you're giving Libby a chance. Willard seemed less than enthused about her return. But she might have changed."

She stared off in the distance. "I couldn't deny Dillon and

Chelsey the chance to know their mom. I'm not that mean, despite what you think."

Jared studied her profile. Her long shapely neck, refined nose and cheekbones, and haunting eyes — eyes that had experienced great pain. Overall, the most captivating woman he'd ever seen. "I never thought you were."

"Oh no?" Her thin eyebrows arched. "Just yesterday, you accused me of being insensitive to Dillon's feelings. What did you think? That I was too caught up in my own worries to consider my family?"

Anxiety stabbed his gut. "I thought we'd called a truce. That we were through arguing."

She pinned him with a hard stare. "If I remember correctly, you were the one who called the truce. I never agreed to anything."

Jared's face heated at the truth in her words. He had questioned Natalie's compassion toward Dillon and had implored her to recognize the boy's pain. "I apologize for second guessing you. That was ill mannered of me. I'm sure you have your brother and sister's best interests in mind."

"Their welfare is all I've thought about for days. It's all I've thought about for most of my life."

The young woman put up a tough front, but Jared had seen Natalie at her most fragile state, and her eyes, though cold and determined, couldn't always conceal the pain. "Don't you have family? Aunts, uncles, grandparents?"

She released an exasperated breath. "Our grandparents are dead. Our only other relatives are too old or live too far away. And I'm not moving the kids from their home. No matter how you look at it, the burden's mine."

"You have Willard ... and me." He held her gaze, unblinking.

"So you've said." She paused as though considering. "You mentioned before that you helped your granddad on his farm when you were a boy?"

"Every summer."

Her gaze traveled past him to the barnyard. "You probably did your share of haying, then?"

"I've done it all—mowed, raked, and baled." Jared noticed the tractor parked inside the open machinery shed and recalled that Mr. Adams' death had been tractor-related. He suspected that Natalie needed help but would rather eat worms than ask for it. "I'd offer my assistance, but I'm sure you'd prefer someone with more experience than a city boy like me."

She uttered the softest snort.

"Of course, then you'd have to worry about them taking advantage of you," he went on, "like that Tom fellow."

Her eyes narrowed. "What about your congregation? Wouldn't another job interfere with your church duties?"

The unguarded hope in her voice came through loud and clear. "I'd be happy to oblige with whatever you need. Haying, fixing the fence—laundry." Jared grinned. "I'm sure I could work around my schedule at church. It'd give me something to look forward to. Get me away from my desk and paperwork."

She seemed to study him. "Why did you choose to be a pastor? I mean, if you enjoy farm life so much?"

Jared marveled at the woman's skill in manipulating a conversation. Somehow she'd managed to turn the wheel away from herself and point the arrow directly at him. "My dad was a pastor, as was my mother's father."

"And you wanted to keep it in the family?"

"Something like that." His jaw tightened. The subject still caused his nerves to bristle, even after all this time. He thought he'd surmounted the problem in seminary, but if that were the case, why did he feel such guilt now? "It seemed the right path for me to take."

She bit her lip. "You don't sound very sure."

"No, I am." Jared straightened to his full height, calling on every ounce of confidence he owned. "I loved my granddad and his farm, and I'll always treasure the time we had. But that chapter's over."

"Sounds like it must have been an important chapter."

"It was a good one." Some days his granddad's gruff voice tracked him every step like a faithful hunting dog. Jared hated that he'd turned against the man in the end and wished he could redo that part of his life. He cast the futile thought away and stared out at the distant pasture. Lush green bluestem covered the hills, making the white outcroppings all the more noticeable. A Scissor-tailed Flycatcher perched on a nearby fencepost, its sharp raspy chirp drawing his attention.

Second chances were for the living. Better to learn from his mistakes and find purpose in today. "In the end, I felt called to the ministry."

Natalie groaned and stepped away from him.

"What? Haven't you ever felt God's call?"

She sunk onto the porch step and stretched her legs. "Maybe God doesn't look out for everyone the way he does you. Maybe our family isn't good enough to deserve his interest."

"No one is good enough in God's eyes. We don't earn his mercy."

"Well, I don't remember him ever talking to me, let alone directing my steps." She stared up at him. "Where was he when my mom died? Or when Libby left? Or how about when Dad was caught under that tractor? Seems if he was going to show up, those would have been good times to do so, don't you think?"

"I understand your anger." Jared sat beside her on the step. "Sometimes it may seem like God has abandoned us, but we aren't always able to see the big picture. When we do, we realize that he's been with us all along."

The frown on her face showed she wasn't convinced. "If I hire you to do the haying, will you be able to round up your own work crew?"

Amused that they'd circled back to the topic of her needing assistance, Jared grinned. "I think some boys from church would be willing to help out."

"All right then. Let's discuss the plans over dinner tonight."

Jared hesitated. "Are you sure? Tonight's a big night for your family."

Her forehead wrinkled as she peered at him from the corner of her eye. "I could use the support. It's not like I can invite Willard, considering his aversion to Libby." She pursed her lips in appeal. "Please?"

Unable to take his eyes off her full lips, Jared raised his hands in submission. "When you say it like that, how can I refuse?" Only after the words were spoken did he comprehend the amount of leverage this woman had over him. That, if asked, he would probably do anything for her.

TWENTY-THREE

"GOOD, THEN MAYBE YOU'D BE WILLING TO HELP WITH ANOTHER problem as well?" Natalie headed to the front door, not taking time to consider Jared's deer-in-the-headlights expression. Expecting him to follow, she bounded up the living room stairway. "I've been cleaning my dad's bedroom, and everything is packed in boxes—mostly work clothes, but there are a few western suits. Maybe you know someone who could use them?"

A quick glance inside the room gave Natalie a moment of satisfaction that her chore was almost done. It also left a hollow pit in her stomach, that their father's personal possessions would soon be gone. Her eyes pricked with tears, and she hurriedly swiped them away as Jared caught up to her.

"I'm sure I can find a home for them," he said at the top of the stairs, a bit winded. "How much do you have?"

She widened the door to reveal a dozen cardboard boxes. "Think we can fit them in your car?"

Jared scratched his forehead. "Sure, no problem."

Natalie wondered if Jared always displayed such a positive attitude. From what she could tell, the man was optimistic to a fault.

What she couldn't decide was whether this trait was a good thing or a nuisance. She lifted one of the boxes and headed for the stairway.

"Let me carry that." He took the bulk from her with ease, and it became apparent that he possessed more strength than she realized.

Her hands fell to her hips. "I'm not helpless."

"I never said you were." He glanced back with a smirk.

Fifteen minutes later, they'd managed to fit half the boxes into his small car.

"I guess we should have loaded them in my pick-up." Natalie studied her black Ford, debating whether to transfer everything into the bed of her truck.

"This will do." Jared closed the car trunk. "I can deliver these to the church and then when I return tonight, I'll get the rest. What time is dinner?"

Natalie watched her brother chase after a goat, swinging a rope over his head. "Libby's supposed to be here around seven," she said as Dillon abandoned his game and came running toward them.

"Hey, whatcha doing?" His forehead glistened with sweat. "Are you leaving already?"

Jared opened his car door. "I'll be back in a little while to eat dinner with you."

Dillon's loop dangled at his feet. "Can I go with you?"

Jared shrugged and glanced at Natalie. "It's all right with me, if it's okay with your sister."

Her brother's eyes darted to Natalie's, begging her to say yes. "I've finished my chores. Can I go, please?"

"Don't you want to be here when your mom arrives?"

His eyes slid to Jared's. "We can be here, can't we?"

Jared studied his watch. "Is six-thirty early enough?"

Natalie nodded, wondering at the fondness these two shared. She supposed Dillon needed the male companionship, especially now that their dad was gone. "I guess that'll be okay, as long as you promise to clean up as soon as you get back."

Her brother almost knocked her over with a hug. "Thanks, sis." He then handed her his rope and charged for the passenger door. The two waved good-bye as they drove out of the lane.

THREE HOURS LATER, NATALIE STOOD OUTSIDE AT THE GRILL, WAITING FOR their company to arrive. With her eyes peeled on the gravel road, she watched for Jared and her brother, who were late.

As she turned the sizzling T-bones, Libby's yellow car pulled into the driveway.

The woman stepped out of the sedan, dressed in a pink shirt and jeans that would make any other woman in her mid-forty's look like a bag of cotton candy. Oddly enough, the outfit wasn't unappealing on her stepmother.

Libby lugged her suitcases to the grill and deposited them on the ground.

Natalie glanced at the luggage. "How long do you plan to stay?"

The woman flapped her hand in the air. "You know me. I don't know how to pack light."

Natalie's question remained unanswered. "I've invited Jared Logan to join us for supper. I hope you don't mind. He took Dillon into town, but they should be back any minute."

A grin molded onto Libby's face. "The young pastor? How delightful. The two of you are quite friendly."

Natalie didn't miss the suggestive undertone in the woman's voice. "He's been a good friend to all of us."

The back screen squeaked open, and a few minutes later Chelsey joined them. Natalie handed her sister the long handled utensil. "Here Chels, will you finish cooking these steaks while I help Libby get settled?"

Her sister frowned, her eyes on Libby. "Sure, order me around like a slave."

Natalie sent her an apologetic smile and amended her request.

"I'm sorry, will you *please* finish these steaks while I help Libby with her suitcases?"

The girl shrugged and poked the meat with the stainless steel fork. With a sigh, Natalie carried the two heavy cases to the house, then up to her father's bedroom. She'd done her best to make the room attractive by adding fresh sheets and a more feminine blanket for a bedspread, and Chelsey had gathered some wildflowers to put in a vase. She wasn't sure why she was trying so hard to please the woman, except that maybe there was a small part inside that still longed for her love.

Libby followed her into the room and bounced on the covered mattress. Her tanned face cracked into a smile. "Seems like just the other day I shared this bed with your father. We had some good times, he and I."

"All I remember are two crying babies wondering why their mama left," Natalie said. "Kind of makes those good memories fade in the background." She peered at the woman masked in heavy make-up. "Why did you leave, Libby? Where did you go?"

"I understand you're perturbed with me. And that's okay." Libby scooted off the bed and braced Natalie's shoulders. "I can't get over how much you've grown. Why, you've turned into a beautiful lady, Nat, just beautiful. What can I do to make things up to you? I'd like for us to be friends. Do you think that would be possible?"

Natalie stepped away from the woman. "How about if you answer my question? Why did you leave?"

Her stepmom's forehead wrinkled. "I don't expect you to understand. You were so young back then. You didn't know how things were between your dad and me. When we married, it was more for convenience than love. Don't get me wrong. He was a good-looking man, and I was plenty attracted." A thin eyebrow shot up as though remembering.

"But he tended to be ... how shall I say ... overbearing?"

Natalie agreed that her dad had been strict, although she'd

watched some of that strictness wane as he'd gotten older. After all, he'd allowed Chelsey to date a senior in high school, something he would never have done when she was that age. "What are you saying? That he didn't love you? Or that you didn't love him?"

Libby pulled out a pack of cigarettes from her purse and held one between her fingers. "Mind if I smoke in here?"

Natalie scowled. "Yes, I do, actually."

"Well, I've been trying to quit, anyway." The woman smiled awkwardly as she tucked the cigarettes back in her purse. "What I'm saying is, our relationship was complicated. After your father and I had been married a while, we decided we wanted different things."

Natalie scoffed. Yeah, her dad wanted to be married and Libby didn't. Her dad wanted to raise a family and she didn't. The comparison could go on. "What I remember is that you came home one day from shopping, and you grabbed your suitcases and left. You never looked back. How could you do that to us?"

Libby pressed her lips together and went in search for something else in her purse. After a few seconds, she drew out a piece of gum. "Like I said, I don't expect you to understand."

Natalie was quickly tiring with the discussion. If they were going to manage this temporary living arrangement, she would have to get a handle on the situation. "For the record, I agreed to let you stay here for Dillon and Chelsey, so they'd have a chance to know you. I never had a second chance with my mom, and I couldn't refuse them theirs. But I'm not going to pretend that everything's okay. If I sense even a hint of trouble, you'll leave. I don't want the kids to carry the pain I've had. I won't do that to them—just so you know."

Libby wandered to the dormer window and looked out at the pasture. "Tell me about this Jared guy. You say he's joining us for supper? If you ask me, the young pastor has his eye on you."

Natalie balked at these words. Agitated, she spotted some folded towels on a chair and moved them to the dresser. "He wants to help our family. He considers us his little mission project."

"Seems overly fascinated, if you ask me."

"Generous with his time is more like it." Natalie checked her defense of the man. Jared didn't need defending and certainly not from her.

"You're a beautiful young woman, Nat. I've been around enough to know when a man is interested ... and believe me, this man's interested."

Natalie pursed her lips. "That's ridiculous. He's a friend — a pastor."

"You don't think pastors fall in love? If you don't watch out, pretty soon you'll be going to Bible studies and making food for bake sales."

Natalie shook her head. "I don't do bake sales."

Libby leaned back in a hearty laugh. "One thing I've learned in this life, is never say never."

Natalie checked her watch again and glanced out the window toward the gravel road. "I have no idea what's taking them so long."

"Maybe you've put too much faith in this new pastor, letting him whisk Dillon away on a whim."

"It was hardly a whim." Natalie again found herself defending the man, but she did wonder where he was. Jared assured her he'd be back in plenty of time. Which meant one of two things — he'd forgotten, or there was trouble.

TWENTY-FOUR

JARED PRAYED OVER MR. WILSON IN THE HOSPITAL BED. THE ONLY OTHER people in the room were his wife and daughter, weeping beside their newly departed loved one.

Though his heart went out to the woman, he thought briefly of Dillon waiting patiently in the room outside. A noise stirred from behind, and Jared turned to see the boy watching from the door. He patted Mrs. Wilson's shoulder before leaving. "If you need anything, you have my number."

"Thank you, Pastor Logan. I could never have gotten through this without you."

"I'm glad I could be here. I'll call again tomorrow to see about going over the service arrangements."

When he reached Dillon's side, he checked his watch. "Your sister is going to kill me." He groaned but took comfort in knowing he had a good excuse for being late — and for not calling, though he'd tried the house two times.

The boy continued to stare at Mr. Wilson's body. "Is that what you do as a pastor? Be with people when they're dying?"

Jared prodded Dillon down the corridor. Hospitals were always so cold and sterile. As a new pastor, Jared had spent only a few hours in hospital waiting rooms, and they weren't his most pleasant experiences, although sending one of his members off to meet his maker was indeed an awesome responsibility.

"Did that man know he was dying?"

Jared opened the exit door of the Charris County Hospital and inhaled the fresh air. "Yes, he knew. We visited several times while he'd been in the hospital."

Dillon turned quiet and sober. "What's it like to die?"

Jared studied the boy. "Are you thinking about your dad?"

"Natalie never wants to talk about it, but sometimes I wonder if Dad is watching over me, if he can see me here, and if he's in heaven. You believe in heaven, right?"

It never ceased to amaze Jared the many reactions people had about heaven. Some even thought the dead were transformed into angels — or worse, into animals. "Of course, I believe in heaven. And if your dad believed in Jesus as his savior, then he's in heaven. It's that simple."

He ruffled the boy's hair and unlocked his car door for him. "Tell me something, Dillon. Do you believe in heaven? Do you believe in Jesus?"

Dillon got into the car and thought about it for several seconds. "We don't go to church, but I've heard people talk about it," he said as Jared climbed into the driver's seat. "I remember Willard and Dad talking about church stuff. Do you think Dad believed in Jesus?"

"I don't know, Dillon. We can hope so." He started the engine and headed for the edge of town just as the sun began its descent in the west, casting a reddish glow against the hills, with the purest blue sky above. A good day for going home.

Images of the grieving family and all the plans necessary in arranging Mr. Wilson's funeral soon overshadowed the peaceful contemplation. Jared swallowed the knot that formed in his throat and forced his mind to concentrate on the sunset, glad to call this place his home, for however long God intended him to stay.

"Can I ask you something?"

Jared nodded, learning to brace himself for such questions, as they almost always provoked a deep reaction.

"Do you like my sister?"

Jared eyed the boy in the passenger seat of his car. Dillon's question had been sincere, not an ounce of teasing in his expression.

"Yeah, she's all right—for a girl." Jared winked, trying to lighten the mood.

"She's pretty, don't you think?"

The boy didn't fight fair. "I'd say she's about the prettiest woman I've ever seen."

A wide grin spread on Dillon's face, and he nodded in agreement. "You don't have a girlfriend, do you?"

Jared cleared his throat, fearing where this chain of questions might lead. "No, I don't. What about you? Do you have a girlfriend?"

Dillon wrinkled his nose.

"Good answer. You're too young to like girls."

"But you like girls, don't you?

"I like them just fine." Jared grinned. "As a pastor, I have to be particular about the women in my life. I can't date like other men. You understand that, right?"

Dillon stared out the window, silent. "I wish you could date Natalie."

Perspiration gathered on Jared's back. "Why don't we listen to the radio? How about the oldies?"

Dillon shrugged. "Dad liked country music. His favorite singer was Merle Haggard."

Jared tuned in to a country station and turned the volume down. "You miss your dad a lot, don't you?"

The boy didn't answer, quiet for a moment. "And now our mom's coming back. Did Natalie tell you?"

"Yeah, I heard. How does that make you feel?"

His mouth tilted to the side. "I've been trying to imagine what it'll be like having her around, but I can't figure it out. Natalie's the closest thing to a mom that we've ever had."

Jared patted Dillon's narrow shoulder, thinking a lot of weight rested there. Maybe what the boy needed most was someone willing to listen. "It'll be all right. If you ever want to talk, I'll be around. Your sister asked me to help with the haying this summer."

"Really?"

"Yeah, and there's always fishing. If you need to get away — you know, from the *girls*, you can come hang out with me."

A wide grin spread on Dillon's face and his mood lightened. "If you're a preacher, how come you know so much about farming?"

Jared shook his head. "I don't know much. What I know, my granddad taught me — like your dad taught you."

"Do you miss him?" The young boy sought Jared's eyes, his own pain raw.

"More so now. Seems there are a lot of reminders here in the country."

With the understanding of someone much older, Dillon pushed the radio dial to its previous station and cranked up the volume to a John Mellencamp song.

The heavy bass vibrated in Jared's ears, but he knew the lyrics and they were good. "I was born in a small town," he sang out, believing music often served as the best medicine for a hurting soul. Soon Dillon joined in loud and strong.

A GLIMMER OF CHROME SHOWN THROUGH THE KITCHEN WINDOW AS Natalie prepared to serve the dessert Chelsey had made. She checked the clock above the refrigerator. Over an hour and a half late. She stormed out the kitchen door and down the back steps to meet them.

"Where have you been? Do you have any idea how late it is?" She caught her brother as he climbed from the car and finding nothing physically wrong, turned her wrath on Jared.

"You said you'd bring him home early. Did you forget?"

"No, of course not," Jared said without his usual smile. "Something came up that I couldn't walk away from. I tried to call, but your phone was busy."

Natalie groaned, wondering if Chelsey had been on the phone. "I don't know what it's like where you come from, but out here, if you tell someone you're going to do something, you do it. Besides, you could have called my cell."

Dillon tugged on her elbow. "It's not what you think, Nat. Mr. Wilson died."

She shook her head at the alleged misunderstanding. "What?"

"We were getting ready to leave when Jared got the call from the hospital. Don't be mad. It wasn't his fault."

Natalie turned to Jared, aware of Libby lingering on the porch. "Is that true?"

The dark shadows under his eyes stood out now. "It's no excuse for not contacting you. We couldn't remember your cell number, but I should have kept trying the house. I'm sorry we worried you."

At his apology, remorse washed over her. Swallowing her anger, she went straight to the kitchen to collect the extra plates on the table. "We were just getting ready to eat the dessert Chelsey made, but I can warm your supper in the microwave. You must be starving."

Jared followed her to the counter. "Thanks for understanding." He took the white stoneware from her hands, and their fingers brushed against each other.

Conscious of his touch, Natalie set the dish in the microwave, recalling the words Libby had spoken in the bedroom. Her cheeks flushed with heat as she waited for the food to warm. Could Jared be interested in her? At the microwave's ding, she stabbed the T-bones and set each on a plate, careful to avoid the man's face. "Was Mr. Wilson a friend?"

"A member of our congregation. A nice old man, and a man sure of his destination." Jared's voice came to her soft and fatigued, and wrapped around her like a warm embrace.

"All this talk about death gives me the creeps," Libby said from the table, having apparently overheard their conversation. "It lingers over us like the smell of dead fish."

At the woman's voice, the warm embrace evaporated, leaving Natalie cold and unattended. "Really, do we have to discuss this while we eat?" She busied herself with wiping off the counter.

Jared took the plates to the table and sat down with Dillon. After a quick prayer, he and her brother tore into their food as though they hadn't eaten all day. "Death isn't something to fear," he said. "We'll all die one day. What's important is that we not waste the time we're given. To live the life we're called to live." He winked at Natalie and smiled. "Some people are called to be pastors, and some are called to be pageant queens."

Natalie tossed the dishrag into the sink, wondering if he was making fun. She turned her attention to Chelsey's cake displayed on a glass pedestal. Her sister had outdone herself, creating a real work of art with curls of grated chocolate scattered on top of the three-layer dessert. It looked almost too pretty to eat.

"If that's true then I must have been called to be in rodeo," Libby said.

The woman's boastfulness grated on Natalie's nerves and she tried to hold back her condemnation. Had God not called Libby to be a mother? Or had he called Natalie to be the mother instead? The entire situation irritated her to no end. She ran a sharp knife through the chocolate layers, then licked the fudge frosting from her finger. "Who needs more ice?"

"I'll have some, thank you." Libby held out her glass and glanced around the room. "Where did Chelsey go, anyway?"

"She's probably on the phone." Dillon answered with his mouth full. "I thought you were going to ground her for that?"

Libby stared up as Natalie dropped a piece of ice into the woman's glass, causing the tea to splash onto the table. "Ground her? From talking on the phone? Surely not."

Natalie added a few more cubes to the glass. "Chelsey is grounded, but not from phone calls—yet."

Jared cleared his voice. "Not to interfere, but it might be wise to at least monitor who she talks to."

"Yeah, I bet she talks to Lucas ten times a day," Dillon said.

"You think?" Natalie's hand stalled in the air. What good did it do to ground the girl from the boy if she was just going to talk to him on the phone all day ... or night? She returned the container of ice to the freezer, and feeling incredibly inept, slipped out of the kitchen to find Chelsey.

Her sister lounged on the stairs talking on the phone, just as Dillon suspected. Natalie motioned for her to end the conversation.

Chelsey rolled her eyes. "I'll have to call you back," she said to the person on the other end. "My warden is giving me the look."

After a few seconds, she closed the connection and stared up at Natalie with a vile expression that bordered on hatred. "What's the matter? Can't I even talk to my friends now?"

"Jared and Dillon are here. We're ready to serve your cake."

"So what? You could eat without me."

Natalie clenched her teeth, tempted to strangle the mouthy teenager. "We have guests, Chelsey, and one of them is your mother. I don't think it's too much to ask for you to give us your attention for one night," she said, hating the sound of her voice. When had she turned into such a disapproving nag?

"How come you invited Pastor Jared, anyway? Aren't we around him enough, without him eating with us? Besides, I didn't think you liked him."

"Why do you say that?" The question lingered in Natalie's throat.

"Whenever he's around, you end up arguing. All you do is fuss.

You didn't used to be so mean. What happened to you, anyway?" Chelsey rose from the stair step and moved past, clipping Natalie's shoulder in a huff.

Natalie couldn't argue with the truth. She'd been angry a lot these days. The fact that she'd been angry, angered her even more.

TWENTY-FIVE

JARED LOOKED UP AS CHELSEY ENTERED THE ROOM, FOLLOWED BY NATALIE. It didn't take a crystal ball to realize the two females had exchanged words, the air as thick as his mom's custard pudding. He savored another bite of his juicy steak, determined not to let the dour mood spoil his appetite. It'd been years since he'd eaten farm-raised beef—probably since before he went to seminary. Too long, and he wasn't about to waste a minute of his enjoyment.

"I understand you made dessert for us, Chelsey." His gaze traveled from the frosted cake on the counter to the young girl fuming at the end of the table. She sat with them, but judging by her grim expression, she didn't want to be there.

"Who else would bake it?" Her lids narrowed. "Not the beauty queen. That chore is too far beneath her."

Jared sipped his iced tea and studied Natalie's reaction. The sweet scent of chocolate clashed with the acrid vibes bouncing off the people in the room. "Not everyone is blessed with culinary skills, but it obviously agrees with you."

"You didn't get it from me, that's for sure," Libby said. "What do you kids have planned for your summer vacation?"

149

Chelsey's frown deepened. "Thanks to Pastor J, I'll be helping with Vacation Bible School every night next week."

"It won't be that bad." Jared grinned at the teen as Natalie began serving thick slices of cake to everyone.

He reached for a plate and passed it to Dillon. "I talked to Mrs. Trevor today. She said you'd be able to help with the first and second graders."

Chelsey folded her arms across her chest, her expression unchanged. "Oh goody. I can hardly wait."

Libby bit into her piece of cake as soon as she received it. Dark chocolate smudged her mouth. "Let me get this straight. All of you attend New Redeemer Church?"

Natalie sniffed and shook her head. "Not exactly."

"Then I don't understand." Her lips smacked with chocolate, and her mouth curved upward. "You're so involved with Natalie and the kids. What's the connection?"

Dillon hopped up from the table and returned with a glass of milk. "Chelsey got in trouble last week, so now she has to do time at Pastor's Jared's church."

Chelsey glared at the boy and he stuck out his tongue.

"What Natalie said is true, then. This family is your mission project." Libby took another bite of cake and licked the frosting from her lips.

Jared straightened in his chair. "I wouldn't say that." He shot a look at Natalie and recognized her unease — wondered if that's how she really felt.

Natalie cleared her throat. "Why don't we take our dessert to the living room where it's cooler?" She rose from the table, and Jared followed her lead.

"Wanna play checkers?" Dillon asked as they entered the next room.

"Sure, set them up." Jared figured a little laughter might ease some of the anxiety that had collected the last few minutes.

Libby settled on the couch with her plate in hand. "You've befriended Dillon, you're counseling Chelsey, I can only imagine what your plans are for Natalie, her being single and the new owner of this ranch." Though she'd directed the comment toward Jared, her eyes remained fastened on Natalie.

"I'm only part owner," Natalie sat in a nearby rocking chair. "Dad split the property between all three of us."

"All the more reason for you to have an advisor in the matter." Libby took another bite of her cake. "Perhaps that's the role Pastor Jared wants to play—like in *The Thorn Birds* with Meggie Cleary and Father Ralph. I loved that movie. Kind of gives you a whole different perspective on things, doesn't it?"

"Ah, but this isn't Australia, and I'm not a Catholic priest." Jared eased into a chair and drew a line in the condensation on his glass.

Natalie pitched back and forth in the wooden rocker across from him, her gaze intent. "Just because we both happen to be single doesn't make us candidates for a steamy romance. Besides, that movie was ridiculous. A priest falling in love with a child."

Jared couldn't agree more and chuckled. All this talk about romance reminded him of Dillon's matchmaking efforts in the car and caused him to wonder what kind of woman he wanted for a bride. Certainly a virtuous one who commanded respect, who was gentle and wise. But wouldn't he also need to be physically attracted to her? He noted Natalie's tan, slender legs and the shapely arch of her bare feet. When he realized he was staring, he quickly looked away and turned his attention to the chocolate cake on his plate. He took a bite. Rich and moist, with just a hint of bitterness on the tongue. "Chelsey, this cake is delicious."

Chelsey sat cross-legged on the floor. "It's my own recipe. I tweaked the ingredients until it came out just right."

"Well, it's very good. You should share it with Clara at the café. Maybe she could sell it to her customers."

The young teen blushed, but her mood seemed to lighten at the compliment.

"Chelsey's been cooking for us since she was a little girl," Natalie said. "Of course, everyone was thrilled when she took over my job. I'm not much good at the stove—unless you like your food burnt."

Jared studied the sisters, wondering what it must have been like growing up without a mother. His gaze slid to Libby. He would have thought this conversation would make her uncomfortable, but it didn't seem to faze her at all.

"Goodness knows I like to eat," Libby said. "But if I had a choice, I'd rather be out working or riding a horse to being in the kitchen."

Dillon finished setting up the game of checkers and nudged Jared to make the first move.

"Speaking of work, when do you want to begin haying?" Jared moved one of his pieces and waited for Natalie's response.

His question garnered several stares. "Are you hiring Pastor Jared to work for you, Nat?" Libby asked.

Chelsey fell back on the couch. "Tell me it's not so."

Natalie's gaze darted around the room and landed on Jared. "I can't do everything myself."

"We'll help you," Dillon assured her, more interested in his next move than in the conversation.

"And I expect your help. Now that Tom's gone, you're all going to have to pull your weight, including you, Libby, depending on how long you stay."

After that, the mention of work didn't come up again. Instead the conversation centered on crowning kings, fishing trips, and future rodeos. When Jared caught Dillon yawning, he realized he'd overstayed his welcome. "I should be getting home." He stood, his legs stiff from sitting so long.

"Let me help you with the rest of Dad's clothes." Natalie rose from the rocker and led him to where she'd stacked the remaining boxes on the porch. She slipped the satin ribbon from her hair, and her long mane tumbled down her back in one liquid motion. "I'm sorry for being angry before."

Mesmerized by the gleaming hair, Jared found himself speechless, wondering what it might be like to catch the fine strands between his fingers. "Believe me, I understand," he said when he'd gained control of his thoughts. "I'm sorry for causing you to worry."

They each lifted a box and carried them to his car, followed by two more loads. "What did you think of Libby? Do you think she's changed?" Natalie asked on their final trip.

Jared leaned the box against his car, reminded that he'd been put in this woman's presence for a purpose — not to ogle her beauty but to offer her Godly instruction. "I don't know. They say leopards cannot change their spots, but in terms of people, we can always hope. She certainly seems interested in getting to know the kids."

Natalie stared at him perplexed and wary. He fought the urge to reach out to her and instead dropped the heavy box into the trunk of his car. "You're not a little girl, anymore, Natalie. You're smart and kind enough to give Libby another chance. And that's all it takes. Let God do the rest."

She dipped her head with the faintest smile, and he took her box and set it beside the other. As he did so, he caught sight of a red satin ribbon on the floorboard and recognized it as the one Natalie had worn in her hair. He casually picked it up and tucked it in his pocket.

"Maybe you could come by next weekend to discuss our plans for haying?" Her gaze traveled to his eyes, their blue depths glimmering in the yard light with expectation, hope. "Maybe you and Dillon could even go fishing?"

Jared had seen many expressions on Natalie's face, angry stares and smiles that made his knees quiver, but the gentle appreciation that shone in her eyes now made his heart hammer within his chest. Could he trust himself to be around this woman and not fall in love with her? The thought scared him half to death.

"Sure, I'll call you later this week ... if that's all right," he said, and at her nod, he got in his car and drove away.

TWENTY-SIX

THE NEXT MORNING, NATALIE BRACED JACKSON'S FOOT ON HER KNEE AND picked a piece of chert from his hoof, preparing him for their daily trek through the pasture. A strong south breeze blew in through the barn and brought with it a singing whistle. Natalie glanced up from her work to see Dillon heading off to the pasture with his fishing rod.

"Hey," she hollered. "Have you done your chores already?"

Dillon stopped midstride and shuffled toward her, his boots scraping against the gravel drive. "I fed the goats and horses. I thought I'd catch us some fish for supper."

"Did you forget you were supposed to ask permission before you traipse off on your own?"

"I told Libby. Besides, I'm only going to the pond. Dad never cared if I went fishing — as long as my chores were done."

"Things are different now." She set Jackson's foot on the ground and smoothed a hand over the gelding's leg. "I hoped you would ride with me this morning to check the cattle — keep me company."

"Why can't Chelsey help? Or Libby? You never let me do anything fun."

"I took you to the rodeo." Natalie frowned and considered Jared's fondness for her brother. "Help me today, and tonight you can call Jared and ask if he'll take you to the river this weekend."

Dillon's brown eyes squinted with hesitance. "You'd let me go? After the trouble we got into last night?"

"What happened last night wasn't your fault—or Jared's either, for that matter." Natalie led Jackson to the tack room to retrieve her saddle and was reminded of the cash she'd found there. "Have you been keeping your eye out for hidden money?"

Her brother nodded. "Yeah, I've looked all over the barn, but so far the only thing I've found is a nest of baby mice." He grinned and propped his fishing rod against the wall.

Natalie made a face, thinking it might be time to buy some rat poison from the farm store. Either that or get more cats.

"Is Libby going with us this morning?"

Natalie hadn't seen anything of her stepmom since breakfast. She knew the woman wanted to spend time with each of the kids and thought perhaps she was with Chelsey. "I kinda doubt it. What do you think of her so far?"

Dillon handed her Jackson's saddle straps and scrunched his nose. "She's alright. She talks a lot."

Never shuts up is more like it, but Natalie kept that to herself. "What do you talk about?"

"Stuff—mostly rodeo. Libby thinks we need another horse, either a barrel racer or one for roping."

Natalie tugged the cinch tight on Jackson's stomach, wondering how Libby planned to pay for such a horse. She didn't waste any time, either, already filling the kids' heads with ideas. "And what do you think?"

Dillon grinned. "I think if we find another stash of money, we should buy one."

Natalie chuckled and then a measure of foreboding formed in her gut. "You didn't tell Libby about the money, did you?"

Her brother shook his head. "Want me to?"

"No, not yet." Natalie's anxiety eased a bit. She then caught sight of Libby hustling toward them, dressed in lemon colored pants and top. The woman had impeccable timing, her radar tuned to perfection. Natalie forced a smile. "Are your ears burning?"

Libby smiled back, cheerful and bright. "Should they be?"

Natalie led the horse forward to meet her at the edge of the barn. "Dillon and I were just discussing our plans for the day."

"Well, I'm glad I caught you," Libby said, out of breath. "I was just getting ready to go into town and wondered if Chelsey could go with me. You don't have anything for her to do this morning, do you?"

Natalie corralled her annoyance. "Dillon and I were about to ride out and check cattle. We do have a ranch to run, and with Dad gone, it's even more important for the kids to lend a hand."

"Oh sure, and I'll do my part, as well." Libby grinned. "But you don't have anything going on this morning, right?"

Natalie clamped her mouth in an effort to hold her tongue.

"I'd like to buy Chelsey some new cowboy boots. Hers are looking worn and shabby. I'm sure you can appreciate that. I've seen the boots in your closet."

A ripple of irritation slinked up Natalie's back. Why had Libby been going through her closet? She glanced down at her own scuffed boots, a heavy film of dust coating them. How long had it been since she'd been shopping? To look at clothes or boots or anything besides grain and groceries? She shook off the thought and checked Jackson's cinch again. "I'd appreciate it if you'd ask me before giving the kids permission to do things. Like Dillon and his fishing."

The woman made a clucking noise with her tongue. "You gotta let the kids be kids, Nat. It's their summer break. They need to have some freedom."

The hair on Natalie's neck bristled. What about her freedom? Sure, she was no longer a child, but it wasn't as though she'd asked for this job. She'd traded her freedom for instant parenthood and land. And for what? More responsibility? She watched as Dillon dug behind a set of wooden panels, probably searching for those baby mice. Her heart warmed at the sight, longing to experience a bit of childhood herself. "I guess you can take Chelsey with you. But tomorrow is a work day—for all of us."

"You should take a little time for yourself, Nat. You're working too hard on this ranch and trying to raise these kids. It's not right, a young woman being tied down. It's good I'm here to take some of the burden off your shoulders."

Natalie's brows arched. How long did Libby plan to stay? All summer? "You never did say if you had a job to get back to?"

The woman patted Jackson's neck. "This here's a mighty fine animal you have, Nat. I bet he's good with barrels, isn't he?"

"He's good at barrels." But not as good as Libby was at evading questions. "He's good at chasing cows too, which is what I need to do now."

"Want us to bring you back some hamburgers or a pizza?"

"I'm sure Dillon will be hungry. Seems like he's always eating something."

"He's a growing boy." The woman gazed at her son with appreciation and pride, causing Natalie to wonder at her ability to abandon him all those years ago.

The back screen squeaked open and drew their attention. Chelsey came out on the porch with the phone. "Natalie, you have a call."

Natalie debated ignoring it as most of the calls she'd received lately had to do with her father's death—from life insurance companies, creditors, or other folks wanting their share of his money. Being the executor of his will had turned into an incredible nuisance. "Take a message, and I'll call them back."

Her sister planted a hand on her hip and sent Natalie a look of indifference she could discern all the way from the barn. "I think you'll want to answer this. It's someone from your royal court."

Natalie's attitude perked at Chelsey's flippant terminology, guessing it was news about the upcoming queen clinic she'd volunteered to help with. "Tell them I'll be there in a minute."

She handed Libby her horse's lead rope. "Would you mind tying Jackson for me?" she asked, unable to withhold the excitement from her voice. Without waiting for an answer, Natalie hurried to the house to take the call. Right away, she recognized the voice of the clinic coordinator.

"I hate to bother you, especially when you have so much else to think about, but I'm in a bit of a panic," the woman stated.

"It's no bother. What's going on?" Natalie had been working with Connie on the clinic plans for months and looked forward to the diversion from ranch work, even if only for one weekend. "We're not canceling, are we?"

Her friend laughed into her ear. "It's not that bad. The preacher we had scheduled for our cowboy church has a family illness. You don't happen to know of anyone in the area who might fill in, do you?"

Natalie instantly thought of Jared. "Actually, I might. When do you need an answer?"

"As soon as possible. If we aren't able to get a preacher, we'll have to rearrange our schedule."

"Well don't worry, I'm sure we'll be able to come up with something. I'll get back with you as soon as I can." Natalie ended the conversation, optimistic Jared would be able to help or at least suggest someone who could. As she returned to the barn to load the horses in the stock trailer, there was a lightness in her step. Maybe Libby was right. Maybe her life didn't have to be all about ranching and the kids. Maybe this clinic was exactly what she needed to give her soul a boost—or at the very least keep her from going insane.

TWENTY-SEVEN

THURSDAY EVENING JARED MADE HIS DAILY ROUNDS FOR VACATION BIBLE school, welcomed by the usual classroom greeting.

"Say hello to Pastor, children," Mrs. Trevor called to her first and second graders.

"Hello Pastor Jared," a dozen kids shouted in unison, waving and jumping up and down in their seats.

"Hey, how are things going?" He waved then smiled at Chelsey who helped at the back of the class. This week, he'd kept close tabs on Chelsey and Sarah, and each of them seemed to take their responsibilities seriously. He hoped their week of church duty would make a difference in their lives.

During the snack break, Jared stopped to visit Chelsey. "The kids seem especially enthusiastic tonight. Do you suppose they've had too much sugar?" He laughed. "You appear to be holding up okay, though."

Chelsey took a sip of her fruit punch. "They're probably nervous about tomorrow's program."

"They should be — we all should be." He grinned, recalling how half the children still didn't know the words of their songs. "I'm glad you decided to help this week. The teachers really appreciate the extra hands."

Chelsey wiped the red juice from her mouth. "It's not like you gave me much choice," she said, but then smiled.

"You have a knack with kids." Jared had watched the young teen work with her students, helping them with their coloring projects and leading them in games. It was a good decision to give her the responsibility. "Will your family attend the program tomorrow night?"

The girl stared down at her boots. "I doubt they'll come. It's not really their thing, if you know what I mean."

Jared frowned in frustration, wanting to understand and help, but not sure how to break through the barrier. "What is their thing, Chelsey?"

She shrugged. "Nothing against your church, Pastor J, but you have to admit, the activities are kind of lame."

"You think so?"

"Yeah, but if it'll make you feel better, I'll ask them one more time." She grinned as a little girl tugged on her hand and drew her off to play.

"COME ON, IF I HAVE TO GO TO THE PROGRAM, YOU DO TOO," CHELSEY told Natalie the next evening, while doing their chores. "Besides, this is my last day of penance. After this, I'm free."

Natalie returned the feed bucket to the barn, mystified by the change in her sister's demeanor and wondering if it had to do with her work at church or if it was because of Libby. "That doesn't mean you can go back to your trouble-making."

"Pastor J will be so pleased to see you at church tonight." Chelsey clutched her chest and fluttered her eyelashes, completely ignoring Natalie's admonition. "He's been asking about you all week."

Natalie disregarded the playful taunt. "What are we supposed to wear to this shindig?" she called after her sister, but Chelsey was already halfway to the house.

An hour later, Natalie trailed her family across the church-yard, lawn chairs tucked under their arms. She glanced through the crowd, on the lookout for Jared in his clergy attire. She spotted him speaking to a group of children, but he wasn't dressed in black. Instead, he wore a white T-shirt with a colorful design printed on the front. Unaware of her presence, he gestured with his hands and flapped his arms like a chicken, causing the kids to explode in laughter.

"Kinda makes you see him in a whole new light, doesn't it?"

Startled by Willard's sudden appearance, Natalie nearly toppled over a youngster running in front of her. "What are you doing here?"

The man reached out to steady her balance. "Pastor invited me. Said there'd be ice cream." His eyes twinkled.

"I should have known." Natalie giggled, glad for her friend's company. She gazed at Jared, realizing for the first time what his job entailed—teaching little ones, visiting the sick, working with Bible study groups, and preparing sermons. In the last few days, she'd grown to accept him as their friend, but seeing him now surrounded by his congregation, she couldn't deny his profession any longer. The realization gave her pause and left her feeling a bit out of her element.

Chelsey split off to be with her classroom, while Natalie and the rest of her group found a place to sit. For the next thirty minutes, she watched as the kids went through their program of songs and skits, showcasing everything they'd learned that week. She applauded when the parents applauded and laughed when the others laughed, thoroughly enjoying the evening. Afterwards, Jared came up to them, beaming with pleasure.

"I see Chelsey talked you into attending the program."

Natalie grinned. "Your puppet skit was quite entertaining, especially your lion routine. The children loved it."

He took a generous bow. "What can I say? Perhaps I missed my calling and should have gone to Hollywood."

"No, trust me, you're much better suited for Diamond Falls."

Jared chuckled and shook Willard's hand. "It's good to see you too, even though I know you're only here for the ice cream."

Willard pointed to the church awning where several women were serving dessert from behind a row of tables. "Yes, and folks are already getting in line. We should too, don't you think?" He nudged Dillon, his eyes bright and animated.

"By all means, go right ahead." Jared stepped out of their way. "I've heard we have thirteen flavors tonight."

"All I need is one." Willard winked at Natalie, then led her brother and Libby to the tables, not sticking around for chitchat.

"Shall we join them?" Jared held out his arm, and Natalie latched onto his elbow, enjoying the relaxed camaraderie.

"Let me guess," she said. "Your favorite flavor is—"

"Vanilla," he offered before she could finish.

She giggled. "Men are so boring."

"Oh really? I suppose your favorite is Tropical Peach Mango or some other crazy concoction."

She smiled at this rare playful side. "Actually my favorite is chocolate chip. Chunky, chunky chip if you want to get technical."

"Do all women crave chocolate? My mom loves the stuff."

"Pour on some thick hot fudge, and I might float away on a cloud."

He wrinkled his nose and stared up at the evening sky, not yet twilight. "Pour too much on and you'll sink the cloud."

Natalie jammed her elbow into his side. "Not funny."

They reached the tables and an elderly woman served them. Natalie noticed the woman didn't smile.

"Thank you, Mrs. Hildebrand," Jared said. "Did you make this ice cream yourself?"

She practically gushed at his attention. "Yes, and I hope you enjoy it. It's an old family recipe, brought down from three generations."

"I'm sure it'll taste delightful."

They moved through the line, and Jared helped himself to three more flavors until his bowl could hold no more. "Shall we sit over there?" He motioned toward an empty picnic table.

Natalie felt the stare of several congregation members as they walked by. "I think we're being watched."

Jared followed her gaze, then waved to a few of the people. "They're probably wondering why a pretty lady like you is sitting with a geek like me."

"I doubt that." Natalie's face grew warm at the compliment. She couldn't help but notice how the woman behind the serving table still stared, still frowned. "Perhaps they don't approve of the company you keep?"

Jared flashed a disapproving look. "Why would you think that? This church is a friendly bunch, open to anyone who wants to hear God's Word or have fellowship with us."

Natalie wanted to believe him. She thought of their phone conversation earlier that week. "Thanks again for agreeing to lead cowboy church for us at the clinic. You really helped us out of a pinch."

"It's my pleasure. I'm glad you called. Maybe one of these days you'll join us for church here—I hope so, anyway."

Oddly enough, the idea didn't sound as distasteful as it once had. "Chelsey enjoyed Bible school this week. I guess your plan wasn't so bad after all. I've already begun to see a change in her attitude." She offered a slight grin. Then her stepmom's cackle filled the air, and the hairs on Natalie's neck bristled with dread. Her gaze tracked the raucous laughter to the other side of the churchyard, and to her horror, Natalie witnessed the woman in lime green press provocatively close to the man next to her. The middle-aged man seemed to enjoy Libby's flirtation and laughed right along with her. Did the woman have no shame?

A cloud of gloom enveloped Natalie, as once again, she feared what Jared's congregation would think of the wild interlopers who had crashed their party. "Will you excuse me for a minute?" She got up from the table hoping to deter the train before it wrecked.

Within seconds, she reached Libby's side and drew her away. "Are you crazy? We're at a church social, not a cocktail hour."

"What do you mean, Nat? I'm just having a little fun with this gentleman. We were about to get us some ice cream, weren't we?" She grinned back at the balding man whose interest hadn't waned despite the obvious scene Libby made.

"Can you at least turn your volume down so you don't make such a spectacle of yourself?"

Libby tore her arm from Natalie's grasp, taking offense. "I don't know where you get off judging me, Nat. I don't mean anybody any harm. And besides that, Chelsey is the one who invited me to this social, so if anyone is going to judge, it'll be my daughter."

Natalie balked at the woman's attack, realizing for the first time that Libby didn't consider Natalie her family. She cringed as the torrent of words continued, Libby's voice growing louder with each sentence.

"Okay, okay, just lower your voice," Natalie pleaded, wondering if her stepmom had been drinking.

"Don't worry about me." Libby pointed at Jared who stood a few yards away observing the display. "Why don't you go back to your preacher fella? I can see he's anxious for your return."

Natalie's cheeks flamed hot as a branding iron. Not only had Libby embarrassed her and her family, she now implicated Jared. What would his congregation think of him? Eager to leave, she searched the crowd and spotted Dillon with a couple of boys his age. Chelsey sat at a table with Sarah.

On her way to fetch them, she stopped to offer Jared an apology. "I'm so sorry for causing a scene."

Jared's dark eyes shone with compassion. "I doubt people even noticed. Why don't you stay and finish your ice cream." He carried their bowls in his hands.

"I can't. We need to leave."

"No, you don't." He set her bowl on a table and waited for her to join him. "None of us are perfect, Natalie."

Confused by Jared's forbearance, Natalie struggled with whether to leave or stay, wanting nothing more than to return to the light-hearted evening they shared before. Right when she was about to agree, Libby again made her presence known and tapped Jared on the shoulder.

"Pastor Jared, I have something I want to ask you." Her voice slurred, and Natalie was now certain the woman had been drinking.

Jared surely realized it too. "How can I help you, Libby?"

"I wanna know if you like my stepdaughter." She leaned close to Jared and stared up at him. "Do you like Natalie? Cause if you do, I think that's just great."

"Why yes, Libby. I like Natalie very much. I have an idea, though." Jared took the woman by the arm and sent Natalie an unspoken message. His eyes told her to trust him. "Why don't you let Natalie drive you home, and we can talk about this later."

Willard came up to them and buffered Libby's other side. "That's right, we can talk about this at home," Willard said, lowering his voice for Natalie, "where there aren't quite so many ears to hear."

"I don't want to leave," the woman fussed. "The party is just beginning. I haven't even had my ice cream yet."

The two men led Libby through the crowd to the truck and passed by Chelsey and Dillon who watched in stunned silence. Natalie fought back her humiliation, desperately wishing to be invisible, but needing to be courageous for her brother and sister. She opened her arms to them. "The party's over, kids. Why don't you gather our chairs so we can go home?"

Dillon immediately did as told, but not Chelsey. Instead, she rushed to take Jared's place and wrapped her arm around Libby's waist. "Come on, Mom, we have ice cream in the freezer, and it's twice as good as the stuff they're serving here."

Natalie recoiled at the barbed words issuing from her sister's mouth. She exchanged worried looks with Jared. Then Chelsey shot a dagger at her.

"Like mother like daughter, isn't that what you're thinking?"

TWENTY-EIGHT

"No one is thinking that, Chelsey." Jared opened the passenger door for Libby, hating that all their work this week would end on such a sour note and possibly destroy the progress made in the teen's troubled life.

"That's right, young lady. Nobody's going to compare you to this woman." Willard confiscated a near-empty bottle of dark liquor from the floorboard of the truck. "She's been gone so long no one even remembers her. Not even here a week, and already she's causing problems." The man ground the words out through his teeth and set the bottle in the back of the truck.

"You never did like me, did you, old man." Libby climbed into the cab, shoving past any help offered her. "But that's okay, 'cause I never liked you much either." She scooted to the middle of the seat allowing room for Chelsey to join her.

"I know you love your mom and want to help her," Jared told Chelsey as she entered the cab. "We want to help too. You believe that, don't you?"

Chelsey stared back, confused and on guard.

"We'll get home a lot faster if you'll quit jabbering," Libby bellowed, and Jared gently shut the door on the woman's loud mouth.

He caught up to Natalie as she made her way to the driver's side. "You're always welcome here, Natalie. You and your family." He cast a quick glance at his parishioners. A few still watched from the lawn. "Remember what I told you, none of us are perfect—we're all sinners and all in need of Jesus' forgiveness and salvation."

Natalie turned to him and exhaled. "I don't know, Jared. Somehow I get the feeling we don't fit in with this crowd."

Jared clasped her hand within his own. "I'm not here to judge you, Natalie."

"Can you say the same about them?" She nodded toward his congregation.

"Test us and see. Come to church on Sunday. Bring Chelsey and Dillon, Libby too, if she has a mind to attend."

Dillon appeared at Natalie's side, his arms loaded with lawn chairs. She helped stack them in the bed of the truck, then waited for her brother to squeeze in beside Chelsey. "Thanks for inviting us tonight," Natalie situated herself behind the wheel and rolled down the window. "But I wouldn't count on seeing us in church on Sunday."

"I'm not giving up that easy." Jared watched as Natalie backed out of the parking lot and called out to Dillon. "I haven't forgotten about our fishing trip, either. Best start digging some worms."

Willard patted Jared's shoulder as Natalie drove off. "Don't give up on them. Remember, the prayers of a righteous man availeth much."

Jared nodded, glad for the man's support. "I'm sure by now my ice cream has melted. Want to join me for seconds?"

Willard let out a deep chuckle and patted his stomach. "Does it look like I've ever turned down seconds?"

LATER THAT EVENING, NATALIE RUMMAGED THROUGH THE VAST ARRAY of queen clothing in her closet. Her fingers lingered on the leather gown she'd worn at the Miss Rodeo America coronation, a red dress with fringe and sterling sequins. Of all her outfits, this had been her favorite—along with her sunflower vest designed especially for her by Rickrageous. Was it time to put all of this behind her and sell her pageantry outfits?

Her throat tightened with tears as she scanned the row of hangers. There were plenty of girls who could use the clothing, and she certainly didn't have much need for leather dresses out here on the ranch. Her boots were another story though, as she didn't think she could part with them.

She pulled two dresses from the closet, and a knock sounded on her bedroom door. "May I come in?" Chelsey asked in a muffled voice.

Natalie opened the door, still irritated about the evening. "What do you need?"

Chelsey traipsed into the room and sat on the bed. "I wondered if we could talk? About what happened tonight? About Libby?"

"You know you can talk to me anytime. I miss that about us—how we used to stay up chatting and giggling into the wee hours of the night." Natalie draped a powder blue gown on the bed to study. "What do you think of this dress? Should I try to sell it at the queen clinic?"

Her sister fingered the soft, supple leather, and Natalie showed her the second gown on a hanger, a pink two-piece that complimented Chelsey's complexion more than it did her own. "Want to try this on before it goes to auction? We could fix your hair and makeup ... just like old times."

Chelsey shook her head, but Natalie caught her hesitation. "Come on, it'll be fun." She dangled the dress in front of her sister as bait.

"Okay, if it means you'll stop nagging." Chelsey snatched the outfit and took it to her room, returning minutes later dressed in the pink leather.

Natalie noticed right away that her sister had taken the time to accessorize and wore the new heart necklace Libby had bought her the other day on their shopping trip. "Now all you need are some pink boots."

"Does everything always have to match?" Irritation spouted from the girl's lips.

"You bet." Natalie dug in her closet through her stash of boots. "And you must always blacken the heels and bottoms of your boots because the judges are eyelevel with your feet when you're on stage—It's one of the first rules you learn in modeling." She grinned and handed her sister a pair of pink ropers, dyed to match the dress.

"Sure seems like a lot of nonsense." Chelsey slipped into the boots with ease, her feet a size smaller than Natalie's.

"A rodeo queen represents the sport of rodeo," Natalie said, "and there's nothing foolish or sissy about that." There were plenty of cowboys who made fun of rodeo queens, thinking they were all about style and beauty and didn't have a brain, but they were wrong, and so was Chelsey.

Her sister pulled her hair back into a sloppy bun. "Okay, how do I look?"

"Let me help you with that." Natalie guided her to the oak vanity and brushed the girl's long blonde strands. "Are you mad at me for what happened tonight? You think I should have controlled Libby? Kept her from getting drunk?"

Chelsey stared back at her in the mirror, her hazel brown eyes made all the more vibrant by the pink collar on the dress. "Did you even know she'd been drinking?"

Natalie shook her head and frowned. "By the time I realized it, it was too late. Have you talked to her since we came home?"

Her sister gnawed on a fingernail. "She said she was nervous about being around all those church people. That she'd needed something to calm her nerves."

Natalie groaned. A little Jim Beam would do that every time.

She made a few more swipes with the brush. "What about the comment you made to me?"

The girl shrugged. "It was what you were thinking—that we were both drunks."

Natalie twirled the teen's hair, tempted to manipulate it even more with a good yank. Instead, she formed it into a chignon at the back of her head and set it with a clip. She gazed into the mirror at her sister and smiled. "I never thought that about you, Chels. I know you're having a hard time dealing with Dad's death. We all are. And we all make mistakes—goodness knows I've made my share of them."

Chelsey sprung from the vanity chair and pulled the clip from her hair. "You never make mistakes. You're perfect—Dad's favorite little girl. He always said so." She went back to the bed and fiddled with the pink fringe on the dress.

"Is that what you think?" Natalie joined her on the bed. "Because I assure you Dad and I had our difficult moments. What is this really about, anyway?"

Her sister's bottom lip quivered.

"Are you mad because I've forbidden you to see Lucas? Is that it? You don't want me controlling your life?"

"You don't know what it's like to be in love."

"I've had plenty of boyfriends." Natalie gazed down at her lap, thinking of one guy in particular.

"I mean someone you really love, who you want to spend the rest of your life with."

Natalie recognized the raw emotion on her sister's face and remembered all too well her own misguided feelings for Ryan. "You think you're in love, but it's just a phase you're going through. Like puppy love. You're too young to have those kinds of feelings, Chels."

Her sister set her jaw hard and tight. "What about you and Pastor Jared?"

Natalie faltered at the mention of Jared's name. "I don't know what you mean."

"Do you like him?"

"I guess so . . ." She shrugged, not caring for where this interrogation might lead.

"Oh, I get it. We can talk about my love life, but yours is off-limits?" Chelsey crossed her arms in front of her chest and frowned. "You say you want to be close, to talk like we used to, but you don't really mean it, do you?"

Trapped by her own words, Natalie gave in. "Okay, what do you want to know? Let's talk about men or love or whatever." She snatched a pillow from her bed and hugged it to her chest.

These must have been the magic words, as Chelsey turned all gushy and cheerful. "How do you know when you're in love?"

Natalie's face flushed with warmth. "I suppose it happens over time, when a man you like becomes your friend, and you enjoy spending time with him, or maybe you think about him when you're not together."

"Or your hands get all clammy, and your heart beats like a herd of horses inside your chest?" Chelsey stretched out on the bed and seized a pillow of her own.

Natalie grinned. "Yeah, I suppose it's something like that."

"Is that the way you felt when you fell in love?"

Natalie had to consider what it had been like with Ryan. She'd enjoyed spending time with the man, and he'd certainly made her heart thunder. Nearly every queen contestant drooled over the guy, so Natalie felt especially favored when he'd shown her attention. "I don't know for sure . . . maybe."

"That's what it's like for me and Lucas." The girl rubbed the silver heart pendant that dangled from her neck as though it were a charm.

"But Chels, he's so much older than you."

"What does that matter, if we love each other?"

Natalie resisted throwing her pillow at the girl. "And what makes you think he loves you? Has he said as much?"

Her sister didn't answer, and Natalie knew why. Though Ryan had declared his love to her, his words had been empty. He'd used her, like Lucas was using Chelsey. The boy probably just wanted to get as much mileage from her as he could.

"I don't want to condemn the boy when I don't even know him." Natalie tried to give Lucas the benefit of the doubt. "But if it's really love like you say, then some time apart isn't going to hurt anything. Let's do it this way. You agree to keep your distance from Lucas this summer, then if you both have the same feelings when school starts in the fall, we can discuss him coming over for visits when you turn sixteen. Sound fair?"

"I don't know if it's fair, but it's better than nothing. Does this mean I'm not grounded?"

"I didn't say that."

"How about a cell phone? I'm going to be a sophomore. Don't you think it's time I get one?"

Natalie shook her head. "Are you ready to get a job so you can pay for it?" Chelsey's mouth drooped, then just as quickly tilted into a conspiring grin.

"You never answered my question about Pastor J. Libby thinks he likes you. She thinks you went to church tonight to impress him."

"I assure you, if I attend church, it's because I want to, not because I'm trying to make an impression." Natalie's skin burned as she remembered the easy camaraderie she and Jared shared earlier that evening, the attraction she'd felt. She clutched the cool pillow to her neck.

"He seems a nice enough guy, for a pastor, that is."

Natalie closed her eyes. If only Jared weren't a pastor, she might allow her attraction for the man to grow. "We're friends, that's all."

Chelsey's eyes flickered with mischief. "Well, that's how it begins, isn't that what you told me? You start out as friends."

TWENTY-NINE

Sunday morning, Jared looked out at his congregation and scanned the pews row-by-row, hoping to see Natalie and her family seated among the members. But they were not there, just as Natalie had warned. Disheartened, Jared put the woman out of his mind and focused instead on his parishioners and the sermon he'd prepared. Afterwards, Mrs. Hildebrand cornered him in the receiving line to invite him to dinner.

"I refuse to take no for an answer. You will join us, won't you?"

Jared peered over the heads of the congregation members filing out of the sanctuary. Why shouldn't he have lunch with this family? Had he really been so optimistic as to think there might be some hope for Natalie and him? At best, the idea was ridiculous. The two had so little in common. "Yes, of course, I'll join you for dinner. Thank you for thinking of me."

Two hours later, Jared checked his watch, having spent a good portion of his afternoon warding off Mrs. Hildebrand's attempts to match him with her daughter. And to be fair, there was nothing wrong with Clarice, though he couldn't help but compare her to Natalie. Both quite pretty, Clarice had a sweet innocence about her, while Natalie exuded confidence — whether she possessed it or not.

"Thank you for a delicious dinner, but I should probably be going, as I promised to take Dillon Adams fishing this afternoon."

"You spend a lot of time with those people, don't you?" His secretary sniffed.

He wiped his mouth with a napkin, trying not to take offense at the comment. "They've had a lot of problems to work through since their father's death."

"I should say so." She huffed. "That woman at the ice cream social certainly had problems. I fear what sort of impression she left on the children. It makes me wonder if the older sister is mature enough to be Dillon and Chelsey's guardian."

Jared tried to hold back his irritation. "I assure you, Miss Adams is quite capable of raising her brother and sister. I'm not going to condone her stepmom's behavior, but let's not forget that Jesus hung out with, and forgave, even the worst of sinners. We could all learn something from that."

Upon escaping the Hildebrands' home, Jared loosened his tie, eager to put on his old clothes and enjoy an afternoon of fresh air and fishing. It irked him that his secretary had questioned Natalie's ability. Sure, Natalie had more than her share of trouble, but she loved her brother and sister, and he had every confidence that she could handle the job.

A short while later, he drove the familiar road to the Double-A Ranch. With his window down, he stretched out his arm to soak in the sun. He considered taking Dillon pond hopping, but by the time he arrived at the Adams' house he'd decided on the river, which would be more exciting for the boy and for him.

Dillon met him on the doorstep with his fishing rod and a glass jar in hand. Libby followed right behind. She wore a purple outfit today with her hair pulled back in a bun. "Dillon tells me you're taking him fishing this afternoon."

Jared checked the clouds in the sky — slightly overcast. "I think it might be a good day for getting bites. Not too hot, either."

"Would you like to come in for a glass of lemonade before you go?"

He glanced at Dillon, who seemed ready to be on his way. "Thanks for the offer, but if we leave now, we should get there right about feeding time."

"I wouldn't want to interfere with that." Her grin faltered. "About the other night at your church. I wasn't myself. I'm sorry if I caused you any embarrassment."

Jared recognized the humility on her face. "I appreciate that, Libby. You're welcome to join us again. All of you."

"Well, don't let me keep you," Libby said. "Maybe you can join us for supper when you're done. I'm sure Natalie would like to see you."

Jared's brow furrowed, tired of everyone's matchmaking. "I'll try to have Dillon back before dark," he said, ready to shake the uncertainty from his mind and get on with simple pleasures. If Natalie wanted to see him, he felt sure she'd do so on her own terms and without the help of a woman like Libby.

THIRTY

JARED PARKED HIS CAR NEAR THE BEND IN THE RIVER, AND HE AND DILLON made their way down the steep riverbank. The water had receded since the last time he'd been here, and he made note of a fallen log upstream where a channel cat might lie in wait behind the current breaker.

"Do you ever go home empty-handed?" Jared asked Dillon, stopping at the river's edge to prepare their lines.

The boy stared up with a cheeky grin. "Nope, never."

Jared set his line with a barrel swivel and an egg-shaped slip-sinker, then added a foot to the other end hoping to get a better snag on a fish. He ran the hook over his fingernail to test it, and it dug in plenty sharp. He glanced over at Dillon and noticed the container he held.

"What's in the jar?"

Dillon opened the lid, and Jared could smell the foul contents from where he stood. He wrinkled his nose and fanned his hand in front of his face. "Don't tell me that's your secret weapon?"

"Dad taught me how to make it." Dillon's voice cracked with amusement. "He always used chicken livers, but hotdogs work just as well." He pulled one from the jar and put it on a treble hook.

Jared had heard of homemade baits but had never tried them. "Works better than worms?" He wasn't convinced.

"Test it and see." Dillon handed him one for his hook. "We also used dough balls made from cornflakes and cheese. That works pretty good too. Guess it depends on what you have in the cupboard."

Jared studied the bait with skepticism. "Does Chelsey know you're pilfering her hotdogs?"

The boy giggled. "Think she'll want them back?"

"How long have they been fermenting?

Dillon scrunched his brow, and Jared could see his calculator working.

"Two weeks or so. I added a little garlic and salt too. Dad always said fish will eat just about anything as long as it smells bad."

Jared bated his hook with the piece of hotdog and cast it into the river. "Well, here's to fishing with dogs."

They both laughed, but it wasn't long before Dillon had a bite on his line.

NATALIE SWAYED BACK AND FORTH IN HER DAD'S WROUGHT IRON ROCKING chair and stared at the tall elm branches above. This was her favorite time of evening—when the sun gave up its heat to the cicadas whirring in the trees. Beyond her in the pastures, the windmills squeaked and the grass waved quietly like the sea while the sky turned a red-violet indigo. She watched as Dillon and Jared strolled in with their day's catch. Jared's face beamed with pleasure.

"I take it Dillon told you his secret." She nodded toward the string of fish in Jared's hand. "You've got a lot of work ahead of you."

"You mean we have to clean them too?" Jared whimpered as though abused.

Natalie chuckled. "If you're not careful, you'll be cooking them as well."

"I'll have you know, I'm a good cook."

She noted the healthy glow of Jared's skin and had to admit the fresh air and sunshine was having a nice effect on the man. "I'm sure Chelsey would surrender the kitchen for one night."

His eyes flashed at the challenge. "Are you inviting me to make supper?"

"Fish-and-chips?"

"And coleslaw too, if you have the ingredients."

She rose from the chair and pointed at Dillon with a smile. "You heard the man. Run and get a knife. I'll tell Chelsey she has the night off." Sensing Jared's eyes on her as she sauntered toward the house, she turned and caught him staring. Excitement fluttered in her chest.

Thirty minutes later, Natalie sat on a kitchen stool and watched as Jared prepared the meal. The others had abandoned them to play a game of cards in the living room. "Are you sure I can't do anything to help?"

The man sliced chunks of fish and dropped them into a cornmeal batter as though he'd done it every day. "Nope, I have it all under control." He spun to fetch an item from the refrigerator.

"Why haven't you ever married?" She picked up a carrot and crunched it between her teeth, amazed that she'd had the nerve to bring up such a personal subject, especially when everyone in her family seemed to be throwing them together. "I'd think they would encourage young pastors to marry before assigning them a congregation."

He seemed caught off guard by her question and stood frozen at the refrigerator. "They do encourage it ... I mean, there aren't any laws that say a pastor has to marry."

"Then why isn't there a Mrs. Logan?"

"There is." He carried a bottle of lemon juice to the counter and squirted some into the bowl where the fish soaked. "My mother."

"Very funny."

"I guess I just haven't met the right one yet."

"And what would the right woman look like?" She enjoyed the easy banter, but also wondered if the right woman might look anything like her.

Jared's eyes narrowed, as though trying to see inside her mind. "I'm sure I'll know her when I see her."

Natalie fanned herself and cleared her throat, thankful for the explosion of laughter in the next room. "You must have certain qualities you're looking for—a man your age isn't single unless he has a list a mile long."

"You think so?" He began placing the pieces of fish into the hot oil, causing it to sputter and bubble to the top of the kettle.

"I don't blame you. I'd be particular too."

His chocolaty brown eyes called her bluff. "You're a former rodeo queen. Your list must be long, as well."

"I'm not going to settle for just anyone." Especially after what she went through with Ryan.

"You should be picky," Jared said, sounding a lot like her father. "In fact, find yourself a good Christian man, who'll love you and make honorable decisions. That's what you should want in a husband."

Natalie squirmed at the lecture. "Women must come to your church in droves to listen to your sermons. Not only are you the new preacher in town, but you're good-looking and single." She hoped this might make him squirm some too. Instead, he laughed.

"If anything, my being a pastor scares women away. Few want the job of a pastor's wife—bake sales and all that."

Warmth crept up Natalie's neck as he'd repeated her earlier thoughts almost verbatim. "I'm sure the right woman's out there."

"Maybe so, but I'm not in any hurry—despite the weekly calls from my mother." He removed the golden chunks of fish from the deep fryer and placed them on a tray lined with paper towels. "She wants grandchildren and says she's tired of waiting for them." He chuckled.

Drawn by the zesty lemon seasoning, Natalie snatched a piece from the tray and silently wished she could laugh and share such moments with her mom. "Does it bother you being single? I mean, are you ever lonely?" Her teasing mood shifted to one of genuine interest, as she weighed the probability of any man marrying her now that she bore such responsibilities. After all, flirting with Jared was one thing, marrying him was quite another.

"You're full of questions, aren't you?" He grinned. "But there are some things a man must refrain from answering, lest he bare his soul too much."

"Now you sound like Willard."

"Speaking of Willard, he's been wondering how you're getting along." Jared motioned toward the other room where Libby and the kids played cards, effectively changing the subject. "He's worried. And, perhaps he has reason to be?"

"I'm keeping a close watch on her." Natalie broke the piece of fish apart and watched the steam rise from the white flakes. "I wanted to thank you for your help the other night — and to apologize again. That couldn't have been easy, dealing with such a display in front of your congregation."

"We all have problems — some more than others." He sliced a few potato wedges to go with the fish. "I'd hoped to see you in church this morning."

Her eyes darted to his. The man was persistent. But could he also be romantically interested in her? Was that why he kept prodding her to attend church? "I told you not to expect us."

He shrugged. "And I told you I haven't given up."

THIRTY-ONE

JARED BERATED HIMSELF, HOPING HIS WORDS HADN'T SOUNDED FLIRTATIOUS. While that hadn't been his intent, this entire conversation about wives and marriage was getting too close for comfort.

Dillon came into the kitchen and snatched a piece of fish from the platter. "Is supper about ready? I'm starved."

Glad for the interruption, Jared transferred the dish to the table and watched as the others filed through the door.

"This smells so good," Libby crooned. "You are a man of many talents, aren't you? Better snag this one before he gets away, Nat."

The kids giggled, and Natalie's face turned a lovely shade of pink, like a summertime peach from his mother's orchard. At this thought, Jared's chest grew warm, and he checked the clock above the refrigerator. "No wonder you're starving, Dillon. I'm sorry for making you wait so long to eat."

"Don't worry about it." Libby passed the plate of fish to her son. "This way we'll have lots of energy tomorrow morning. I'd like to get an early start and show you kids a thing or two about barrels. Thought you might like to compete in a few rodeos this summer."

"That'd be cool." Chelsey's face lit with enthusiasm, but not Dillon's.

"Barrels are for girls." Dillon streamed ketchup over his fries.

"Well okay, after I'm done with Chelsey, I'll work with you on roping. I used to be a decent roper in my day. Course, if you really want to excel, you'll need to buy a trained horse that has some experience."

"Not much chance of that happening," Natalie scooped some coleslaw onto her plate. "We can't afford a horse like that—not yet anyway."

"They can be expensive, but there are deals to be had." Libby winked at Chelsey. "You just have to know where to look—which I do."

"Maybe we'll find another stash of Dad's money." As soon as the words came out, Dillon cupped his hand over his mouth and peered at Natalie.

Jared noted the instant tension this caused.

Libby's gaze bounced between the two. "What stash of money?"

"It's nothing." Natalie shrugged. "You know how boys are. They find some money and imagine pirates and hidden treasure." She scrunched her face at Dillon and smiled.

Libby huffed. "The way your dad liked to horde his money, it's a wonder you haven't found a hundred treasures."

Natalie's fork paused in midair as she stared at the older woman. "Considering the gifts you've been showering on the kids, I'd say you know a thing or two about hording money yourself."

Libby wiped her mouth on a napkin and cleared her throat. "If you have a problem with me buying things for the kids, just say so, Nat. I didn't realize it bothered you so much." Her cheek twitched as she ran her tongue along her bottom lip.

Sensing a time bomb about to go off, Jared attempted to change the subject. "Natalie, how are your plans coming along for the queen clinic?"

Chelsey groaned. "No more queen talk, please. I've heard enough this past week to last a lifetime."

"You should join us, Chelsey." Natalie tried to sound upbeat, but Jared heard the irritation lining her voice. "There'll be several girls your age, and you could probably help with the horse event."

"I already told you I'm not interested." The teen refused to give in to Natalie's persistence.

Natalie drew a deep breath and turned her attention to Jared. "The clinic starts next Saturday, so if you want to stop by the fairgrounds then, we can run through your service."

"Is there any particular subject you want me to cover?" Having never attended cowboy church, Jared wasn't sure what to expect.

"Whatever you come up with will be fine."

Jared grinned, surprised that Natalie had given him such freedom. He knew God would provide suitable material for the event and silently prayed there would be a particular message in it for Natalie—something that would help her or speak to her heart. "I'll see what I can do."

THIRTY-TWO

THE NEXT WEEK PASSED QUICKLY AS NATALIE AND THE CLINIC COMMITTEE finalized their schedule for the queen workshops and activities. Saturday morning, Natalie strolled toward the exhibit building at the fairgrounds, having left her brother and sister in Libby's care to look after the ranch while she was gone.

Jenny Stiles, the current Miss Rodeo Kansas met Natalie inside the metal building and gave her a hug. "It's so good to see you again. Are you ready for this big weekend?"

Natalie recalled the many clinics she'd attended through the years and grinned. "I almost forgot how intimidating these workshops can be." Especially the mock interviews and impromptu questions — her most grueling sessions by far. Some girls whizzed right through them, but for Natalie, the very thought of them brought on a cold sweat. "I like it much better on this side of competition. But what about you? Have you started gearing up for Vegas?"

The younger girl's blonde curls bobbed as she made a distressed face. "Only in my dreams and my every waking hour."

"Well, don't worry about it too much." Natalie offered Jenny an encouraging smile and watched as three high school girls wandered into the exhibit building, looking as unsure and incompetent as she had once felt. "This weekend is all about learning and asking questions. Ask me anything you want. I know you'll do terrific," Natalie stated without envy or resentment. She'd expected awkward moments now that her era of competition had ended but was pleasantly surprised by the mentoring experience, as though she'd returned to her element or had even come into her own.

When everyone arrived, Jenny and Natalie welcomed the participants and went over the weekend schedule. Afterwards, they escorted the girls to the arena where two clinicians were set up to help with horsemanship skills, the riding stock furnished by the cowboys, as well as from the Double-A-Ranch. One man stood in the middle of the arena with a saddled horse, and the second came walking in from the arena gate leading Natalie's horse, Jackson.

Natalie caught her breath when she saw the man. What was he doing here? How could she have missed his name on the staff roster?

He strode past her and grinned. "Good to see you, Nat."

Natalie's knees nearly buckled. She tried to mumble a hello, but the greeting vaporized in her throat. Ryan Frazier was the last person she wanted to see or say hello to ever again.

Ryan took his place beside the other cowboy and spoke into a cordless microphone, offering introductions and going over the day's agenda. "One of the first things we want to cover this morning is proper riding etiquette, so watch closely as Miss Adams demonstrates for you."

Natalie plastered a smile onto her face, hoping to hide her stunned reaction at Ryan's sudden appearance. Her hands trembled as she gripped Jackson's reins.

"Always check your riding gear before mounting and never let your reins touch the ground," he said as Natalie stepped into the saddle. She forced herself to listen to the rest of his directives, though her emotions threatened to run away.

"Sit straight in the saddle, with your toes up and your heels down. You should be able to draw a line from the back of your ear to the back of your heel." He indicated an imaginary line from Natalie's head to her boot, and his fingers brushed against Natalie's leg on the way down. A shiver of anticipation raced up her spine, and her mind rebelled in irritation. How could there be any attraction left for Ryan, after all the pain and heartache he'd caused? She swiped the imprint of his touch from her jeans, wishing she could do the same with his memory.

While the other cowboy distributed copies of reining patterns, Ryan went over a few tips with the girls. "As you study your handouts, try to remember where the markers are and be sure to make the speed and size variations of your figure eights apparent."

He asked Natalie to demonstrate one of the patterns while he offered instruction. She ran the course effortlessly, the sequence ingrained in her mind from years of drills. It wasn't until the attendees practiced on their own that she had a chance to speak privately with him. She wiped her hands on her jeans, her palms clammy with sweat. "What are you doing here, Ryan?"

His attention followed one of the riders through a sliding stop, the horse's hindquarters digging into the disked ground. "I'm filling in for a man who broke his arm. I hoped you'd be happy to see me. You don't mind that I'm here, do you?" His focus shifted to her.

"It's a free country—you can go wherever you want." Though she wished he hadn't chosen Charris County. The question of why remained to be answered.

"You look good, Nat. Real good." His blue eyes flickered with appreciation, and then his face turned sober. "I'm sorry to hear about your dad."

Natalie accepted his condolences, measuring how much her life had changed since she and Ryan had last spoken. "What have you been doing with yourself? Still following the new queen prospects, I see. Some things never change." Resentment tinged her voice.

"It wasn't like that and you know it." His bangs fell to one side, giving him a boyish charm she'd never been able to resist. "You said yourself we were free to date other people."

"It hardly matters now." She stared at the man whose good looks had a way of taking her breath away, and a heavy weight settled on her chest. She and Ryan could have had such a wonderful future. "From what I hear, they're keeping you busy. I'm surprised you'd have time for our little clinic."

"I'll always make time for you, Nat." He flashed a grin, and her knees went weak. "But you're right. This year I'm booked in forty-eight states with four sponsors to endorse. Who would've guessed my bronc riding days would lead to this?"

Natalie looked away, unable to hold his gaze a moment longer. How easy it would be to slip into the excitement of Ryan's world once more. Her throat tightened as she watched one of the attendees lope a horse in a large figure eight. "I hope it works out for you, Ryan. And thanks for volunteering to fill in for the weekend. We really appreciate it." She turned to walk off, needing to escape. Then his voice called out to her.

"If you're not busy, maybe you could join me for dinner tonight — after your workshops?"

Natalie closed her eyes, her back to the man. Could she trust herself to be alone with Ryan and not fall into the old familiar trap? Then she considered the long days she'd put in at the ranch this past month and of the kids and their ongoing turmoil. Didn't she deserve a night out? How could one night hurt? One dinner, and then Ryan would be out of her life for good. "I should be free after the clothing auction this afternoon. Pick me up at the house, so I can freshen up first?"

His confidence never wavered. "Sounds good to me."

The rest of the morning flew by in a haze as Natalie replayed their conversation in her mind. Did Ryan still care for her? Was that why he was so friendly and had asked her out for dinner? She observed him in the arena, appreciating the way he moved, so sure of himself and able with a horse. She and Ryan had made the perfect couple, complimenting each other in every way.

Well ... almost every way.

She tried not to think about his roaming eyes, wanting to believe Ryan had changed, that he'd come to his senses and desired to have her back. Why else would he have volunteered for this queen clinic?

JARED SCANNED THE FAIRGROUNDS FOR NATALIE'S LONG DARK HAIR. Cowgirls of all age and size milled around in the shade, and then he spotted her in a green western shirt. She walked toward him with a stack of clothes in her arms, her hair pulled back in a loose ponytail.

He met her halfway. "Can I help with that?"

She peeked over the top of her load. "Oh thank you. I think my arms were about to give out." She laughed.

Jared took the entire pile from her and followed her to a building where a dozen girls were setting out clothes on hangers. "Getting ready to model?"

"We're having a clothing auction. I've decided to try and get rid of whatever I can." She motioned for him to lay the outfits he carried on a table.

"All of them?"

Her eyes glazed with sadness. "Almost."

Just then he realized how hard it must be for Natalie to put the past behind her. He also had the impression he was intruding on a very busy schedule. "I stopped by to see if you had time to go over tomorrow's service, but I can come back later if you want."

She skimmed the activity in the room and sighed. "It's no problem. Wait here while I tell someone where we're going." She went to talk to another worker and returned within seconds. "I don't know why I'm so rattled today. Too much excitement, I guess."

Jared had never seen Natalie so unstrung, as though she were a completely different person from the woman he knew. "Don't worry about it. Where are you planning to hold your cowboy church?"

She led him outside to a covered show ring surrounded by bleachers. "We thought this might be the coolest area tomorrow morning."

"And you have a microphone and speaker system, right?"

Natalie nodded, clearly distracted. Her attention slipped toward an outdoor arena about a hundred yards away. Jared followed her gaze. A blond-haired man was giving a demonstration to a group of girls using Natalie's horse. Jared wasn't sure if Natalie was concerned about her horse or about the young man leading it. Even from this distance, Jared could tell he possessed a ton of charisma as testified by the band of females hanging on his every word.

"Who's the guy in the arena?"

Natalie's eyelashes fluttered. "That's Ryan Frazier. He's helping with some of the horsemanship classes today. Maybe you've heard of him?"

Jared shrugged. "I don't get around much in the rodeo world, remember?" He scrunched his mouth, getting the feeling Ryan Frazier wasn't an ordinary cowboy—at least not to Natalie.

"I'm sorry, Ryan is a rodeo commentator—an announcer. He travels to all the major rodeos in the country. He's even been to Australia."

"You and this Frazier guy are friends?"

Natalie nodded, confirming his suspicions. "You could say that." Sadness shadowed her voice, and Jared decided he didn't want to know the details of their history. "Would you like to meet him?"

Jared shoved his hands in his pockets. Natalie was obviously too preoccupied to go over the service details. And that was okay. Jared could handle preaching off the cuff. "He looks kind of busy."

Ignoring his observation, Natalie took off for the arena, her boots kicking up puffs of dust as she went. By the time they reached the gate, the crowd had dissipated, and Frazier was leading Natalie's horse out of the arena.

"You timed that perfectly. I was just getting ready to return Jackson to his stall."

Natalie gathered her horse's lead rope in her hands. "Ryan, I'd like you to meet a friend of mine. This is Pastor Logan. He'll be conducting tomorrow's cowboy church."

With a flick of his head, the man tossed his blonde hair to the side of his face. "Nice to meet you." He held out his hand.

Jared noted the strong grip. "It's always good to meet another friend of Natalie's. Have you two known each other long?"

Frazier's grin widened and his blue eyes crinkled. It was no wonder women fawned over the guy, he could have been a Greek Adonis. "We go back a few years. It's been a while since we've seen each other, but I'm hoping to get reacquainted tonight." He winked at Natalie, and her face flushed a bright pink.

She cleared her throat, her gaze shifting between the two men. "Ryan and I are going out for dinner later—as friends. Perhaps you'd like to join us?"

Jared rubbed the back of his neck. Why would Natalie invite him to accompany her when, from the looks of things, this friendship with Frazier went much deeper? "I'd better pass. I'm sure the two of you have a lot of catching up to do."

"You got that right." Frazier eyed him warily and again reached out his hand. "It was good meeting you. I look forward to hearing your sermon tomorrow."

Jared nodded, taking that as his signal to leave. "If there's nothing else to go over, Natalie, I should let you get back to your clinic." He forced a smile to his lips, wanting nothing more than to leave the fairgrounds and erase the image of Natalie and Frazier from his mind. Something about the two together didn't set well in his stomach.

"Oh, okay." Natalie's voice quivered with uncertainty. "Well, thanks for coming out. We'll talk again tomorrow, before the service?"

"Of course." He stared at the ground, feeling inadequate and weak compared to the cowboy beside him. In Natalie's estimation, he would never measure up, but why should he care? Swamped by a myriad of undesirable emotions, he bid them good-bye. "Enjoy your dinner."

THIRTY-THREE

Ryan appeared on Natalie's doorstep right at eight, looking terrific in a pair of black jeans and a western shirt.

"You've met my brother and sister," Natalie said, feeling confident in her favorite pair of Lucchese boots made from goat leather that fit her like a soft pair of moccasins. "And this is Libby ... our house guest." For some reason, she couldn't bring herself to introduce Libby as her stepmom.

Chelsey ogled him, which didn't surprise Natalie. Ryan was the best-looking man she'd ever seen, and Natalie had met a lot of men in the last two years. Libby, too, had a hard time taking her eyes off him.

Ryan shook Libby's hand and revealed his dimpled smile. "Nice to meet you." He ruffled Dillon's hair, and her brother backed off as though affronted.

"Are you two going on a date?" Dillon crossed his arms over his chest, looking a lot like her dad.

Natalie's nerves betrayed her in an awkward giggle. "No silly, Ryan's just taking me to dinner."

Her brother cracked his knuckles and then tore off for the kitchen. The back door slammed shut causing the walls to shudder.

"Don't mind him." Natalie waved off his rude behavior. "He's probably already roping a goat or steer."

"That's what I would have been doing at his age. Watch out, though, when he moves on to riding bulls and steers. That's when you need to start worrying." Ryan rubbed his backside to show he'd suffered plenty.

"Concussions and bruises, right?" Libby chuckled, and he nodded in return.

After a few minutes of small talk, Ryan walked Natalie to the truck and opened the door for her. He helped her inside, and at his touch, her skin tingled, the attraction as strong as ever. She gave him directions to Charlie's Steakhouse, and a short while later, they were seated at a corner table for two.

Ryan studied her, his blue eyes intense and unwavering. "I've missed you, Natalie. I didn't realize how much until I saw you today. Being a queen suits you."

"I'm a past queen, Ryan. Even if I had won the national competition it would have been short-lived. The dream doesn't last forever."

"Ah, but your grace and beauty surpasses a crown. They just don't make queens like you, Nat."

Not a man to blow smoke for no reason, Ryan was up to something. She could feel it. "Why did you agree to help with this clinic, Ryan? And don't tell me it was to help us out, because you're not that thoughtful."

He gripped his chest as though wounded. "Your words cut like a knife."

"Save the theatrics for your groupies ... and don't pretend you don't have them. I saw the way the attendees watched your every move."

"That's the funny thing, Nat. These last few months, I've learned that I only have eyes for you."

"Really?" She didn't believe him. Not for a minute. Yet her heart pounded inside her chest, wanting to believe his words. "The last time we spoke was what? Six months ago? That doesn't sound too endearing to me."

"Ah but it is. I've come to realize that my rise to fame in rodeo, although amazing right now, isn't everything. Hearing about your dad made me grasp that even more. It's made me think about my future and about settling down. Maybe we should consider that, you and I?"

"Haven't you heard? That's what I've done already," Natalie scoffed at his insensitivity. "I'm not free to roam the country. I'm a landowner now, in charge of my brother and sister. I have responsibilities."

He reached for her hand and squeezed it beneath his own. "We could do that together, Nat. I'm not asking you to come away with me. But would it be such a bad idea to start seeing each other again? See where it takes us?"

She pulled her hand away. "What makes you think I'd want to risk taking a chance on you? Do you have any idea how much you hurt me in Vegas?"

"I'm sorry about that." His fingers slid the length of her arm and wandered to her cheek. "Let me make it up to you."

Natalie closed her eyes, relishing his touch against her skin. With a little work, she could almost remember the joy of his kiss.

"'O! that I were a glove upon that hand, That I might touch that cheek!'" a gravelly voice spoke nearby, and Natalie's eyelids sprung open. Willard stood before her at their table wearing a straw cowboy hat, all dressed up for the evening. "It's about time you enjoy a night out, Natalie. And who's this young man with you?"

Natalie reached for her sweet tea, the glass cold and wet beneath her fingers. "This is Ryan Frazier, a friend from my days as Miss Rodeo Kansas."

"The sports announcer?"

She blinked her surprise. "You've heard of him?"

Willard nodded, his eyes watchful and keen. "I remember your daddy talking about Ryan."

Natalie sipped her tea, imagining all too well the stories her dad might have told. "Ryan, this is Willard Grover, a good friend of our family. Willard is the one who saved my grandpa in Vietnam."

"Nice to finally meet you." Ryan shook Willard's hand. "Natalie's told me a lot about you. How you and your wife took care of Natalie and the kids when they were young."

Willard grinned, his teeth bright against his dark skin. "Yep, they're like my own family. And what about your family, Ryan? Where do you hail from?"

Ryan relaxed into his chair. "Clearwater, Oklahoma."

"That's a good drive from here. What brings you to Diamond Falls?"

"Ryan's here for the clinic we're having this weekend. He taught the horsemanship classes." Natalie cleared her throat. "Jared's helping too."

Willard's eyebrows arched. "You don't say."

"He's leading our cowboy church." She offered a slight smile, able to see Willard's mind churning.

"That's real interesting. Has Jared met Ryan yet?"

Natalie took another drink of her tea, hoping to quell the anxious butterflies in her stomach. It wasn't as though she and Jared were romantically involved, so why did she feel guilty for being here with Ryan? The young pastor had made it perfectly clear he wasn't interested in anything more than friendship. And Natalie certainly wasn't interested in marrying a preacher. "Actually, I introduced them this afternoon."

"The preacher man?" Ryan grinned. "Not exactly rough stock material, but he seemed like a nice guy."

"You can't always judge a man by his appearance," Willard said. "Some men you have to look deep inside to read what they're all about, isn't that right, Natalie?"

Natalie gazed up at Willard. "And then again, some men are as easy to read as the desserts on a menu."

"Touché, my girl, touché." Willard smiled and tipped his hat toward her. "I've bothered you young'uns long enough. I think I'll head back and see if they've brought my order yet."

They said good-bye, and Ryan's smile didn't waver. "Who is this Jared guy again?"

Natalie drew a line in the condensation on her glass, unable to keep from comparing Jared to Ryan. Complete opposites, yet they both held a certain attraction. "I told you, he's a friend of the family."

"And a preacher? I didn't realize you were so religious."

"I'm not." The words came out defensively. "Although I admit, I've been thinking about certain things lately."

Ryan's eyes softened. "Like death?"

She nodded. And God's plan for her life — if there was such a thing. "Enough about that, though. Are you going to save room for dessert?" She flipped open a menu and forced herself to study it.

He did the same. "I don't think so. I need to watch my girlish figure."

Natalie giggled as the waitress approached their table. "Not me. I'll have the top sirloin with a salad and baked potato and then if there's room I want the brownie a-la-mode." She handed her menu to the waitress after ordering.

Ryan cringed. "And you call yourself a rodeo queen?" He laughed then and slapped the menu on the table. "I'll have the same."

Once the waitress left, he leaned in closer and took her hand. "You know, I've been hearing things."

Natalie tilted her head. "Such as?"

"Rumors."

"Well, you can't trust a rumor."

"Even still, you might be interested in what I've heard." He squeezed her fingers, his own strong, yet smooth.

Her eyes narrowed, wondering if Ryan had finally gotten around to the real reason he'd volunteered to help with this clinic. "I'm listening."

"I've been hearing a lot of commotion about Lisa's health. That Miss Rodeo America's not doing so well."

Natalie had already heard the rumors, and her heart went out to the girl. She swallowed the sadness welling inside. "Why are you telling me this?"

"They're saying she might have a brain tumor. That she might not finish her term as queen."

Natalie pulled her hand from his. "That's not even funny, Ryan. There are some things you don't joke about."

"You know what that would mean, don't you?"

Disgust erupted within her, that Ryan would mention this, let alone, think it. "You don't wish bad things on a person in hopes that something good might come of it for yourself. I can't believe you brought this up. It's just bad manners."

Ryan raised his hands at her attack. "Hey, I'm just telling you what I've heard. You can do whatever you want with the information."

"Is that why you came here? Because you thought there might be a chance for me to return to the spotlight?"

"Why do you think so poorly of me?"

"What else am I supposed to think? Our past tends to color our future."

"Listen, forget I even mentioned it because you're right. It doesn't matter. You know I wouldn't wish Lisa any harm, even if it meant you'd get to take her place. I'm sorry I said anything."

Natalie tried to read the sincerity in his eyes, but it was impossible. Reading Ryan was like reading a menu written in German.

THIRTY-FOUR

JARED SAT ON HIS PATIO, ENJOYING THE NIGHT AIR AND GOING OVER HIS Bible verses for the next day. Fingering the red satin hair ribbon he now used as a page marker, Jared thought of Natalie and her dinner date with Ryan. The two had a lot in common. They were both involved in rodeo, enjoyed ranching, and seemed to have a physical connection. All of this combined spelled out a perfect future. And Natalie's odd behavior around the man led Jared to presume that she cared for him.

The realization left a quiet, lonely ache in his heart. What did God have in store for his future?

Lord, help me be content with what you give and help me serve you—only you.

A rustling noise from the bushes drew Jared's attention. He expected a rabbit to zip from the undergrowth, but to his astonishment, Dillon rose from the greenery and took a seat beside him.

"What are you doing here?" Jared put his notes down in surprise. "And what's more, how did you get here?"

The boy stared at his lap, troubled. "I hitched a ride in the back of Ryan's truck."

Jared's eyes widened. "Ryan's truck? You mean your sister's date?"

"It's not a date." The boy shook his head indignantly. "She said it wasn't."

"Does Natalie know where you are?" Jared couldn't believe Natalie would allow her brother to ride in the back of a truck all the way to town.

Dillon remained solemn. "I couldn't stand being there. I had to get out of the house."

"Tell me what's going on." Jared tried to understand. "Why did you feel you had to get out of there?"

"It's Natalie. She's making a mistake."

Jared's pulse skipped. "Is Natalie in trouble? What do you mean?"

The boy pressed against the back of the chair, his feet barely touching the floor. "She's going out with that Ryan guy, but she ought to be with you, Jared. I've tried to tell you, but neither of you will listen."

Jared scooted closer to the boy. "I met Ryan this afternoon. He seems like a nice enough fellow. Why don't you like him?"

Dillon wrinkled his nose. "He's a worm."

"Besides that?"

"He broke up with Natalie before. He'll do it again."

"You mean he's her old boyfriend?"

Dillon nodded, his mouth scrunched in a frown. "Why did she go out with him again? Why would she do that? She has you. She ought to be with you."

"Hold on, there. First off, she doesn't have me. Remember, I explained that to you. I have to be careful who I date. And although your sister is a lovely woman, and I like her very much, she's missing the one thing I can't live without."

The boy studied him. "What's that? Love?"

Jared shook his head, hating to spell it out so boldly. He didn't doubt for a moment that love could be gained. He'd felt the signs, his spirit warmed when he was around Natalie, he enjoyed her company, longed to hold her in his arms. Love wasn't the problem. "The woman I fall in love with must love Jesus. Do you understand that?"

"You mean she has to go to church?"

"That always helps." Jared offered a gentle smile. "But more than that, she needs Jesus in her heart. Right now, that's something your sister fights, though I pray for her every day." *Morning and night.*

"Why does she fight it?"

"I'm not sure. Some people just do." Jared marked the gospel of John in his Bible with a piece of paper and handed it to the boy. "I'd like you to have this, Dillon. It'll help you get through tough times, like what you and your family are going through now, and it'll help you appreciate the blessings when times are good."

Dillon reached out with hesitance.

"Go ahead," Jared assured him. "I have another Bible inside."

He accepted it then and clutched it to his stomach. "Natalie says we're your mission project."

Jared grinned, having heard those words before. "Well, Dillon, I want good things for your family, and I want you to know Jesus. If that means you're my mission project, I guess it's true."

The boy peered up through thick lashes. "Are you going to take me home, now?"

"Don't you think your family might be worried?"

"They were watching TV when I left. I doubt they even know I'm gone."

Jared rested his forearms on his knees. "How are you getting along with Libby? Do you think of her as your mom?"

Dillon shrugged. "I guess. Mostly she likes doing things with Chelsey, but sometimes she helps me with chores."

"What about Natalie?"

"She doesn't do much with Libby and us. She's either working outside or in Dad's office." The boy's lip curled as he popped his knuckles. "I miss how it used to be."

"I'm sure she misses it too." Jared stood and waited for the boy to join him. "Give her some time. It'll get better."

"Are you mad at me? For wanting you and Natalie to be together?"

From the moment they met, the boy had carved a niche in Jared's heart. Not only did Jared enjoy Dillon's company, but he recognized a bit of his childhood in him. He couldn't be mad at the boy—at least not for very long. "Promise never to do something like this again?"

Dillon nodded. "I promise."

Jared acknowledged the boy's honesty, never knowing him to tell a lie. "I realize it's hard without your dad, and that some days you want to run away and hide. But sometimes you have to stand up and face your problems—like David did with Goliath. If you want I'll tell you about David in the car."

Jared grabbed his keys from inside the house and drove Dillon back to the ranch. "Think your sister's home yet?"

"I wish."

Deep in his heart, Jared wished Natalie was home too. The thought of her being out on a date with her ex-boyfriend caused his stomach to writhe.

THIRTY-FIVE

NATALIE LOOKED UP FROM HER GAME OF DOMINOES AS THE KITCHEN DOOR screeched open. She exchanged glances with Chelsey and Libby seated on the floor around the coffee table, wondering if it might be Willard. But it wasn't.

"Jared, what are you doing here?" Ryan had brought her back after ten, so she knew it had to be late.

"I came to drop off a visitor." He pulled Dillon to stand beside him in the doorway. "Do you want to tell them, or shall I?"

Natalie rose from the floor, acutely aware of the guilt on her brother's face. "Dillon, what are you doing with Jared? I thought you were upstairs in bed."

Dillon stared at her, and Jared nudged him forward.

She placed her hands on her hips, growing more ill at ease with every second that ticked by. "Will one of you say something, please? You're scaring me."

"Calm down, Nat." Libby stood beside her with a handful of popcorn. "I'm sure you're getting worked up for nothing. Let the boy explain."

"No, I won't calm down. What's going on guys? Dillon, are you okay?"

"Everyone's fine." Jared raised a finger to quiet her. "The problem is your brother hitched a ride to town in the back of Ryan's truck. He walked to my house, and I found him on my patio."

"You snuck into town?" Natalie closed the distance between them and bent down so that she was eye-level to her brother. "Why, Dillon, did something happen?"

"I just needed to get out of here for a while. It was no big deal. I was with Jared."

"And you hid in the back of Ryan's truck? You could have been hurt." Frustration warmed her cheeks. Why was her brother so intent on stealing off on his own? And how was she going to make it stop? "What if Jared hadn't been home?"

"Does it matter? You were off with that cowboy and didn't even know I was in the truck. I don't know why you care. I'm home now, aren't I?"

"Don't sass your sister," Libby scolded, and Dillon stared down at his shoes.

The reprimand only served to irritate Natalie more. She didn't need help raising these kids—especially not from a stepmom who'd been absent most of their life. Natalie tilted Dillon's chin and gazed into his hazel eyes. "Of course I care what happens—to you and Chelsey. Ryan and I went to dinner, but now I'm home." She caught Jared's gaze, and her lower lip trembled.

"Where's Ryan now?" Dillon moved away from her touch.

"He went back to the hotel. I asked him to take me home so I could spend time with you guys—only I thought you were sleeping."

"You're not mad?"

She thumped him on the side of the head. "I ought to give you a thrashing. What did I tell you about going off on your own? I swear, you kids are going to give me an ulcer."

"Don't blame me. I didn't do anything this time," Chelsey said, still seated on the floor, but obviously listening to their discussion.

"Yeah, and you didn't even know I was gone," Dillon added.

"That's not the point." Natalie raked his bangs to the side of his face. "Will you promise to never pull a stunt like this again?"

Dillon nodded, and Natalie let out a deep breath, wanting to put the incident behind them.

"Pastor, would you care to join us for a game of dominoes?" Libby asked. "It's not too late for us to deal you in."

Jared shook his head and gazed at Natalie. "I better get back home. I have dual services tomorrow."

"Can I walk you out?" At his nod, Natalie trailed Jared out the back door and shuffled along beside him, staring at the thousands of stars that lit the sky. "Why do you think Dillon snuck out tonight?"

Jared stopped at his car and sat against the front hood. "You're smart, Natalie. What do you think?"

She hugged her arms to her chest. "He hasn't been himself since Dad died. Hiding in outbuildings, traipsing off to the river, and now sneaking into town in the middle of the night. I'm afraid to think what he might try next."

"Your brother's had a lot of change in his life, and he's on the verge of his teen years. That's scary for a boy, let alone a boy without his dad."

"And now he's stuck in a house full of women. No wonder he wants to run away." Apprehension twisted Natalie's gut. Maybe she did need help raising these kids. She hadn't even considered Dillon's age and the changes he'd soon go through. "What should I do now?"

"Listen to him, be his friend, and don't be afraid to discipline him when he needs it, because I guarantee there will be times he'll need it." Jared grinned. "Other than that, just take one day at a time."

Desiring to understand the difference between this man and Ryan, and why her attraction for Jared seemed to grow each time he came around, Natalie reached out and touched the rough stubble of his cheek. "Is that what you do? Live one day at a time?" She traced the line of his jaw and heard the intake of his breath.

"It's the only thing we can do." Jared cupped his hand over hers and gently lifted her fingers from his skin. "Anything else, and God tends to laugh at our plans."

Oh, how well she'd learned that lesson. She tucked her hands behind her back and considered her father's estate. He'd worked all his life to make the ranch profitable and on his death, none of it mattered. The money he'd saved *and hidden* would only go toward taxes. All of his plans seemed such a waste.

"Thank you for bringing Dillon home." She tried to make sense of the one thing she knew—that Jared was always there for her and her family. "I'm sorry if I made you uncomfortable. You're a good friend. I shouldn't ask for more." She lowered her eyes, embarrassed to have succumbed to such curiosity.

Jared let out a long sigh. "I wish things were different. That I could tell you what I'm feeling."

"What?" The word came out a whisper. "I'd like to know."

"Lots of things. Too many things. Things I'm not supposed to feel." He tilted his head toward the starry sky. "What about you and Ryan? Dillon said he was your ex-boyfriend. Has that changed? Is that why he's here?"

Natalie stared out at the pasture, the moon casting an ethereal glow on the hills beyond. "We dated for about a year, and then after I lost the national competition he broke up with me. My not winning apparently ruined his plans."

"Were you going to marry him?"

"Lots of plans were ruined." She shifted her gaze to Jared. "I'm not sure why Ryan came here. I'd like to think he's changed, but I can't shake the feeling that he's up to something."

"It's usually wise to listen to your intuition. God gave it to us for a reason." Jared brushed a strand of hair from her face, and she leaned into his hand. "And for the record, it might be a good idea to talk to Dillon about Ryan."

"Is that why he ran away?"

"I'd rather you find out from him." Jared caressed her cheek with the back of his fingers, and Natalie closed her eyes, relishing his gentle touch. Two men had caressed her cheek this night, two men as different as night and day. But there was something about Jared that made him stand out to her—his kindness, his generosity ... or was it his honesty? Whatever it was, she wanted to know more ...

JARED DROVE TO THE END OF THE LANE, THE SOFTNESS OF NATALIE'S SKIN clinging to his fingers. He stopped the car. What was he doing? Messing with fire? Challenging God? He thumped his head on the steering wheel ... hoping to rattle loose some common sense. Stupid, stupid man.

He knew better than to get involved with Natalie, to allow himself to become infatuated with her. But oh, the pleasure of her smile. If only she would stop denying God's presence in her life. She'd attended church as a girl with her mother, had attended cowboy church and would go again tomorrow. Was it such a big stretch to think she could change? That she might move toward a life of faithfulness? She was so close—seemed on the brink of it every time they talked. But something always held her back.

Then a cold hard realization hit him like a slap on the cheek. His desire for Natalie's conversion had somehow become a means to an end—a way for them to be together. He dipped his chin in remorse. What kind of pastor was he to allow such selfish thoughts? To put his own needs and desires before those in his care. He shook his head, knowing exactly what kind.

A miserable one.

THE NEXT MORNING JARED ARRIVED AT THE FAIRGROUNDS WITH HIS BIBLE, wearing khaki pants and loafers, certain he was breaking some cowboy code of attire. He took a seat at one of the bleachers to go over his notes. Natalie sat beside him a few minutes later with her hair draped over one shoulder, smelling sweet and fresh like the honeysuckle that bloomed outside his office window.

"I hope the incident last night didn't keep you from your studies."

Jared patted the note cards against his palm and straightened. "Not at all. I'm more concerned that I should have worn my boots and hat." He grinned, half-joking.

"You'll do fine. Here, let's get you wired." She clipped a microphone to his shirt collar, and her fingers grazed his neck. A chill of excitement shot down his back, and he warded it off, determined to show more discipline than he had the night before.

"Are we ready?" he asked.

At her nod, Jared crossed the sandy arena to the podium set up for him. After a few familiar hymns, he situated his Bible and surveyed the small crowd of women, a handful of men dotted among them. Ryan Frazier stared back at him, his legs stretched out on the bleachers and his arms folded across his chest. Jared tried not to let the man's presence unnerve him and prayed for God's peace and wisdom.

"Good morning." He breathed an audible sigh. "I knew I forgot something when I left the house this morning—my hat and boots." This statement triggered a few giggles, and the mood lightened.

"This is the first time I've led cowboy church, so please forgive me for that oversight. I have to admit, when Natalie asked me to fill in for this service, I wondered what topic to cover. Now looking out at all of your beautiful faces, I can't believe my struggle." He lifted his Bible for all to see. "In God's Word, there is one story that seems particularly fitting for the queen clinic you're holding today. Some of you may know it already—the story of Esther."

Jared continued and as he reached the close of his sermon, his gaze drifted over each listener until it landed on Natalie. "God used Queen Esther to save a nation—an entire race of people. Many of you may go from here and win queen titles. And so I ask, how might God use you? Maybe it will be in serving the rodeo association with grace and dignity, or perhaps it will be in supporting your community or a special cause. You may never win a title, but God may use you as a witness to your fellow queen participants, or to your friends, or even your family. So think on this as you leave here today. How might God use your talents and your beauty in serving his kingdom? May God grant you the courage to accept the challenge as Esther did."

Jared closed with another hymn and a prayer. With little time to spare before his next service, he gathered his notes and Bible, thankful the sermon had gone without a hitch. Two girls came up to express their appreciation, and he thanked them, always amazed at how God could speak through him to touch a person. Natalie stood at the edge of the arena visiting another girl. Perhaps his words had affected her as well—at least he could hope.

Not wanting to bother her, he waved and headed for his car parked on the opposite side of the fairgrounds. On his way, he passed Frazier, once again encircled by a group of young ladies. The man seemed to prize the female attention. Jared didn't miss how Ryan's hand rested comfortably at the curve of one girl's waist, possessively so.

As he strode to his car, he lifted a prayer to heaven. "Please Lord, watch after Natalie, and protect her from men with wandering eyes." If he couldn't have Natalie for his own, he at least wanted her to be with someone who would honor and cherish her, and from what he could tell, that someone was not Ryan Frazier.

THIRTY-SIX

Natalie caught up to Jared, out of breath from running. "Were you going to leave without saying good-bye?"

Jared scowled an apology. "Sorry, I needed to move on to New Redeemer, and you looked busy."

She glanced back at Ryan surrounded by a dozen females then returned her attention to Jared. "You wouldn't have disturbed me."

"I remember a time not so long ago when you didn't care so much for my company." Jared rubbed his jaw. "In fact, you ordered me off your property. I guess we've come a long way since then."

"We're friends now." She grinned and picked a piece of dead grass from his shirt. "I liked what you did with your sermon. I've received a lot of compliments."

He stared down at his shoes, appearing uncomfortable with her praise. "Maybe now you'll be more inclined to join us on Sundays ... to hear more. I'm certain everyone in our congregation would welcome you."

"Like a family, huh?" Her eyes drifted again to Ryan and his groupies. She'd once considered Ryan part of her family. But those days were gone—she knew that now.

Jared gazed at her unflinching, his brown eyes bright and sincere behind his glasses. "Yes, like family, we all make mistakes and none of us are perfect."

Natalie considered his invitation, at war between opening her mind to God's Word or continuing on her own as she'd done most of her life. Unlike the story about Esther, Natalie had never felt God's call, unless of course, he was calling to her through Jared. When she failed to comment, Jared proceeded to his car.

The clinic coordinator came up to her as he drove away. "That pastor of yours did a great job this morning. I wanted to thank him for his time, but I see I've just missed him. Can you give him his check or should I send it in the mail?"

"I can give it to him." Natalie swept her hair from her face, ready to put it into a ponytail as the morning temperature had already climbed into the nineties. "What do you think of the clinic so far?"

"I think Ryan Frazier turned out to be a particularly helpful draw." Connie nodded toward the cowboy commentator and his groupies. "I understand the horsemanship classes went especially well this year."

Natalie frowned as the woman's words confirmed what she already knew to be true.

"The two of you aren't still seeing each other, are you?" When Natalie shook her head, Connie went on. "I had to wonder when he volunteered to fill in for our other clinician. I thought maybe there was another reason he wanted to visit Kansas."

Natalie pursed her lips. "Ryan has no shortage of females in his life, but I'm not one of them."

"That's a relief. I understand he took one of the girls to a bar last night and kept her out till the wee hours of the morning."

Natalie hid her surprise, though her mind reeled at the news. Ryan had gone out after he'd dropped her off at her house? *The nerve.* It made her wonder even more what he was up to—*the snake.* Why had he taken her out if he wasn't interested in getting back with her? And how dare he mess with her clinic participants—or with her mind. Natalie fanned herself, her body smoldering with hostility.

Connie offered a sympathetic shrug. "It might be good to go over appropriate conduct this afternoon. Remind the girls that with the crown and title comes responsibility and an image to uphold."

"I'll be sure to add that into my talk this afternoon." Natalie wondered which girl Ryan had taken to the bar.

"Raising teenagers is one of the toughest jobs a mother can have. Believe me, I know. I have three of them." Connie smiled with affection. "What you're doing for your brother and sister goes way beyond generous. Not many young women would strap themselves to such an obligation. I applaud your efforts."

Natalie shook off the compliment, unworthy of such admiration, especially when her mind rebelled at the decision every chance it got. "I really had no choice in the matter."

"Everyone has a choice." Connie tore a check from her bankbook and handed it to Natalie, then ripped out another. "Do you want me to pay Ryan or would you like to do the honors?"

Natalie's gaze shifted to Ryan and his dwindling crowd. "I'd be happy to give it to him." She smiled, thinking part of his payment should include a good kick in the pants. Minutes later, she walked up to Ryan and handed him his check. "Connie wanted me to thank you for coming to our clinic."

He took the check and whisked the blond bangs from his face. "I'm glad you caught me before I took off. I had fun last night. We should try that again ... soon."

She caught the expectant tone in his voice and a violent shiver raked down her back. "That'll be hard, unless you're planning to pass through Kansas on your way to and from rodeos."

"What if my prediction for you comes true?"

Natalie scowled. "You're not going to start that again, are you?" Tired of his nonsense, she turned to walk off.

He shuffled beside her. "What if Miss Rodeo America has to step down, and they offered you the position? Would you take it?"

Natalie swallowed the disgust she felt for this man. What had she ever seen in him? "I guess I'll cross that bridge if it comes, but I'm not going to spend any time thinking about it. It's been nice seeing you, Ryan." She held out her hand and waited for the familiar rush of longing to hit as he took her hand. Only it didn't.

THIRTY-SEVEN

AFTER THE SERVICE AT NEW REDEEMER, JARED ESCAPED TO HIS FAVORITE fishing hole in an old shirt and jeans. His boot heels dug into the moist slope of the riverbank, the overhead sun hot on his back. A south breeze whipped the new straw hat he'd purchased at the local farm store, and he smiled, wondering if Natalie would approve. Upon reaching the gravel bar, he located a shady spot to prepare his line. Earlier that week, he'd concocted some of Dillon's secret hotdog bait and although it had only fermented a short time, he planned to see if it would work for him today.

The tall cottonwoods swayed high above, their leaves whispering in the wind as though they had hundreds of stories to tell. Although Jared enjoyed the physical activity of his Sunday outings, he found himself most looking forward to the peaceful quiet the river afforded—a place to sit and think or listen without human interference.

Beyond him, bullfrogs croaked and waited at the edge of the muddy current as it gushed and gurgled over rocks and fallen limbs. Jared attached some of the stink bait to his hook, his thoughts drifting to Natalie and her family. Of how he'd met Dillon right here only a month ago, alone and troubled, and how the boy searched him out the night before, still troubled and running. Looking for something stable, someone he could depend on.

Jared cast his line into the deepwater bend, hoping a big cat might be hiding in the underwater debris, despite the afternoon hour. All boys needed a role model — someone to look up to for guidance and support. He supposed in a way, he'd been a lot like Dillon. His own father had been very active and busy with his pastoral duties, leaving Jared alone and searching most of his childhood. And just as Dillon had found Jared, Jared had marked his granddad as his champion, his teacher, his friend.

A tree branch floated down the river, bobbing and spinning as it crossed over the riffles. Jared drew in his line, and the click of his reel took him back to his last fishing trip with his granddad over ten years ago.

"Where you going to college, boy?" Granddad sat on an overturned bucket as they fished side-by-side on the wide waters of the Republican River near Concordia, Kansas.

A senior in high school, Jared had his whole life ahead of him — and wanted only one thing. "I'm not going to college."

The old man's mouth wobbled in surprise. "Why not?"

Jared concentrated on the rippling water. "You didn't go to college. I'm going to farm, like you." Deep inside, Jared hoped for an invitation, that his granddad would ask for his help. They could be partners. "You could hire me to work on your farm." He smiled then, satisfied that he knew what he wanted in life.

His granddad shook his head. "You gotta want more than that, boy. Farming's hard work, and there's no guarantees. You might lose everything to drought or flood. And if those things don't get you, the market will. I don't want those worries for you, boy."

Jared knew the arguments, he'd heard them before. But in his mind, it didn't matter. "The only guarantee we have in life is that we'll die. I love the land, just like you. I can't see myself doing anything else."

"You ought to go into the ministry, like your dad. I know that's what he wants for you."

"See these calluses?" Jared held out the palms of his hands. "These are a working man's hands. I don't want to sit behind a desk all day." The thought of being in an office and wearing a suit made him nearly hyperventilate.

The old man chuckled. "You don't know what God has in mind for you. He might want you to use those callused hands as a missionary in some foreign country."

Jared laughed at that and cast his line into the water, fully expecting to spend many more summer days fishing with the man who'd been everything to him. He hadn't counted on his granddad getting sick with cancer and giving the farm to his uncle—the eldest son, ripping Jared's future right out from under his feet.

The tree branch drifted to the edge of the river and became lodged in the muddy silt, its forward motion blocked just like Jared's plans had been all those years ago. He flexed his fingers and examined the palms of his hands, noting how calluses had begun to form there again.

AFTER LUNCH, NATALIE AND JENNY HELPED THE GIRLS WITH MODELING and appearance, spending time on makeup, hairstyle, and clothing selections. During the last portion of the clinic, they concentrated on the personality aspects of competition and covered impromptu questions, interviews, and speeches.

"You can never be too prepared," Natalie stated to the group of girls seated in front of her, ranging in ages from eleven to twenty-one. She'd seen many contestants who appeared sure and confident, but when it came time for the interview, they didn't know their facts and had floundered with the questions. "This afternoon, we're going to review possible questions that might be asked in competition. Go over these papers until you can answer without a hint of hesitation. Study your current events and learn everything there is to know about the sport of rodeo from brand names and sponsors, to the names of judges, stock contractors, announcers, and clowns—if there is a link to rodeo, you better be aware of it."

The girls divided into two age groups, and for the next hour, Natalie and Jenny questioned attendees and listened to speeches. When the clinic ended, Natalie was exhausted.

"I guess this means so long." She gave Jenny a hug, knowing the challenges that awaited the young queen. "If there's anything I can do to help you prepare for Vegas, I'm only a phone call away."

"You're not getting off that easy." Connie placed her hands on her hips in a stance of authority. "We expect you to join us at the Dodge City competition, and we'd like your help at another clinic we're having this fall. Just because you have a ranch and a few extra responsibilities doesn't mean you can wipe your hands of us," she teased.

"I'd like that." Natalie's heart swelled at knowing she was still needed. It made facing her unknown future a bit easier to swallow.

"And of course I'll accept any help you're willing to offer for the pageant in December. I know that's more than six months away, but I'm already so nervous, I can hardly stand it." Jenny laughed, but Natalie knew her words to be true.

The queen clinic officially over, they said their good-byes, and Natalie hauled her things to the truck. When she pulled out of the fairgrounds, her dad's words echoed in her ears.

It's time to get back to the real world.

She rested her elbow on the window frame of her truck, the warm air whipping her hair about her face as she drove down the gravel road to her home. The weekend had given her a taste of old times, watching the young girls prepare for competition and learn the skills necessary to do well. And although her dinner date with Ryan hadn't turned out as expected, she'd walked away from him with a smile—something she'd never thought possible.

She knew it was mostly due to Jared.

Natalie couldn't help but compare the two men. Ryan had been born into the rodeo world, and Jared was a stranger to it. Jared was thoughtful, caring, and honest. He would never hurt Natalie. This she knew as certain as rain. She also knew that Jared would never use her. He'd never take advantage of her or compromise her reputation, something Ryan wouldn't think twice about, only interested in serving his own needs.

Maybe Jared was right. Perhaps God wasn't ignoring her. Maybe like Esther, he did have a plan for her life — one that she couldn't see right now, but in the future would be clear and visible.

A mile past Coover's Bridge, she noted a white vehicle parked on the side of the road. Jared's Toyota. Realizing he must be fishing, Natalie pulled behind his car and shut off the engine. She debated whether to stop and visit, thinking of all the work waiting for her on the ranch. Then she remembered the check in her pocket.

She stepped from the truck and looked down the marshy bank, reminded of the first time she'd set eyes on the preacher. Once again, he stood at the river's edge, with an aluminum pole in his hand — and a cowboy hat on his head.

"Catching anything?" She called out to him and made her way through the brush and rocks.

Jared waved back. "What are you doing here? Is your clinic over?"

"It is." She continued down the slope until she stood at his side. "What about you? Are you catching supper?"

"Trying to, but not having much success."

"If Dillon finds out you were here, he'll be so jealous. He loves fishing on this river."

"Well, don't tell him I borrowed his bait recipe — because it's not working." He squatted to retrieve another piece of the smelly meat from a jar. "Care to join me? I have another pole in my car."

"No thank you." She scrunched her nose at the stench. "Fishing is Dillon's passion, not mine."

His eyes crinkled in amusement. "Did the clinic go well?"

"I think so."

"And what about Ryan?" He searched the bank, as though anticipating the man to walk over the horizon at any minute. "Is he still around?"

Natalie cleared her throat, embarrassed to have fallen for Ryan's act even once and glad she hadn't made the mistake twice. She remembered what Jared had said about Libby and applied it to Ryan. "You were right. A leopard doesn't change his spots."

"I'm sorry to hear that." Jared's mouth tilted in concern as he peered at her beneath his hat. "But maybe you're better off without him?"

Feeling suddenly self-conscious, she pulled the check from her jean pocket. "Connie wanted me to give you this. She wanted you to know how much she appreciated your service. We all did."

Jared indicated his filthy hands. "Could you put it in my shirt pocket?"

Natalie tucked the folded check into Jared's shirt, aware of the taut muscles beneath the thin cotton material. She caught herself admiring the man's rugged appearance, enhanced by the hat he wore and the dark shadow on his face. Realizing where her thoughts had strayed, her mind scurried to something safe.

Work — and a job that needed done.

"I know you only agreed to help with the haying, but I wondered if you might have time this week to give me a hand with our windmills." She'd been putting off this particular task for weeks and for good reason. "Dad always took care of the maintenance before ... I'm not sure I can handle it myself." The mere thought of climbing the thirty-foot towers caused her palms to sweat.

Jared cast his line into the middle of the river seemingly unaware of her turmoil. "Would tomorrow work for you?"

Natalie nodded, determined to overcome her weakness despite the dread building in her stomach.

THIRTY-EIGHT

The next afternoon, Natalie tucked a coil of wire into the saddlebag on her father's horse as Jared strolled into the barn sporting a pair of Wrangler jeans and the cowboy hat he'd worn the day before. His effort to fit in with ranch life amused her. "I see you finally broke down and bought yourself a hat."

Jared tipped the straw brim in gentlemanly fashion. "I decided it was time to make a trip to the farm store."

"It suits you." She liked this new cowboy look. His dark brown eyes gleamed beneath the yellow brim, causing her brooding fear to almost melt away.

"There are three windmills in the North Pasture," she said. "I thought we might ride out and check cattle while we're there. That is, if you don't mind going on horseback." She hoped the ride would calm her nerves—depended on it, even.

He rubbed the back of his neck, giving no sign of protest. "Which horse are you giving me?"

A grin settled in the corner of her mouth as she recalled the many bronc rides her father had taken on his snorty horse. "Dad's sorrel hasn't seen much action for a while. He'll likely be feeling fresh, so you'd better take Jackson." Natalie tied a lariat to her saddle horn, confident the well-broke animal would look after Jared.

She handed him Jackson's reins, her spurs jingling. "You might want to wait here for a bit," she said, then climbed into her saddle, prepared for anything.

As expected, her dad's gelding made it halfway through the yard before he planted his feet and sprung high, a low grunt issuing from his belly. Natalie pulled up on both reins to stay in the saddle as he continued bucking, his hooves flinging chunks of sod into the air. On the second jump, she wrenched his head around in a tight circle. Round and round they went.

"Come on, old boy, this fun of yours is too much work," Natalie muttered, the muscles in her stomach, arms, and legs growing tired of the strain. Then after what seemed like minutes, the horse finally gave up his fuss. Satisfied, Natalie sat quiet for a moment and patted his neck.

"I had no idea you were such a horseman." Jared rode out to her in the yard.

"I'm not." She chuckled. "I've just had my share of wild rodeos."

"If they were as wild as the one I just witnessed, I'm impressed. You have grit, Natalie Adams — true grit."

She laughed at Jared's deliberate drawl. "You've been watching too many westerns."

He smiled back. "Maybe, but I'm still impressed."

A few minutes later, the sun beat down on Natalie's thin cotton shirt as she and Jared passed through the gate headed for the pasture. It was a pretty day, the sky blue, the grass a brilliant green. Together, they trotted over the hills of bluestem and crossed multiple gullies, all the while Natalie keeping watch over Jared's progress. For an inexperienced rider, he carried himself well in the saddle, accepting the rough terrain and each low-water passage with ease.

They maneuvered through a small grove of burr oaks edged by a large cluster of flint rock, and farther on, the trail meandered over a tall mound. Before reaching the other side, the distant sound of clanging metal echoed from the next ridge. As they neared, the awful racket grew in intensity until Natalie spotted the cause.

High overhead, one of the windmill blades had dislodged from its support, and with each rotation the loose fixture struck the tower.

Natalie slid from the saddle then collected her supplies. Gathering her leather gloves ... and her courage, she recalled the many times she'd helped her dad with such things, always dreading the climb. "Have you ever been to the top of one of these towers before?"

Jared shook his head. "My granddad had a silo. Does that count?"

Natalie grinned and strapped the rope around her shoulder. She unfastened Jared's cantle bag, which contained some gear oil and a few other items they might need, and handed it to him. Tucking a pair of pliers in her back pocket, she then struggled to pull the lever at the base of the tower, which would shift the direction of the wheel and set a manual brake. Unable to budge the metal device, she stepped back and removed her ball cap, wiping the perspiration from her forehead.

"Here, let's try this." Jared picked up from the ground a discarded pipe and struck the lever, freeing it from the rusted corrosion and enabling its movement. Once the blades stopped spinning, the screeching noise ceased as well. All was silent except for the strong gusts of wind and the clear, hopeful *bob-white* call of a pair of quail nesting in the grass nearby.

Jared waited by the ladder. "Want to go first, or shall I?"

Natalie drew in a deep breath and resituated the cap on her head. "I'll start. That way if I fall, you can catch me," she teased, but her hands betrayed her, cold with dread.

"After seeing how agile you were on that horse, I can't imagine you having a problem climbing a ladder, but if you insist, I'll gladly play the hero."

"Ha, ha, very funny." Determined to overcome her weakness, Natalie took the initiative and began climbing the metal tower. Her long sleeved overshirt billowed and flapped in the air. Halfway up, Jared howled.

"There goes my sun block."

Natalie glanced down and caught sight of the straw hat as it landed on the grass below. The bluestem seemed to quiver and mock her. "You can get it later." She swallowed her anxiety, thankful to have Jared below her.

When they reached the top, Natalie braced herself on the oiling mount and immediately went to work to realign the dislodged blade. "Can you hand me a piece of wire?"

Jared waited below the platform and passed her a coil of baling wire. "You doing okay up there?"

"I'm fine." Her reply came out more tersely than she intended, as she blindly searched for the pliers in her back pocket. Finding them, she snipped a length of wire long enough to begin securing the blade to its support, all the while holding fast to the tower with her other arm. "Here, will you cut a few more pieces for me?" She handed him the wire and pliers.

As she did so, she happened to look down at the grass below, the green blades rippling like the sea. Her vision blurred and the prairie swirled and undulated, throwing off her equilibrium and triggering a cold sweat. The sudden dizziness caused her legs to go weak, and she sunk onto the metal platform to a sitting position.

"Hey, Jared, you might have to finish this for me." She gasped and clung even tighter to the bar.

JARED'S EYES DARTED TO NATALIE'S FACE, PALLID AND DRAWN. AND looking as though she might faint. His legs reacting faster than his mind, he scrambled the rest of the way up the tower to hold her steady. He yanked off one of her gloves, her skin clammy and trembling. "Look at me, Natalie. Come on, this isn't funny."

She squeezed her eyes shut, her respiration heavy and deliberate. "Do I look like I'm having fun?" She licked her dry lips.

He patted her hand in an effort to claim her attention. "Nah, I think you might be doing this on purpose, to play a game on me," he teased, but she wasn't reciprocating. "Why do I get the feeling this has happened before? Are you afraid of heights? Is that why you wanted my help?"

"Do you have to ask so many questions?" Her mouth barely moved.

Fear gripped his stomach as he assessed the real meaning to her avoidance. How was he going to get her down from this tower? "Hey Natalie, you can't pass out on me—not up here." *Lord, please help me get Natalie safely to the ground.*

He waited a few minutes, wishing he had some water to splash on her face. "Do you think you can follow me down the tower?"

She nodded, but her eyes remained closed. At that moment, Jared wanted to be strong and stout like Ryan so he could carry Natalie down. But he wasn't. He noted the rope slung over Natalie's shoulder.

Cautiously, he took the soft nylon rope from her arm and figured it to be at least forty feet. He fastened the loop to the tower and tugged on it. Satisfied it would hold her weight, he wrapped the other end around Natalie's waist, securing it with a bowline knot, something his granddad had taught him well.

Natalie's eyelids fluttered opened, and she relaxed her hold on the metal bar. Her pink color seemed to be returning as well. Good signs. "I need to finish my repairs," she said, her voice barely audible.

Jared chuckled. "Don't worry about the windmill. I'll take care of that as soon as we get you on the ground." He squeezed her hand, and then a Bible passage came to him, comforting words he hoped would calm her as they began their downward journey.

"The Lord is my shepherd, I shall not be in want," he said. "I'm going to go first, Natalie, and I want you to follow me. You'll be safe,

I promise." His words came out bold and sure, with more confidence than he could claim.

"He makes me lie down in green pastures, he leads me beside quiet waters, he restores my soul—And it's really important that you don't look down. Do you think you can do that?"

She nodded, her eyes on him, trusting.

"He guides me in paths of righteousness for his name's sake." Jared maneuvered into position on the ladder and helped Natalie do the same. "Even though I walk through the valley of the shadow of death, I will fear no evil, for you are with me."

Together the two of them began their descent, one rung at a time. "Your rod and your staff, they comfort me—you're doing great, Natalie. Keep going," Jared instructed, careful to use his body as a shield in case her feet should falter.

"You prepare a table before me in the presence of my enemies," Jared went on, allowing the words to soothe and give him peace. When they reached the halfway mark, he lifted up another prayer of thanks and continued protection. "You anoint my head with oil; my cup overflows."

As they approached the bottom, Jared had to be careful not to move too quickly in his haste to reach the ground. "Surely goodness and love will follow me all the days of my life, and I will dwell in the house of the Lord forever."

His feet touched the hard soil, and he grabbed Natalie by the waist and took her into his arms, thankful she'd made it without harm. She surprised him by wrapping her arms around his neck, not yet fully revived but much stronger than before.

"You saved me," she whispered against his cheek. "I could have killed myself up there, but you took care of me."

Jared closed his eyes, longing to take the credit for such things, and desiring the admiration she wanted to give. But he couldn't. "I didn't save you, Natalie. I was merely going through the motions. It was God who held you."

THIRTY-NINE

In the shade of the water trough, Natalie rested as Jared climbed the tower and reattached the broken blade. He continued with the maintenance of checking for loose fasteners and oiling the gearbox, his movements sure and effortless. Humiliation swelled within that she'd not been able to finish the task on her own. Had God really saved her? Was he an active participant in her life as Jared repeatedly claimed? The viable evidence seemed to grow stronger every day.

When Jared returned, he shifted the brake lever on the tower to set the device back to the wind. The blades began spinning and soon beads of water trickled from the pipe into the large round trough, the musical notes beckoning her from her seat on the ground. She rose on wobbly legs, her throat parched and thirsty. Cupping her hands, she eagerly drank the clear, cold liquid.

"Tastes good, huh?" Jared joined her and dipped his hands in the trough to splash water on his face. Water dripped from his chin, and his brown eyes shimmered with pleasure.

"I don't remember anything tasting so good." From this perspective, the young pastor looked mighty appetizing too. She caught sight of Jared's cowboy hat where it had landed on the grass and went to retrieve it. Her steps now steady and sure, Natalie placed the straw hat on Jared's head and clasped her hands behind his neck. Feeling bold and wanting to express her gratitude before she lost her nerve, she reached up and pressed her lips to his.

She closed her eyes and savored the tender kiss, how his lips yielded to her own, gentle yet certain. The slight scratch of his damp chin grazed against hers, and she opened her eyes. Waited for a reaction.

Jared stepped away, his mouth tilting into a timid grin. "What was that for?"

Natalie smiled back and shrugged. "I wanted to thank you. You're always coming to my rescue — with the kids, Tom, and Libby. I can't even count how many times you've helped me this past month." She swallowed the emotion quivering in her throat.

He looked down at his boots and shoved his hands in his pockets. "I don't want you to get the wrong idea, Natalie." His face contorted and her hope skidded to a halt.

She could have sworn Jared was interested. Or had her dizziness warped her senses? "I'm sorry, I thought you enjoyed it." *At least that's how it felt.* For the past few weeks, the two of them seemed to be on the verge of something more than friendship. She'd sensed it in her backyard and was aware of it now. "Is it me? That you're not attracted or interested in me?"

He kicked at the grass with the toe of his boot. "If I told you that, it'd be a lie."

"Well, what then?" She crossed her arms over her chest, horribly exposed yet needing to know.

"I have feelings for you, Natalie, but it's not that simple."

Her eyes searched his for the truth. "Because you're a pastor?"

"That and so much more." He took her hands and massaged her fingers. "The woman I give my heart to is the woman I intend to marry. And that woman will have to share my faith in God. If she doesn't, she'll never know who I truly am — or more important, who she is."

She lowered her gaze at his hard words, and yet this unwavering commitment was what drew her most to Jared. "But you feel it, don't you?"

Jared lifted her chin with his finger. "Practically since the first day I saw you on the river. How could I not be attracted—you're beautiful, sensitive, and so caring. I've never known a woman more determined than you."

A cautious grin belied the fluttering of her heart. "What do we do? Ignore it? Hope it goes away?"

He put his arm around her shoulders and walked her to where the horses were tethered. "As much as you might not want to hear it, the answer is simple," he said. "We pray."

THE WEEK PASSED AND WHEN SUNDAY MORNING ARRIVED, NATALIE WOKE to her previous night's resolve to attend church, desiring to learn more about Jared's faith. She'd informed Libby and the kids of her decision, and despite their arguments and groaning, they all agreed to go with her.

Wanting to fit in with Jared's congregation, Natalie took her time dressing. She fastened a belt around her denim skirt then checked her image in the mirror. Her dark hair hung limp at her neck, and she fluffed it to life, wishing she had Chelsey's natural waves. She slipped on a pair of leather sandals and dug from her jewelry box her favorite silver earrings. Her fingers shook as she put them on, and she chided herself. It was only a church service—a small step toward knowing Jared better. It wasn't as though she was entering a competition. Tired of feeding her anxiety, she strode out the door and knocked on the kids' rooms on her way to the stairs. "Hurry along. I don't want to be late this morning."

Dillon stepped out with his dress shirt partially tucked in. He shoved the shirttail into his pants, the same outfit he'd worn to their father's funeral.

"You look spiffy. You might want to run a comb through that hair of yours, though." She smiled at the cowlick that refused to stay down.

Her brother pulled a comb from his back pocket and followed her to the kitchen where she poured them each a glass of orange juice.

Libby and Chelsey jostled down the stairs minutes later, laughing like high school friends. Natalie frowned at her sister's choice of clothing, a tight pair of jeans and a tank top. Libby's casual outfit surprised her too, as she figured the woman would want to impress everyone with her fashion sense. "Is that what you're wearing?"

Their smiles faded. "We've decided not to go to church this morning."

Natalie tried to hide her surprise. "Why not?"

Chelsey exchanged looks with Libby as though they shared an intimate secret.

"I decided to take Chelsey to Junction City this morning," Libby said. "We're going to look at a barrel pony. This morning was the only time we could meet with the owners."

"Really?" Natalie's mouth quirked in suspicion, wondering why her stepmom hadn't mentioned this last night.

Dillon jumped up from the table, sloshing his orange juice. "Can I go too?"

Natalie shot him a look that pinned him to the chair. "No, you can't. You're going with me."

His mouth pulled into a frown. "How come Chelsey gets to do the fun stuff, and I always get stuck working? And now I have to go to church."

"I thought you wanted to go? To see Pastor Jared?"

He shrugged. "Buying a horse is more fun."

Natalie's eyes narrowed. "You're not planning on buying the horse today, are you? We talked about this. We don't have that kind of money to spare."

Libby waved off Natalie's concern. "Don't fret, Nat. We're just going to look. But if we like what we see, we'll have to figure out a way to buy him—won't we, Chels?" The woman elbowed the young teen, charged with excitement.

Dillon returned to his chair. "We've got the money we found in the barn."

Natalie raked her brother with a cold stare. "We need to save every dime we have right now. Besides, we have plenty of horses … and plenty of work to do." Her gaze drifted to Libby and her sister. She couldn't make Chelsey want to go to church, but that didn't mean she was ready to relinquish her control. "I guess you can go, but I expect you to return this afternoon. No fooling around in town. Is that understood?"

The two giggled. "We'll be back in time to help with the chores, don't you worry." Libby assured her.

Natalie had heard those words before—and the woman had failed to live up to them on each occasion. She checked the clock above the refrigerator and realized it was time to leave. "I guess we'll see you later then."

Dillon shuffled to the door, his earlier excitement gone. Natalie's had diminished as well, and she briefly debated staying home. Something called to her though, and a wave of guilt rushed over her. Whether due to the incident on the windmill or from Jared's talk about God, she chose to heed her intuition. Twenty minutes later, she and Dillon entered the small sanctuary of New Redeemer with its tall ceiling and stained glass windows. Not wanting to draw attention to their last minute arrival, they took a seat in one of the back pews.

Jared saw them, and his eyes lit with pleasure. Natalie realized then that his clergy robe didn't cause her a moment's hesitation but instead gave her a measure of comfort, like a well-worn boot.

She relaxed against the pew as the prelude music from the pipe organ consumed the room, its rich haunting melody sending chills up her arm. Captivated by the beautiful composition, Natalie's chest

swelled as the notes reached their pinnacle, the resonate tones causing her to soar and meet them, as though it were just her and God
in this small sanctuary.

The song brought back a forgotten memory, one that Natalie
had packed away and stowed after her mama's death along with so
many other cherished items. She'd sat beside her mama on a wooden
pew much like this one. She'd held her mama's hand and listened
to her sweet soprano voice sing about Jesus' love. And Natalie had
claimed that love for herself—she'd embraced it in her heart and
had felt his arms about her—so long ago, so many years ago.

How had she forgotten?

Drawn to a stained glass picture of Jesus holding a lamb, a sense
of peace washed over Natalie and reminded her of that love. Tears
sprang to her eyes, and as the opening hymn played, she heard her
mama's voice, and the words came to Natalie as though she'd always
held them on her tongue. "What a friend we have in Jesus." For
the next forty minutes, Natalie clung to that precious childhood
memory.

"You came." Jared clasped Natalie's fingers as she and Dillon
were ushered out of the sanctuary.

She nodded, conscious of his hand on hers. "And I'm glad I did.
It was a memorable service."

"Will you stay for lunch?" Jared moved on to welcome her
brother. "It's the last Sunday of the month—Potluck Sunday."

She glanced at Dillon and shrugged. "I didn't bring anything to
share."

"Believe me, there will be plenty of food." He winked at Dillon,
undeterred.

Natalie gazed at the people congregating in the fellowship area.
Their friendly chatter drifted into the sanctuary, as did the savory
aroma of beef and noodles—the combination smothering. Her fear
of not fitting in crept back with a vengeance, but more than that,
she had an overwhelming desire to go home and sort through the

memories that had erupted during the service. Her mind spun with uncertainty. "Maybe next time."

Disappointment creased Jared's brow as he walked them to the door. "I overheard a few ranchers who planned to cut their hay this week. If you'd like, I could come out and start on yours tomorrow."

Her eyes drifted from his collar and lingered on his lips, her confusion growing by the minute. Here she was, attracted to the man, yet not sure she could fit into his world, though she found herself wanting to — very much. "That sounds good," she said, falling back on what she knew best. Work. "I'll have the tractor and mower fueled and ready."

FORTY

NATALIE CLIMBED FROM THE SADDLE, HAVING SPENT MOST OF THE afternoon riding fence in the pasture. Seeking a break from the penetrating sun, she led Jackson to the shade of a cottonwood tree, her mind filtering through childhood memories — or at least those that had anything to do with faith.

The day they'd buried her mama in a lonesome prairie cemetery, Natalie had picked a bouquet of black-eyed Susan's to put on her grave. Days later, she'd lain on her soft mattress, reading her mama's Bible, the pages so thin she feared they might tear and be forever destroyed. Natalie had prayed for God to bring her mama back, and when she realized that would never happen, she'd gazed out her window at a crescent moon and cried in anger, feeling abandoned and alone.

Had that been the moment she'd turned her back on God, on Jesus' love? Her eyes landed on a cluster of black-eyed Susan's, and she stooped to pick one of the bristly stems. Twirling it in her hand, tears trickled from her check onto the yellow petals. Oh how she longed to feel his comforting arms around her once more — to know that gentle love again. But how? How could she take back all those years of denial and give up her control?

She wiped the tears from her cheeks, knowing she couldn't. Not with so many things and people depending on her.

As Natalie rode in from the pasture, she spotted Tom's pickup at the barn. She glanced about the yard for Dillon and noted Libby's car parked in its usual place. At least she and Chelsey had made it back from their horse shopping.

But why was Tom here? With trepidation, she flicked Jackson's reins and entered the shadowy recesses of the limestone barn, her eyes trained on any movement. Laughter erupted from her dad's tack room, then her ex-hired hand stepped from the doorway, followed by Libby.

"What are you doing here?" Natalie was in no mood for trivial conversation.

Tom held a wooden crate in his arms and grinned. "Hey there, your stepmom was just catching me up on the news around here. Sounds like you've been busy."

Natalie scowled, her senses on alert. "What's in the box?"

"Don't get excited. I only stopped by to pick up some shoeing tools I left. And I'm glad I did. Otherwise, I wouldn't have met your lovely stepmama."

Her mouth pulled down even more just thinking of the trouble those two could get into if they put their heads together. Not a good combination, and yet another reason for her to keep hold of her control. "Well, you have your belongings, so I guess you can leave."

"I'm heading out now." He shoved the crate in the back of his truck then paused before opening the driver's door. "I'm curious. Did you find yourself another hand for the summer?"

Natalie peered at Libby, wondering how much the woman had divulged. "We're managing. What about you?"

His shoulders relaxed. "My brother has a connection with a ranch south of here. If that deal works out, we'll be sitting pretty."

He let out a harsh laugh and crept closer, his hand reaching out to stroke Jackson's mane. "I guess that means I should thank you for firing me."

"No need for that." She nudged Jackson forward, fully intending to knock the man down if he didn't back off. "It's been nice talking to you, Tom, but I have work to do, and I'm sure you have somewhere you need to be."

Tom took the hint. "You're right, I do." With a brisk wave of his hand, he retreated to his truck and started the diesel.

Chelsey traipsed into the barn as his truck sped down the lane. "What was Tom doing here?"

"He came to pick up some tools he'd left behind." Natalie dismounted, wishing she'd checked the items in his crate.

"Why'd you have to be so rude to him, Nat?" Libby came to her side and hooked a stirrup to the saddle horn, then began loosening the straps. "He seemed like a nice enough guy."

"You would think so." The woman practically drooled on every male she saw, including Jared. "What did you tell him, anyway?"

Libby's bottom lip tightened. "You always think the worst of me. I didn't tell him anything."

"Why don't I believe you?" Natalie took the leather strap from her hand. "Tell me about this horse you took Chelsey to see. Was he everything you hoped for?"

"Oh yeah, he was that and more, which is something I need to talk to you about."

Already jumping to conclusions, Natalie braced herself against Jackson's ribs. "If it's about buying the horse, I told you we can't afford him."

"That's just it, Nat. I made an offer, and the guy took it. Can you believe that?" She went to stand beside Chelsey as though for support. "It was a really low number. I never thought for a moment that he'd accept."

"Call and tell him you've changed your mind." Natalie curled her fingers into a fist, biting back her agitation. "Tell him you have to renege on the deal."

Libby's chin jutted forward. "I can't do that. I gave him my word."

Natalie forced a grin. "Then I guess you'll have to come up with the money yourself."

FORTY-ONE

THE SUN BEAT DOWN ON THE CAB OF THE JOHN DEERE TRACTOR AS JARED circled the hayfield with the baler. All week they'd worked in the fields to get the hay put up before the predicted thunderstorms that weekend. Now Friday, the air was so humid, the sweat poured off Jared like rain. The day before, he'd mown the native grass in this field, and Chelsey had followed behind hours later with a tractor and rake. This afternoon the hay had cured enough for him to bale.

Mindlessly following the windrow laid out for him, his thoughts drifted to Natalie and Dillon's surprise visit to church last Sunday. He'd watched her slip into the back pew, quiet and unnoticed, and hadn't been able to hide his pleasure. That she'd stopped fighting God long enough to attend church caused his heart to swell.

As though beckoned, Natalie came driving up in her black truck and parked beneath a tall cottonwood tree. He set the brake and jumped from the tractor, his feet hitting the ground with a thud. The last few days, he'd spent a lot of hours behind the wheel of a tractor, and it felt good to stand and stretch.

Natalie met him with an ice jug and a smile. "I thought you might like some cold water and some of Chelsey's cookies."

Jared reached for the container and took a swig of the icy liquid, thinking he could empty the entire contents. By the time he came up for air, his stomach bulged, and he had no room for cookies.

"Looks like you're about finished."

Jared removed his cowboy hat and raked his hands through his hair, dirty and grimy from being out in the sun and dust. "I hope we can get the hay off the ground before the storm comes."

"That's why I came by. One of the boys on your crew called and said he couldn't work tonight."

Jared cringed at the news but should have expected as much. Considering it was the start of the Fourth of July weekend, he was fortunate to get anyone's help.

"I could take his place." Natalie peered at him through long lashes.

He shook his head, not interested in having a woman on his hay crew, no matter if she was the one funding the job or not.

"It's not like I haven't hauled hay before," she argued.

"I don't doubt your ability, but I'm not about to have you working alongside a bunch of hot-blooded boys."

"You're kidding, right? I've been working beside cowboys all my life." She lifted her hair off her long slender neck, as though placing an exclamation point on Jared's reason for not wanting her there.

"That may be, but if you're on the wagon, the guys will be looking at you instead of doing their work." He knew he spoke the truth as he'd been watching her all week. He took another drink and handed the jug back to her with a grin. "I'm sure we'll figure it out."

"Suit yourself, but don't say I didn't offer." She placed the jug in the shade and headed to her pickup. "I'll see you at the house when you're done," she called out with a wave.

Jared watched her leave and, after all these days, could still feel her lips on his, as though branded for life by the rodeo queen.

An hour later, Jared's shirt stuck to his back and the acrid stench of dried sweat rose to his nostrils. Finished baling, he let the tractor idle and headed for the cooler, already tasting the sweet water on his tongue.

A gust of air thrashed his hat and the tang of freshly mown hay surrounded him as a meadowlark fluttered on a nearby bale. He gazed at the line of trees bordering the creek with the blue sky above and the hills beyond. Along the fence where the mower couldn't reach, the bluestem grew tall, its slender stems blooming into what looked like a turkey foot and in another month would begin to turn to seed.

All of a sudden, homesickness hit Jared so raw and heavy that his throat clenched. Memories of his boyhood flew back to him as though transported on one of the fluffy clouds above. Jared recalled working in the hayfields with his granddad and sharing drinks of water from the glass thermos his granddad insisted kept the water cold even on the hottest day.

In that moment, Jared questioned why he ever left the life he loved so much. Why hadn't his granddad given him a portion of his inheritance so he could enjoy a vocation like Natalie's? Was God testing him?

He shook the traitorous thoughts away and hung his head, grateful for the life God had given him in the ministry. A fulfilling life — and one he should appreciate — not begrudge. He picked up the thermos of water and carried it back to the tractor, the thoughts heavy on his mind.

NATALIE WATCHED FROM THE PORCH AS THE GUYS FINISHED LOADING THE bales into the haymow. Lightning flashed in the west, and the stillness in the air filled with anticipation. She met Dillon at the barn as he leapt from the hay trailer, the others appearing one by one from the lighted mow.

"You boys got done just in time," she called up to them, the hay elevator clanging to a halt.

Jared stared up at the sky where the stars still twinkled—not yet overcome by the approaching storm. "It looks like we're in for a good one."

"If you're hungry, we've fixed some food up at the house." She waited for Jared and her brother to accompany her back.

Chelsey and Libby had the picnic table ready with a tray of barbecued beef sandwiches, two bags of potato chips, and a cooler of iced tea. The boys tore into the meal, bathed by yard light. But not Jared. He hung back in the shadows, his shoulders slumped with fatigue, drained of energy.

"You look bushed." She handed him a plate already filled.

"The work's been good for me, in more ways than one."

Natalie fought the urge to run her fingers over his temple and ease the weariness from his face. "What do you mean?"

He crouched on the ground beside her dad's wrought iron rocker and took a bite of the sandwich. "It's helped me consider the decisions I've made. Made me appreciate all the things God's given me."

Lightning bugs twinkled in the pasture while crickets chirped from under the tree. Natalie sat in the rocker, tempted to voice her own questions. "I think I'm beginning to understand."

In taking care of the ranch and spending time with her brother and sister, she'd started to see life in its most basic form. Natalie missed her dad and ached for his presence every day, but she was getting used to the way things were—even though it meant giving up certain freedoms. And her recent jolts with faith had caused her to view things from a more heightened perspective, though she wasn't yet sure what to make of this vantage point.

A sudden flurry blew dust and particles in the air, the storm's approach nearly on top of them. The sky crackled above and ended with a boom.

Jared rose from his position. "You boys should be getting home. I don't want your folks blaming me for you getting caught in this storm."

The hungry teens shoved the last of their food into their mouths. Then they thanked Jared and Natalie and rushed for their truck, the first large sprinkles dotting the soil.

"Want to come in for a while?" She began gathering the food from the table.

His movements were awkward as though his muscles were sore. "I'll help carry this inside, but then I'd better head to town. Sleep will come easy tonight — storm or no storm."

Natalie understood completely. "The sleep of a laborer is sweet," she said, having been in that position more nights than not since her dad passed away.

Another strike of lightning lit the sky and then came the downpour. Jared grabbed the jug of tea and hauled it to the porch. Natalie followed close on his heels, the onslaught so sudden it left them soaked and breathless. They stood under the safety of the porch and watched as the deluge created instant puddles on the ground.

"Do you have plans for the Fourth?" She raised her voice over the torrent of rain.

"I'll probably go downtown and watch the fireworks from Clara's. I've heard she's planning to serve cake and cookies." He set the jug of tea down and held the screen door for her. "What about you?"

Natalie carried the tray of leftovers to the kitchen counter where a large watermelon waited to be sliced. "I thought we might have a wiener roast and toast marshmallows. It's a tradition we used to do with Dad." She seized a towel and mopped the rain from her arms and face, poking further into her memory. "He liked to tell stories around a fire and pick out constellations. If it's a clear night, we should be able to see the fireworks from town. You're welcome to join us if you want." She handed him the towel, and their fingers brushed. Uncertainty coursed within her. Longing for Jared's support, to feel his arms around her, yet afraid to ask for fear she might overstep her boundaries again, Natalie dug herself deeper into the hole. "Sometimes it's hard to believe he's really gone." Her words came out little more than a whisper.

Jared draped the towel over a chair then covered her hand with his. "What time should I arrive?"

"Whenever you can get here," she managed to say, caught in a storm greater than the one outside.

FORTY-TWO

THE STORM RAGED ON THE REST OF THE NIGHT, BUT BY NOON THE NEXT day, the sun finally peeked through the clouds. As the day wore on, Jared prepared his last minute sermon notes and visited two elderly members in their homes. He also fielded a phone call from his mother.

"I know you're busy with your new congregation, but your father and I wondered if you'd care to drive up tomorrow afternoon and have supper with us?"

Jared flipped through his planner. He normally kept his Sunday afternoons free from obligation. "Thanks, Mom, I'd like that. How's your garden this summer? Getting lots of produce?"

"Oh my yes," she said, and Jared grinned, savoring the trill of her laughter as it came through the receiver. "I've already canned several batches of sweet pickles, and your dad picked corn this morning."

"Does that mean we'll be eating corn-on-the-cob tomorrow?"

"Of course. And feel free to bring a friend if you want—to keep you company on the long drive. A lady friend, even, if you have one you'd like us to meet."

Jared cringed at the hopefulness in her voice. "You ask me that every time we talk. I assure you I'll be arriving alone tomorrow."

The timing of this visit actually worked out well, as Jared had a few things he wanted to speak to his dad about regarding church and female relationships. But no way was he going to admit that to his mother.

"You can't blame me for asking. You know I only want what's best for you," she said, and he envisioned the smile that accompanied those words.

"I know, Mom. I'll see you tomorrow." He closed the connection, looking forward to an afternoon with his folks.

Toward evening, he took his time shaving and slapped on an extra douse of cologne, unable to deny his excitement at spending an evening in Natalie's company. He considered her sorrow from the night before when she'd spoken of her father and knew, without a doubt, he'd feel the same if he had to face life without his parents. He sent up a prayer that he'd be able to ease her grief this evening and that his actions would be pleasing to God.

Thirty minutes later, he pulled in to the Double-A-Ranch. Dillon and Willard were poking logs in a fire pit dug into the ground. They both waved and greeted him as he crawled from his car.

Natalie came out the back door with an armload of food, and Jared met her at the steps. "Need some help?"

She handed him two packages of wieners. "You made it. No last minute voter meetings or emergencies to deal with?"

"Nope, my life's been pretty boring lately." He grinned, admiring her in a pair of cut-off shorts and a sleeveless button up shirt, her long hair tied back with a wide red ribbon.

"I'm glad." She went to give Dillon the roasting sticks and set the package of buns on the picnic table. While they worked to pierce the hot dogs, Chelsey and Libby strolled out of the house all dressed up and wearing makeup.

"You ladies look nice." Natalie shooed Jessie away from the table. "Kind of fancy for a cookout though."

Chelsey peered at her sister with a guilty expression Jared had witnessed before. "Mom and I have been invited to a barbecue in town. We're going to watch the fireworks from there."

"Didn't Chelsey tell you, Nat? We've been planning this for days," Libby said.

Jared sensed Natalie's agitation and wondered how things were going with the kids and Libby. There seemed to be a lot of tension in the air.

Natalie's lips pulled into a frown. "I guess it must have slipped her mind."

"Or maybe you were too busy to hear," Chelsey quipped.

"But this is a tradition, Chels." Natalie poked another hot dog on a stick. "It won't be the same without you."

"Dad's gone. What good are traditions without him?" The young girl stared down at her flip-flops.

"There's nothing wrong with traditions, Nat. Just not this year." Libby made her way to her car and waited expectantly for Chelsey. "Ready to go?"

Chelsey cast a look from her sister to her mom as though torn. She then chose the yellow Impala.

Natalie returned to the roasting pit after they'd driven away and glanced about. "Where's Dillon? I suppose he's decided not to take part in this tradition too?" She bit her bottom lip, appearing to be on the verge of tears.

Willard sat in a lawn chair turning his stick. "He probably went to the house for something."

A trail of smoke issued from the fire, the scent of burning wood and sizzling hot dogs filled the air. In an effort to console her, Jared squeezed Natalie's arm. "I'm sure Willard's right. If you want, I'll go look for him." At her silent nod, he went in search of her brother and found him in the machine shed.

"Hey Dillon, what are you doing in here? Don't you want to help Willard cook the hot dogs?"

The boy didn't say anything. He sat on an overturned bucket, drawing circles in the dirt with a stick. "I'm not hungry."

"You seemed hungry a few minutes ago. Is this because of Chelsey?"

Dillon tapped the stick on the ground. "How come Chelsey and Nat fight so much? And how come Mom and Chelsey never do stuff with me? They always go off on their own. I don't think Libby likes me very much."

"Why do you think that?" Jared noted the boy's indecision on what to call his mom.

"She's more interested in Chelsey. The two of them are always working on barrels or going shopping or giggling about girl stuff."

Jared pulled up a bucket and sat beside Dillon. "I'm not an expert on women, but I think your mom is trying to get to know you kids in whatever way she can. She does things with you too. You've done chores together, and you both went fishing at the pond."

"Yeah, but she hated it."

"But she tried. She probably feels more comfortable doing girl things. I'm sure it'll work out if you give her some time."

Dillon stared at the drawing on the ground. "It won't be the same without them tonight."

"Look at it this way, tonight the females are the minority. You should be happy."

It took a few moments for this to sink in, but then Dillon's face expanded into a smile. "If you want, we can have a seed spitting contest. Natalie's pretty good, but I think I'll beat her this year."

Jared chuckled and followed the boy back to the fire, unable to erase the image of Natalie spitting watermelon seeds on the ground. The four of them sat under the stars that night, stuffing themselves with hot dogs and watermelon. Jared sipped his coffee and watched as a burst of colorful sparks exploded on a distant hill.

"Awesome, did you see that one!" Dillon pointed in the opposite direction spotting yet another display of lights.

Natalie squatted next to the fire rotating her stick until her marshmallows were crispy and charred on the edges. She waved her creation in front of Jared. "Want one?"

"No more." He'd already eaten four.

She giggled, and her eyes danced by the firelight. "Come on, one more, you can do it."

He shook his head, not giving in to her persuasion.

"Dillon, what about you?"

"No, Nat. I've had enough. Feed it to Jessie. She'll eat it." He tried to get the dog to come to the fire, but even she didn't want any more.

"Fine, I'll eat it myself." Natalie pulled off the gooey marshmallow and popped it in her mouth. She licked her sticky fingers and sat beside Jared. "Mmm, I love toasted marshmallows."

"I can tell. I've never seen a girl eat so many." He'd never seen a girl spit watermelon seeds as far as she could either, having beaten her brother by at least a foot. He wondered how many more surprises this woman hid behind her back and studied her in the glow of the campfire, wrapped in a jacket to keep the night chill from her arms.

The bright eruptions in the sky appeared further and further apart until finally Willard stood from his lawn chair. "Dillon, how about a game of checkers before I head home for the night?"

"But what about the fireworks?" Dillon protested.

The man winked at Jared and Natalie. "I think they're done for the night and so am I. Do you want to play checkers with me, or shall I go home?"

Dillon tossed his foam cup in the fire, and it shriveled to nothing. "I'll play, and I'll beat you this time too."

Jared and Natalie watched as the two disappeared into the house. Natalie smiled at Jared and offered her hand. "Want to take a walk?"

Jared's heart rocketed against his chest like one of Dillon's fireworks. He'd entered this family's life through reaching out to Dillon and had grown to value and cherish their friendship. But the kiss he and Natalie shared at the windmill had catapulted that friendship to another level. One he wasn't sure how to proceed with. Casting a silent prayer for direction, he took her hand within his own.

They strolled from the yard light, her fingers entwined within his own, strong and firm. "I'm glad you joined us tonight."

He walked with her to the corral, and his eyes adjusted to the darkness. "It's been fun." He rested his boot against the bottom rung and the silence between them grew.

"May I ask you something?" Her lips glistened under the starlight.

"If I can do the same."

"Okay, you first."

He hoped his next comment wouldn't ruin the peaceful mood. "I noticed things seemed a bit strained between you and Chelsey tonight. How are you two getting along?"

Natalie released a heavy sigh. "I thought things were better. But this past week, she and Libby have gotten really tight — secretive almost."

"Like their outing tonight?"

She nodded. "I don't recall Chelsey mentioning one word about going into town to watch fireworks. It's nothing for the two of them to take off in Libby's car and be gone for hours."

Perhaps Jared had been wrong to persuade Natalie to give her stepmom another chance. Maybe Willard's instincts had been correct. He hoped not. "Is Libby still drinking?"

"Not that I'm aware of."

"It's only natural for Chelsey to want to bond with her mom. Maybe that's all this is?"

"I hope so." She gazed off as another boom discharged in the darkness, spewing silver into the sky.

Jared wasn't sure when it had happened. Somewhere between fishing with Dillon and dragging calves to Natalie's branding fire he'd fallen in love with this family — and he was pretty sure he'd fallen in love with Natalie. He grazed her chin with his finger. "What was it you wanted to ask me?"

Her eyes came back to his. "I wondered if you'd been praying about us?"

FORTY-THREE

NATALIE BIT HER BOTTOM LIP IN ANTICIPATION OF HIS ANSWER, WANTING to know — believing it somehow mattered.

"Yes, I've been praying." His hand stroked her cheek, and she melted into his touch.

"Have you received any answers yet?" her voice whispered back.

Jared's hand crept to the back of her neck, and he slipped the ribbon from her hair. "Not exactly."

"No?"

"I've concluded that you're one of two things." He combed his fingers through her hair, causing tingles to course through her body.

Natalie closed her eyes. "And what is that?"

"You're either an incredible blessing I need to pursue, or you're a temptation I should run from."

She couldn't contain her smile. "And which do you think I am?"

His hand pressed her closer, so close that she could feel his breath on her face, smell the musky scent of his cologne. "I think you're a temptation and a blessing. And ... I think I'm falling in love with you."

Natalie's breath caught in her throat, and as her eyes opened, Jared's mouth closed down on her lips, soft and gentle. She kissed him back, her heart pounding within her chest. Her mind whirled, unable to remember ever feeling this way before — not even with Ryan. His lips ventured to her chin, her cheek, her nose, his skin smooth as silk against hers.

Then somewhere from within, reality surfaced. Jared was a pastor and a man of God. He'd already told her that he didn't enter into relationships lightly, which meant only one thing. Loving and being with Jared might eventually lead to marriage — which would make her a *pastor's wife*. Was that what she wanted? And what about the kids and the ranch? Was it even possible for a pastor to be a rancher?

She eased from his embrace and smoothed the back of her hand against her mouth. Though she had feelings for Jared and those feelings ran deep, was she ready for such commitment? "Maybe we should slow down a bit."

Jared stepped away and a chasm separated them. "I'm so sorry." He lifted his face to the dark sky, his breath uneven. "I got carried away. I should have known better."

Hating to see him tortured, she pressed her palm against his chest, felt his heart thunder beneath his shirt. "It's okay," she said. "But let's think about this for awhile. Decide if this is what we really want. I mean, there are a lot of questions that need to be considered."

His eyes penetrated hers. "Walk instead of run."

Natalie's attention drifted to a far-off hill where one final blast erupted into the sky, flickering out and flashing like a multicolored kaleidoscope. With each massive detonation, Natalie held her breath in expectant hope, almost the same as when she'd heard the organ music hover from the pipes in the sanctuary — the day her soul soared to meet God.

"And while we're walking," she said, "we can do some more praying too."

THE NEXT MORNING, NATALIE WENT TO CHURCH WITH DILLON WHILE

Chelsey and Libby stayed in bed, insisting they were too tired from their late night of fireworks. She spoke briefly with Jared after the service but then drove Dillon home, needing to sort through some more of her dad's financial paperwork.

When they arrived back at the ranch, the house was quiet. Figuring Chelsey and Libby were still asleep, Natalie opened the office door and found her stepmom still in her pajamas and rifling through the books on her father's shelf.

Startled, Libby's head shot up, and the book in her hand clambered to the floor. "What are you doing back, already? I thought you and Dillon went to church?"

"We just got home." Natalie continued across the room as her stepmom retrieved the book that had dropped. The desk Natalie had tidied the day before now sat in complete disarray with papers strewn from one side to the other. "Have you been going through my things?"

"Of course not." Libby rose from her stooped position. "I know better than to mess with your stuff. Your dad had so many books, I came down thinking I'd find one to read."

Natalie's gaze traveled to her father's book collection, never giving it much notice until now. She inspected it closer and noticed titles such as Shakespeare, Longfellow, Wordsworth, and Poe. She shook her head, wondering how her dad's love for poetry had gone unnoticed by everyone in her family, especially her. Had she really not known him any better than that?

She turned to Libby, her attention caught by a yellow paper in her stepmom's hand. "What's that you're holding?"

Libby waved the envelope in the air, an envelope the same size and color as the one Natalie had found in her father's tack room. "What this? It's just something that fell out of a book." She tried to tuck it into her robe pocket, though it was too big to shove inside.

"May I see it?" Natalie asked.

Libby's nostrils flared and a crimson blush seeped onto her flustered face. "Yeah, sure. Why not?" She withdrew the crisp envelope and handed it to Natalie.

The seal had already been broken. Natalie inspected the item further and opened the flap to reveal a stack of hundred dollar bills.

"Well, what do you know?" Libby eyed the money. "Why do you suppose that was in the book?"

Natalie tried to discern whether the woman was truly surprised or was lying through her teeth. She was inclined to believe the latter. "Dillon told you about the money we found in the tack room. Apparently, Dad hid some in here too." And more than likely, Libby had intended on walking away with every dollar.

"I wonder where else the old coot might have stashed his money." Libby's gaze traveled around the room, dollar signs cha-chinging in her pupils.

"As the executor of Dad's estate, I'm supposed to inventory all the money we find on the ranch."

The woman chuckled. "It's cash, Nat. Who's going to know?"

The same thoughts had crossed Natalie's mind many times. "I'll know."

"You're kidding? You'd rather pay taxes on it than buy yourself something useful — needful even?"

"I'll do what I have to do. You haven't found any more of Dad's money have you, in his bedroom or around the house?" Natalie's suspicions grew by the second.

"You don't think I'm stealing from you?"

Natalie regarded her stepmom with cold speculation. "You and Chelsey have been doing a lot of shopping lately, and you don't have a job."

"I can't believe you're accusing me of this," Libby stammered.

"You're the one who made an offer on a horse. Where does all your money come from?"

Libby sniffed in denial. "You've been putting off a lot of angry vibes toward me lately. I've tried to get along, but maybe I've worn out my welcome. Maybe it's time for me to look for a place in town."

Natalie returned to the mess on her father's desk, convinced Libby had rifled through the papers. "I think that might be a good idea."

FORTY-FOUR

AFTER CHURCH, JARED DROVE TO CONCORDIA TO VISIT HIS PARENTS. AS he pulled up to the house, he met his dad carrying in a bucket of garden corn.

"Hey, you're just in time to help shuck." His dad smiled and patted Jared on the back. "Your mom said you'd be joining us for supper. It's good to see you."

Jared sat at the picnic table where his dad dumped the corn he'd picked. He chose one and peeled back the outer husk. "It looks like your garden is doing well."

His mom came out of the house then and enveloped him in a big hug. "You'll have to take some of this back with you."

Jared smiled his thanks, knowing he'd leave with a trunk full of vegetables. For as long as he could remember, his folks had planted a summer garden — a hobby for his dad and a mission project for his mom as she'd give their produce to anyone who looked like they might be hungry.

"I can't believe it's been two months since your ordination." She pinched his cheek, a habit she refused to give up. "How are things going at your church?"

Jared removed a handful of silk from a golden ear of corn. "I can't complain. We started a men's Bible study and have already finished Vacation Bible School. I'm not so busy that I can't get in a little fishing," he said and winked at his dad.

"You look healthy." His dad took Jared's piece of corn and placed it on a tray with several others. "The women at your church must be feeding you well."

"It's good to see some color on your face too." His mom shooed the flies from the corn piled high on the tray. "You must be getting plenty of fresh air."

Jared glanced at his skin, now golden brown from his time in the sun. "I've been helping a friend with some ranch work. I hoped I might talk to you about that." Jared waited for his dad to take the hint.

His dad caught it like a baseball catcher. "Mother, is it all right if I show Jared the new tiller we bought for the garden?"

She rose from the bench. "You men and your toys. Go ahead. I'm taking these ears inside where I can silk them without any flies. But come in when you're done, and we'll have some blackberry pie. Your dad picked them fresh yesterday morning."

His dad made a face. "Briars and all."

Jared reached over and pecked his mom on the cheek. "I can always count on you to have a pie for me when I come home." He held the back door for her, then walked with his dad to the garage.

"Tell me, son, what's on your mind. While I know your mother's cooking is a great enticement, I also know how precious a minister's time can be. Are you having to take on an extra job to support yourself?"

"It's not like that." Jared attempted to ease his dad's mind. "This friend of mine, her father died, and she needed someone to help with the hay crop."

"She?" His dad's brow curved with reservation.

Jared's ears burned as though he'd been caught in a lie. "She's a young woman, raising her two siblings by herself."

"I'm sorry to hear about her loss. Does she attend your church? Is that how you met her?"

"Not exactly."

"I see." His dad hovered over his new tiller and brushed a speck of oil from the bright red paint. "Does she go to church?"

Jared jammed his hands in his pockets. "She's been a few times, but she's had a lot of roadblocks to her faith."

"Okay, so you're helping a single gal who's struggling with her faith, and you want advice from your old man." He revealed the barest hint of a grin. "If you want my help, you're going to have to offer more than that."

Not eager to admit the problems he'd made for himself, Jared tamped down his pride. "Natalie Adams is a strong and intelligent woman, and the more I'm around her, the more time I want to spend with her. Working on her ranch this past month has brought back a ton of memories. It has me wondering if I made the right choice in becoming a minister or whether I should have stuck it out and tried to work my way into farming." He stared at the rear-tine tiller as though their conversation centered on it. "Right now, I'm confused about a lot of things."

His dad scratched his chin. "This girl, you really like her?"

Jared smiled as an image formed in his mind of Natalie standing on the riverbank with her hair floating long and free. "She's a remarkable woman. She's been through so much, but she always perseveres. I doubt I could have carried her load for as long. Her determination and courage seem to drive her forward. What amazes me is that through all her troubles, she somehow managed to win first runner up for Miss Rodeo America."

"That's quite an accomplishment for a young lady. His dad's eyes perked with interest. "Your friend sounds like a fascinating person — one I'd like to meet someday."

Jared raked his fingers through his hair. "But that's just it. How will I know if Natalie is the woman I'm meant to be with? And, if she is the one God has chosen for me, how will I be both a rancher and a pastor? You and Mom moved to half a dozen churches before you settled here."

"Whoa down, son. These are some mighty big steps you're talking about."

Jared took a breath to settle himself. "I just want to be sure that Natalie and I aren't setting ourselves up for disappointment. Or should I put some space between us and give my full concentration to the church for awhile?" He gripped the handlebars of the tiller. "When I went through seminary, I never questioned whether I would fall in love and marry. I assumed it would happen — expected it to. But I never counted on such an unexpected twist. To fall in love with someone who isn't a member of the church, and who comes with all this extra baggage."

His dad crossed his arms over his chest and frowned. "You mean more baggage than what you've already expressed?"

The garage had turned into a sweltering sauna. "Natalie has a fifteen-year-old sister who has a few problems, and her little brother misses his dad something terrible. Then there's her stepmom who reappeared recently. They thought Libby was dead, but now she wants to be a part of their life. It's complicated."

"Life is filled with complications." His dad turned the key on the tiller, and it rumbled to a steady rhythm. "Take your mother for example. She didn't think we needed such a big tiller and fought me tooth and nail about buying it. But this little darling has an eight horsepower engine and works the ground so fine and soft, a weed won't dare grow in her garden."

After a few minutes, he shut down the motor and patted the machine with satisfaction. "When your mother and I married before seminary, we both understood what we were getting into. We knew we wouldn't always agree, but we also knew God was great enough to handle any problem we would give him. Not all relationships are so easy, though. Your first obstacle seems to be Natalie's faith. Until you get over that hurdle, there doesn't seem to be much future for the two of you.

"Unless, of course, you decide Natalie is more important to you than the ministry. And even then, a marriage between a nonbeliever and one who is faithful is extremely difficult." He moved to Jared's side and squeezed his shoulder. "Maybe you need to step back and look at things from a different view—see if your feelings are as strong when you get away from this gal and her family. Determine how you would feel if Natalie was no longer in your life."

"You're disappointed that I've allowed this to happen?"

His dad shook his head. "No, son, in all my years as a pastor I've witnessed marriages between total opposites that seemed doomed from the very beginning but turned into beautiful, lasting relationships. What's important is that you set God as the foundation for your marriage, and when you do that, everything else will fall into place."

Jared gripped the handlebars tighter. "I know you're right. Maybe I just need to put some space between us." The thought of walking away from Natalie and her family nearly tore his heart from his chest.

His dad sat on a nearby work stool. "Want to talk about the other thing that's bothering you? About your granddad?"

"How'd you know?"

"Let's just say the troubles we had back then have been on my mind a lot lately. I'm guessing God's been working on both of us."

Jared shook his head, recalling the day his granddad informed everyone what his intentions were. The man had lived a long, full life but in the end developed lung cancer. A month or so before his death, he gathered the entire family in his living room. He sat up in his chair braced by a walker, and with a voice so clear and gruff Jared could still hear it to this day, said, "I've decided to give the farm to Jimmy."

The entire room rang with silence, and Jared felt the weight of burning coals heaped on his heart.

"Do you regret arguing with Granddad that night?"

His father winced. "You knew?"

Jared nodded. At the time, Jared had been honored that his dad would stand up for him, but also ashamed that he'd argue with a dying man. "I wish things could have been different in the end. I loved that man so much."

"He loved you too."

Jared wished he'd told his granddad instead of walking away with a bruised ego, thinking the old man had abandoned him. "Do you suppose Granddad deprived me of the farm for a reason?"

His dad braced his hands on his knees. "There was a lot going on back then that you weren't aware of. Your Uncle Jimmy had a mountain of debt and nothing to show for it. My brother needed help. While I'm sure Granddad struggled with his decision, he couldn't abandon his oldest son. What he did gave Jimmy hope for his future." He shifted his position on the stool and seemed to weigh his next words. "Tell me this. Do you enjoy being a pastor?"

Jared considered the time he'd spent with his new congregation counseling, guiding, and teaching them. "I like the challenge and sense God's hand on my work. But I can't deny the satisfaction I receive in the hard physical labor of working the land."

His dad nodded as though he understood completely. "I can tell you this, son, and maybe it'll help. I've known pastors who have stayed at their home parish all their lives," he said. "They've worked farms and held outside jobs, called to do that work as much as they were called to minister. A man has to be willing to listen to God's call and follow wherever it leads him. And that's a lesson for all believers—not just the clergy."

FORTY-FIVE

"I CAN'T BELIEVE YOU'RE RUNNING HER OFF," CHELSEY SHRIEKED AT Natalie from across the kitchen. "I don't know why I even try talking to you. You've been against Mom ever since she arrived. You don't want her here, and you don't want me here either."

Natalie tossed the dishtowel on the table. "That's not true, Chels. Don't you see, she's trying to buy your love? New clothes, boots, a brand new horse that she has no business buying—and we still don't know where she gets her money."

Her sister shook her head in disbelief. "No, Nat, you're just jealous that Mom came back. You're jealous that Dillon and I want her to stay, and because you don't get to be our mom any longer." The girl stormed out of the kitchen.

Natalie forced back searing tears and pursued her up the living room stairs. "You don't mean that, Chels. How can you even think it after all we've been through? I nursed you through colds and flus, and the chickenpox, took you to ballgames and band concerts."

She reached the top of the stairs and trailed Chelsey into her bedroom. "For Pete's sakes, last summer I helped you pass your driver's permit test. How can you believe I don't care about you?"

Her sister jammed another pair of jeans into an already full suitcase. "You brought it on yourself, blaming Mom for stealing Dad's money. That was just cruel, Nat. I can't stand by you after that."

Natalie pressed her hand against her temple, her head pounding. "I caught Libby putting money in her pocket. You can't fight the facts."

"She didn't know the envelope held money," Chelsey defended.

"Yeah right, and I was born yesterday."

"I've had it with your accusations." Chelsey shook her head with bitter resentment and zipped the suitcase closed. "Mom's moving to town, and I'm going with her. Dillon can come too, if he wants."

Her sister's words knocked the air out of her, and Natalie sunk into a chair. "You can't leave. I'm your legal guardian."

"I guess we'll have to see about that, won't we?"

"You can't just leave when things get tough. That's Libby's way. She left when you were a toddler and now she's leaving again. Don't be like her. The only way to get through this is for you to stay and work it out."

"No, Nat. I'm not going to sit back and watch you do this to her." Chelsey lugged her suitcases to the bedroom door then paused. "Libby's changed—she's not the same as she was back then. If you won't allow her to stay, I'm not going to stay either." Her sister raged down the steps with her heavy bags thumping behind.

Natalie fought the urge to go after her. There was no pleading with the girl. Her sister was past the point of listening to reason. When the back door slammed shut, Natalie returned to the kitchen and peered out the curtained window to see Chelsey loading her suitcases in the back of Libby's car.

Minutes later, Libby passed by the counter with her luggage, playing the part of victim quite well. "I never meant to cause such a fuss between you and the kids. I'm sorry it's come to this—that you feel you can't trust me."

She stopped in the doorway and faced Natalie with a puckered brow. "I'll try to talk Chelsey into calling you later, once she cools down. I know you love her."

Her spirit too fragile, Natalie refused to answer and watched as the yellow sedan disappeared down the lane. She crumpled into a kitchen chair. How had things gotten so complicated? She'd begun this journey hoping to get through their father's death and forge a family bond, but somewhere along the way, she'd managed to sever nearly every strand she'd built. The agony inside threatened to pull her apart, piece by piece.

Natalie buried her head in her hands and allowed the tears to fall. She wept for the family she'd tried to hold together, for letting down her dad and destroying all his hard work. And finally, she cried for herself … for losing the two people she cared about most in this world—her brother and sister, for surely it was only a matter of time before Dillon would follow in Chelsey's footsteps.

Without them, it all seemed meaningless—and ironic.

All her life, Natalie had fought to escape the ties and responsibilities that held her, but in reality, those ties and responsibilities were what defined her. Natalie had raised those kids. She'd laughed with them in happy moments and dried their tears when they were sad. How could it all end so hopelessly? Her heart ached with bitterness, and when she could cry no more, a solemn gloom hung over her like a storm cloud.

She glanced out the window and realized darkness had fallen. Then she felt a small hand on her shoulder.

"I won't leave you, Nat."

She shifted her head to see Dillon standing behind her, his own eyes watery.

"How long have you been here?"

Her brother shrugged, and it was then she noticed he held a leather book in his hands. He laid it on the table before her and opened it to a page marked with a red satin ribbon.

"Though I walk through the valley of the shadow of death, I will fear no evil: for thou art with me; thy rod and thy staff they comfort me." Dillon read the words Jared had repeated when he'd talked her down the windmill tower.

"Is this the Bible Jared gave you?"

At his nod, Natalie picked up the hair ribbon bookmark and broke down in tears. God had been with her all along. As a young girl when her mama died, through the years, and especially these past few months. She could no longer deny his existence or his care and felt his presence right now in this room.

For the next thirty minutes, she and Dillon read from the marked passages in Dillon's Bible, and the longer they read, the more comfort Natalie drew from them. Afterwards, she and Dillon sat on the porch and watched the fireflies blink across the yard.

"Are you afraid, Dillon? Do you trust me enough to believe that I want what's best for you and Chelsey? That I want us to be a family and that I'd never deliberately hurt either one of you?"

"I know you love us, Nat. Chelsey knows it too. She's just being stupid right now."

Natalie hugged him to her side. "Tomorrow we'll visit Willard and see if he has any advice for solving this problem. Does that sound like a good idea?"

"What about Jared? He could help us."

Natalie thought so too and couldn't think of anyone she'd rather talk to about this than Jared. She decided to call him before she went to bed that night. Only he didn't answer his phone.

FORTY-SIX

Jared stepped into his study late that night after returning from his parents' home. His answering machine flickered in the dim light. He pressed the button and listened to Natalie's message, her words hushed and lethargic.

"Sorry I missed you. Just wanted to talk to you about something and hear your voice. Call me."

Tempted to return her call right then, Jared recalled the talk with his dad about putting some distance between himself and Natalie. Though difficult, he resisted picking up the phone knowing the best things in life were often the hardest to do. Encouraged by this truth, he pulled a Bible from the desk. He leafed through the onionskin pages until he reached Psalms and began reading the words that quieted his mind and made his troubles seem small.

The next day, the sun shone high overhead as Natalie took a break from her ranch work. Having slept poorly the night before, she completed her chores with sluggish effort, her sister's angry words never far from her mind.

"I'm going over to Willard's for a while," she called to Dillon when she'd come in from checking cattle.

He hurried to her side. "Can I ride with you? And Jessie too?"

Natalie agreed and opened the tailgate for Jessie to hop into the bed of the truck. Minutes later, she arrived at Willard's and parked in front of his leather shop. Her brother and the dog followed her in through the front door.

Willard stood at his workbench, repairing a pair of leather boots. "What did I do to deserve a visit from you this fine afternoon?" He grinned, and it took Natalie back to her childhood, of days spent watching this man craft treasures out of a piece of cowhide.

She sat on a wooden stool, and Dillon found a spot on the floor where he played with the border collie. "You might not think this is such a pleasant visit when I tell you why I'm here."

Willard pulled up a chair and joined her, his attention complete. "What seems to be the trouble?"

Her bottom lip trembled despite her resolve to remain calm. "I tried to take over where Dad left off, but I'm afraid I've failed miserably."

"I'm sure it's not that bad." His friendly eyes consoled her. "Tell me what's going on that has you so upset."

Natalie concentrated on the pile of mismatched boots lying on Willard's floor, never able to understand his sense of order. "Chelsey and Libby moved out. They left last night."

"I see." Willard mumbled under his breath. "Where did they go?"

"They're staying in town, in an apartment by the river."

Willard shook his head and went back to his repair work. "Sometimes I think best when my hands are busy," he said, but Natalie figured it had more to do with needing an outlet for his aggravation. "I warned you it was a bad idea to invite that woman into your home. Libby was nothing but trouble when you were little, and she's not changed, no matter how much we wish it so."

"Libby isn't the only one to blame. I have to accept my share of the fault. I should have known better than to allow her so much freedom with the kids — especially Chelsey. I should have kept a closer watch."

"We can only see what we want to see." Willard tapped the boot's black heel with a plastic mallet, wedging the sole from the upper leather. "Now that you understand the problem, what are you going to do about it?"

"That's why I'm here." Natalie drummed her fingers on the counter. "I need some advice. Should I go after Chelsey and insist she come home?"

He ripped the entire sole from the worn boot. "If you do, she'll only run away again."

Dillon rose from the floor to stand beside Natalie. "Want me to talk to her?"

Natalie opened her arm to him, thankful for her brother's support. "This isn't your fight, Dillon." Despite all their problems the last few months, the two of them remained as close as any brother or sister — or any mother and son.

"How can we get Chelsey back, then?" The sound of his distress tugged at Natalie's emotions.

"As much as it grieves me to say it, your sister's gonna have to come back on her own." Willard stepped from behind the counter and motioned for them with his hand. "Come here for a second. I want to show you something."

He led them to the back of the small room and dug into a cardboard box. Seconds later, he withdrew a rolled piece of paper.

"Sometimes you have to let people figure out things for themselves. I'm thinking Chelsey's a lot like your dad. They're the kind of people who bottle their emotions deep inside. Chelsey's just gotta figure a way to let it out."

"Is that the poem Dad gave you?" Natalie stared at the scroll tied with a string, their dad's signature mark.

The old man nodded. "I found it the other day when I was starting a new project. Completely forgot I'd put it here."

He handed it to Natalie, and she untied the string, hesitant to read another of her father's poems. How could she not have known the depth of her dad's emotion? That he found a release for it in the form of poetry.

"Your daddy gave that to me, about the time you won your Miss Rodeo Kansas pageant. Course you know how I'm always shooting off my mouth, quoting one author or another. I guess your daddy somehow got drawn in. What he wrote there is a Japanese form of verse. It has seventeen syllables and three lines."

"Haiku." Natalie nodded.

"It's not too bad, though why he wrote about an old pair of boots, I'll never know."

Natalie pored over the words, then showed the poem to Dillon. "You think Chelsey just needs to write some poetry, huh?"

Willard chuckled at her attempt at humor. "I believe all she needs is a few days to see her mama with her own eyes. If she's not home in a week or two, we'll all go visit her. But I doubt that'll be necessary."

Natalie leaned against the wall and stared up at the ceiling, wishing she felt comfortable enough to ask for advice regarding her relationship with Jared. Unfortunately, she wasn't brave enough to broach that subject with anyone.

FORTY-SEVEN

FOR THE NEXT WEEK, NATALIE TRIED NOT TO THINK ABOUT HER PROBLEMS with Libby and Chelsey or worry why Jared wasn't returning her calls ... but paranoia crept in. Was Jared ignoring her or giving her the brush off? Had he decided he wasn't interested in more than friendship, or was the explanation as simple as a broken answering machine or an ongoing church emergency? A family emergency even?

When she still hadn't heard from him on Friday, she decided it was time to grab the bull by its horns. That afternoon, Natalie drove into Diamond Falls to pick up some horse grain, thinking she'd stop by New Redeemer to visit Jared before she went home. While at the farm store, a red Corvette cruised in front of her. Though she couldn't make out every detail, she saw enough to know that it was Chelsey in the passenger seat nestled so close to the driver that she had to be sitting on the console.

Natalie shoved the fifty-pound feedbag into the bed of the truck, her eyes trained on the hot little sports car. Should she pretend she hadn't seen her sister? Hold her tongue for fear of making things worse? Or act like the guardian she was and go after her?

Unable to ignore her problems, Natalie slid behind the wheel of her truck and pursued the car. Half a block from the river apartments, she watched as Chelsey and Lucas climbed out, the boy carrying a twelve-pack of beer. To make matters worse, her ex-ranch hand then stepped from the apartment door in jeans and no shirt to take the beer from the boy.

Natalie came to a halt behind the shiny Corvette. "What do you think you're doing, Chelsey?" she called out before her sister disappeared inside. Come here for a second, I want to talk to you."

Startled, the girl inched to the street curb and stared at Natalie with a sheepish expression. "Why are you in town? Where's Dillon?"

Natalie tried to hold her temper. "He's visiting Willard. I see you've returned to your boyfriend." *The namesake of Chelsey's fake tattoo.*

"His name's Lucas."

"Well, tell Lucas he's too young to buy beer. And why is Tom here? Is he living with Libby too?"

Chelsey cocked her hip. "It's not what you think. Mom's having a few friends over after the rodeo tonight, and Tom and Lucas are helping."

A *beer party?* Natalie choked back the knowledge and dread that she'd committed a huge mistake by allowing her sister to stay with Libby for even one night, let alone more. She reached out and smoothed a hand along Chelsey's hair. Concern seeped from her fingertips. "Are you okay?"

Her sister swiped Natalie's hand away. "We're fine. Everything's fine."

"Aren't you ready to come home?" Natalie asked, willing Chelsey to give in and admit her mistake.

"I'm happy here. Mom's helping me with barrel racing, and next summer she's going to take me on the rodeo circuit. As soon as she finds a job, we're going to move into a bigger place. One in the country or on the edge of town. She's going to teach me everything she knows."

That's exactly what Natalie feared most. She'd begun to wonder if the woman had ever held a stable job, or if she'd merely drifted from one rodeo to the next, latching on to whomever would have her. "Don't kid yourself, Chelsey. Willard was right about Libby. She hasn't changed."

The girl drilled Natalie with a cold stare. "For your information, Mom's going to hire a lawyer and file for custody — so Dillon and I can live with her, legally."

Natalie's face pinched. What happened to the sweet little girl she used to read to and make mud pies with? Where had all this spite come from? "Is that what you want? You'd do that to your brother against his will?"

"Dillon loves Mom. Once she gets on her feet, we're going to be a family. Like we should have been from the beginning."

"What about me?" Natalie clenched the steering wheel until her fingers turned white. "I'm your family too."

"Look at it this way, Nat — you'll have more freedom to do what you want and won't have us kids to weigh you down. You can go back to college — live out your dreams." Chelsey stepped from the curb and smiled, offering Natalie a glimpse of the girl she used to know. "I gotta go, but bring Dillon the next time you visit. Just not tonight 'cause Lucas is taking me to the street dance after the rodeo."

Natalie watched as her sister pulled a cell phone from her pocket and traipsed back to the apartment complex. Her stomach roiled with nausea, and she wanted to scream at the girl's defiance. Willard's advice to give Chelsey freedom to come to her senses had been a horrible mistake. If anything, the girl had slipped even farther away than before. Not only was she dating Lucas, she now possessed a cell phone. What might happen to the kids if Libby managed to gain custody? How would Natalie survive? Somehow, she had to stop this maddening ride.

Desperate to see Jared, she turned her truck around and headed for New Redeemer. Once inside the church, she knocked on his office door and it squeaked open. Jared sat hunched over the books on his desk. When he saw her, he straightened and removed his glasses.

"I hope I'm not disturbing you." She noted the flicker of regret that crossed his face.

"Not at all, I've been meaning to call you." He jumped up to clear a chair for her, transferring the books and papers to a nearby shelf. "There's something I want to talk to you about."

Natalie recalled the last time they'd spoken, the words of love he'd offered, his gentle touch, his kiss. Relieved that he hadn't been ignoring her this past week, she sat down, her mood brightening. "I need to talk to you too. But you go first."

He sat against the edge of his desk, his shoulders tense, obviously stressed about something. "I visited my folks in Concordia last weekend."

"Is everything all right?"

Jared nodded, appearing even more troubled. "I wanted to talk to you about the other night — about the things I said."

It was Natalie's turn to be uncomfortable. "Okay . . . I'm listening."

"I went home because I needed my dad's advice." Jared raked his fingers through his dark hair. "I'm afraid I was wrong to be so bold. I should have given it more thought."

Natalie straightened in her chair, the air snatched from her lungs. "I see," she managed to say, but she didn't see. Not at all. Jared's admission of love had been so genuine, so sincere. How could he doubt it now? How could he take his words back? She swallowed the lump in her throat as a cold fist closed over her heart. "Is that why you didn't return my calls?"

He cleared his throat, and the sound grated on her nerves. "I think we should give each other some space — some time," he said. "To see if our feelings are real."

"Your dad gives good advice. I told you the same thing, remember?" But that had been for her protection — to safeguard her heart from becoming entangled. Natalie had never doubted Jared's honesty or his love, and for him to do so now caused her heart to shrivel like a dried up piece of fruit no one wanted.

She stood to leave, her eyes welling with tears.

Jared blocked her advance. "Don't go. Not like this. What was it you wanted to talk to me about?"

Natalie closed her eyes, having forgotten the worries that had brought her here. "It's nothing," she said, and when her eyes fluttered open she saw a woman standing in the doorway.

The female smiled timidly. "Pastor, are you ready for our lunch date?"

Natalie's gaze shifted to Jared, his cheeks blotched with guilt.

"Sure, come on in, Clarice." His fingers caught Natalie's arm. "May I call you later, so we can finish this?"

She shook her head and forced a smile, made her eyes shine bright and cheery as she'd learned to do through the years. "Don't worry, I'm fine. You two have a nice lunch." And with that, she escaped out the door.

Minutes later behind the steering wheel of her truck, Natalie sped down a winding dirt road, trying to process her thoughts. It seemed her life was unraveling at a pace she couldn't control. When she approached Coover's Bridge, Natalie shut off the truck's engine and ventured to the middle of the historic site. She leaned against the chiseled limestone railing and peered at the murky water below. A stick floated out from under the baluster arches and progressed down the river.

"Why, God, why is this happening to me?" Since the night Chelsey left, Natalie and Dillon had been reading the Bible every night and praying together. Though it still felt awkward, somehow in this lonely place, prayer seemed the best form of release. She called to the tops of the green cottonwoods, their thick glossy leaves shimmering in the breeze. "You made me my sister's keeper, but how can I help Chelsey if she refuses my care? Why do you put loved ones in my life, only to take them from me? You took Mom, then Dad, and now possibly Chelsey and Dillon ... *and Jared*. Why?" Tears streamed down her cheeks as her throat swelled with emotion. *Just when I was falling in love with him.*

She hurled a rock into the river and watched the rings echo on the surface. Her soul cried out for comfort and understanding, but the one person who might be able to explain things was the man who'd chosen to distance himself from her—a man who'd gone to lunch with another woman. And judging by her meek appearance and dress, the woman appeared far better suited to be a pastor's wife than Natalie. The sun splashed down on her through the leafy branches above, but inside a thundercloud stormed over her heart.

"O Lord, I'm not strong enough to solve these problems on my own, and I'm tired of trying. I'm sorry for turning away from you. Can you ever forgive me? I need you in my life. Please help me."

FORTY-EIGHT

NATALIE WOKE TO THE RINGING OF HER CELL PHONE. SHE REACHED TO answer it, the full moon lighting the room through her curtained window.

"Natalie, is that you?" A girl's unsteady voice called out in the darkness.

"Chelsey?" Natalie's heart pounded. Why was her sister calling her at two in the morning?

"Nat, can you come get me?" Her teeth chattered.

"Where are you?" She hated to ask, fearing the worst. Was she in the hospital? At the police station? *Was the girl drunk?*

"I need help, Nat. I've been so stupid. I should have listened to you." Chelsey sobbed, barely audible.

"Calm down, honey. Tell me where you are."

"I'm sorry, Nat." The girl sniffed ... and then the line went dead.

Natalie sat up and clicked on the lamp beside her bed. With shaking fingers, she punched in the first number that came to mind, only pausing for a second before she pushed send. Maybe it was wrong to turn to Jared now, but she needed him.

"Answer the phone," she whispered impatiently.

Jared picked up on the fifth ring, and it took a moment for him to respond to her greeting. "Is everything okay? What time is it?" His words came out groggy.

"I'm sorry for calling so late, but it's Chelsey." Her voice wavered, and she feared she might break down in tears—something she'd been doing a lot lately. "I need your help, Jared. She's in trouble."

"Okay, slow down, Nat. Start from the beginning."

"Too much has happened to start from the beginning. We had a huge argument this week. She and Libby moved out. Will you help me find her?"

"Of course, I'll help. You know I will."

Reassured that she'd done the right thing, she explained the situation as she dressed. "I need to call Willard to see if he'll stay with Dillon, but after that I'm on my way. I'll pick you up in twenty minutes."

"WHERE DO YOU THINK CHELSEY MIGHT BE?" JARED CLIMBED INTO Natalie's truck when she arrived, careful to put aside the awkward exchange they'd had earlier that day.

"I don't know." Natalie's voice trembled. "She was about to tell me when we lost the connection. All I know is that she had a date with Lucas tonight. He was taking her to the dance."

"Okay, let's try the side streets and alleys off Main Street." He paused before clicking his seatbelt. "Want me to drive?"

Ignoring his concern, she backed out to the street and ran over the curb, jostling them inside the cab. "You should have heard her on the phone," Natalie said. "She sounded so scared."

"Chelsey's going to be okay. She called you. That's a good indication she's all right." The news that Libby and Chelsey had moved into town surprised him, but he supposed that was what Natalie had wanted to talk to him about today in his office. That she'd taken off in a tizzy before they'd had a chance to discuss it aggravated him to no end. "Did you try contacting Libby?"

Natalie nodded in the dim light of the dashboard. "She didn't have a clue where Chelsey was. I never should have let her stay with Libby. I should have stopped her from leaving."

"You had an argument?"

"I accused Libby of stealing money from the ranch."

With the truck windows rolled down, Jared drummed his fingers on the outside of the door. "Are you certain she did?"

"I caught her sticking money in her pocket."

"Sometimes the truth isn't what it seems."

Natalie pursed her lips and swerved around a corner. "And sometimes the truth is as plain as daylight. Like today, for example."

Jared saw the fight coming and knew it had nothing to do with Libby.

"What you do and who you go out with is your own business," she went on. "Judging by your lunch date this afternoon, I assume you want space to see other people. And that's fine. Just don't drag me along like a calf you intend to brand. I thought you were better than that."

Jared had seen this jealous spark in his office and had refused to feed the unwarranted fire. And he refused to feed it now. "You don't know what you're talking about. Clarice is a friend from church. We had lunch to discuss some mission work she's interested in."

"But she'd make a fine pastor's wife, wouldn't she? Much better than me. Isn't that what you're thinking? What your dad advised?"

He offered up a silent prayer for wisdom and then drew his mind back to their current task, asking for protection over the young teen who needed their help. "Why don't we concentrate on finding your sister? Once that's done, we'll have plenty of time to discuss the traits of a pastor's wife. I assure you, it's not a subject I take lightly — nor should you."

Natalie responded with silence, and together they kept their eyes peeled for any movement on the streets. As they passed an alley, a piece of metal clattered to the ground. Jared's heart hammered inside his chest. Then a tabby cat emerged from behind an aluminum trashcan.

"Maybe we should try some other places," Jared suggested after ten minutes of searching. "Where do teens hang out these days when they want to party?"

Natalie sent him a tormented frown. "Or when they want to be alone?"

Jared hadn't wanted to state the obvious assumption they both feared. "What about the river bridge or the park?"

"We could drive all night and never find her. Maybe we should split up in separate vehicles."

Jared hated to leave Natalie alone, but the suggestion made sense. *Lord, help us find Chelsey. Give us a clue where she might be.* As they turned onto the street back to his house, he noticed a parked truck that had a bumper sticker of a cowboy on a horse roping a steer. It stirred a memory of another bumper sticker he'd seen on Lucas's car the day the boy had dropped Chelsey off at the church.

"Try the rodeo grounds," Jared blurted out. "I have a feeling that's where we'll find your sister."

"I don't know ... that seems too obvious." Natalie slowed the truck in hesitation. "They patrol there regularly, especially on weekends."

He shrugged away her uncertainty. "I might be wrong, but I've learned to trust my instincts. They brought me to you, didn't they?"

"And that's supposed to comfort me?" She frowned, but headed for the edge of town. Minutes later, they pulled onto the arena grounds. Jared shined his flashlight across the bleachers and concession stands until they'd searched the entire area.

"Maybe it's time to call the sheriff." Natalie's distress tugged on Jared's heart. She started to pull onto the road, and then a reflection caught Jared's attention from inside one of the livestock chutes.

"Wait, I see something over there." He pointed in the direction of the movement.

Natalie circled back, her tires spinning gravel as she shined the truck lights into the arena. Sure enough, there inside a metal chute, Chelsey sat huddled in a tight ball with her head bunched up against her knees.

Jamming the truck into park, Natalie bounded from the driver's seat. Jared followed, fearing what they might find when they caught up to the girl.

FORTY-NINE

NATALIE RUSHED TO CHELSEY'S SIDE, HER PULSE RACING WITH FEAR AND adrenaline. The young teen cowered in the darkness. "Chelsey, thank God we found you."

Her sister lifted her head from her knees, her eyes puffy and red. "You came," she said, her voice hoarse.

"Of course we did. Are you okay? What happened?" She braced her sister's chin and tilted her face to examine the bloody scratch marks. "Did Lucas do this to you?"

Chelsey's bottom lip jutted out as tears streamed down her face. Her sister peered up at Jared who stood behind them.

"Answer me, Chels. Did Lucas do this?"

The girl gave a slight nod.

"Oh Chels. Why'd you let it go this far?" Reading her sister's embarrassment, Natalie moved closer.

"I thought he loved me," Chelsey whispered back. "After the dance, he brought me here ... so we could be together. Only I couldn't go through with it. That's when he got all crazy."

Natalie took the girl in her arms. "Oh honey. Did he hit you? Is that how you got those marks on your face?"

Chelsey touched her swollen cheek. "He shoved me, and I hit my head against the dashboard."

When Natalie heard this, she wanted to find Lucas and rope him to a fencepost. "Then what happened?"

"He yelled at me. Called me a tease, and told me to find my own way home. Made me get out of his car."

Natalie sent Jared an imploring look, and as though reading her mind, he pulled out his phone and walked to the truck. Natalie suspected he would call the sheriff, and that they would want to talk to Chelsey to see if she would press charges.

Once Jared left, Natalie gazed deep into her sister's eyes. "Did he hurt you? In an intimate way?"

Chelsey clutched her waist and shook her head, her face rigid.

Natalie sighed and whispered her thanks to God that her sister had not been violated. Her heart soared that she could celebrate such a thing, knowing God was with her family and had not abandoned them.

"I'm sorry I didn't listen to you, Nat. You were right all along. Lucas was only interested in one thing. He didn't care about me." She closed her eyes. "I think you were right about Libby too. I feel so stupid."

"The important thing is that we found you, and that you're okay." Natalie rose from the ground and helped Chelsey to stand. "I should have handled the situation with Libby differently. I thought I was protecting you, but to be honest I was jealous of your love for her. I behaved like a tyrant, running both of you off."

Chelsey rested her head on Natalie's shoulder. "I'm the one who should apologize. I should never have left home. It was horrible living with Libby."

"She didn't harm you?"

"No, it's just ..."

"She's more concerned about Libby than anyone else?"

Her sister nodded. "Mom's not the best listener. And it's not that she doesn't care ..."

Natalie hugged the teen to her side. "I know Libby loves you, Chels. I'm just not sure she knows what it means to be a mom. And as weird as it sounds, sometimes I feel more like a mom to you than a sister." She smiled and squeezed the girl's shoulder.

"Can I come back to live with you and Dillon?"

Natalie scrunched her nose. "Are you kidding? We never wanted you to leave in the first place." With elbows linked, they returned to the truck where Jared handed them a water bottle and a tissue.

"I don't want to go back to Libby's apartment," Chelsey said. "Not after everything that's happened."

"Okay, but we should at least call and let her know you're all right." Natalie wet the tissue and pressed it to her sister's cheek. "We love you, Chels. Dillon and I have been praying for you this week — for all of us." At this admission, she felt Jared's stare and wondered what he would think of her shifting views.

She didn't have a chance to find out, as a sheriff's car pulled onto the rodeo grounds and parked next to Natalie's truck. For the next hour, the three of them went through detailed questioning.

"Are you sure you don't want to press charges?" Jared asked Natalie when they were finished.

Natalie noticed the shiver that passed through her sister's body. "I'll do whatever you want, Chelsey."

The girl hugged her arms around her waist. "No charges. I just want this to be over. I want Lucas out of my life."

THE EARLY DAWN GLOWED PINK AND GOLD ON THE EASTERN HORIZON as Natalie combed Chelsey's hair with her fingers, her sister's head resting on her lap in the truck. Jared had insisted on driving them back to the ranch, and Natalie had willingly agreed, too worn out to protest or apologize for her earlier outburst. Despite their differences, the man seated across from her had been nothing short of a gentleman all night long, a defender and support to her and her family. She owed him a debt of thanks—and she intended to offer it as soon as her mind had enough rest to think straight.

When they arrived at the house, Dillon and Willard were waiting on the porch.

"You're not going to believe what we found." The boy's excitement bubbled over as he raced toward the truck.

"Why aren't you in bed?" Natalie asked Dillon as she woke Chelsey and slid from the passenger seat. She helped her sister from the truck, then wrapped her arms around each of them as they strolled to the house, Jared following behind.

"Willard and I found some more money. But that's not all . . . we figured out where Dad hid the clues."

Natalie's tired mind raced to catch up. "What are you talking about?"

"Dad left us clues . . . we figured out where he hid the money."

"Really?" She glanced at Willard when they reached the porch, unsure whether to believe her brother who seemed to be on some kind of sugar high.

"The boy figured it out." Willard opened the front door for them and smiled. "I see you found Chelsey. I assume everything's all right?"

Once inside the house, Dillon wrapped his skinny arms around Chelsey in a bear hug. "We've been worried about you. Are you home for good?"

Chelsey tousled his hair. "Would that be okay with you?"

He grinned and nodded. "You're not going to believe where we found the money. You either, Nat."

They gathered around the kitchen table, and Dillon could hardly contain himself. Jared found a fresh pot of coffee on the counter and poured a cup for Natalie and him.

"Okay, Dillon, tell us your story," Natalie said after she'd consumed some of the steaming liquid, its rich, bold flavor waking her senses.

"After you left, I woke up and couldn't get back to sleep, so Willard and I played a game of checkers," he said. "Then I got out one of our old puzzles—the one with the running horses, remember?" He dashed to the living room to get it, then set the box on the table as though for evidence.

Natalie remembered the puzzle well. It was one of her favorites.

"Well, we opened it up and there was a yellow envelope tucked inside with two thousand dollars. I couldn't believe it." Dillon giggled.

"Go ahead, son, tell them what happened next," Willard prodded.

"That's when I remembered the poem Dad gave me." He pulled a paper from his back pocket and read it to everyone. "Horses and puzzles. Treasures you never outgrow. Wild Horses Running." He looked up and grinned. "It's a clue. Do you get it?"

Jared's eyes shifted from Dillon to Natalie. "Your dad hid his money and wrote a poem?"

Her brother blew out an exasperated breath. "Several poems. Willard and I tried to remember all of them—and there's probably more we don't know about."

"He gave me one about a cook's cupboard," Chelsey said.

"And Willard's mentioned a pair of boots," Dillon went on. "That's when we realized that all of Dad's poems were about a specific subject—not a person, but an item or thing."

Chelsey's face beamed with understanding. "Do you suppose Dad hid money in the kitchen cabinets?"

"I bet he did," Dillon said. "And Nat, didn't you tell us you'd found one in Dad's room about Shakespeare?"

"Libby." Natalie's eyes widened as she voiced the woman's name. "I found Libby with a book of poetry in Dad's office. She'd found money inside it."

"The day you accused her of stealing from us," Chelsey said.

Natalie nodded, hating to bring the sore subject up again. "I thought it odd at the time. Do you think she knew about the poems? But how could she have known?"

"I wouldn't put it past her," Willard stated gruffly. "The important thing is that we've figured out the key to your father's system. All we have to do now is decipher his poems to find the clues to the hidden money."

"Willard, do you remember the words to your poem?" Natalie asked, unable to recall exactly.

"It weren't very good, but you know me, I don't forget things easily. 'Boots made for walking. Tony Lama leather grain. Well made, well deserved.'"

Natalie gasped and looked at Jared. "Dad's boots. I gave them away."

Jared's eyes widened as he caught on to her meaning. "I delivered those clothes to the thrift shop over a month ago."

"No, you don't understand," she went on. "I gave all of them away ... but one." Natalie thought of the fancy pair of boots her dad never wore. The pair she'd kept for herself. She bolted for the stairway and bounded up the steps to her room. With everyone following behind, Natalie retrieved the elephant hide boots from her closet. *Could the money be inside?*

She stuck her fist into one of the boot shafts and blindly groped with her fingers but came up empty. Realizing her greed, she handed the other boot to Willard. "It was your poem. You do the honors."

Willard studied the pair of Tony Lama's and smiled. "This is a nice pair of boots. You have good taste."

"Just look inside already." She laughed.

Willard dug his hand deep within, and made a big to-do, rolling and squinting his eyes. Then with a big wide grin, he pulled out a yellow envelope. "Bingo."

FIFTY

AFTER FINDING THE MONEY IN THE BOOTS, WILLARD AND THE KIDS WENT downstairs, determined to follow the next clue and search through the kitchen cupboards. Natalie stayed behind and returned her father's boots to her closet. The floor creaked from outside her room, and she realized Jared waited for her in the hallway.

She met him at the door, and he shoved his hands in his pockets. "I should probably be going home."

"You don't want to stay and help?" Natalie noted the dark shadows under his eyes and could only imagine what she must look like after their all-night adventure.

"This is a family moment."

She took his elbow and pulled him to sit with her at the top of the staircase. "A few months ago, I would have agreed that you didn't belong here, but we've come a long way, you and I."

"You've come a long way." He clutched her hand and rubbed his thumb over hers. "You're reading the Bible and praying. Those are big steps for you."

"Dillon helped me see that I don't have all the answers—that it's okay to ask for help, and that I'm not alone—God's with me. He's been with me all along."

"That's what I've been telling you."

She shrugged. "I guess it was something I had to figure out on my own."

"You don't know how happy that makes me." His smile seemed genuine yet guarded. "For the record, though, are we still arguing or did we come to another truce?"

Her mouth titled into a slow grin. After everything they'd gone through tonight, Natalie had nearly forgotten about their argument—the jealous fit she'd thrown at seeing Jared with another woman. "That's right, you said you needed space."

He pulled her close. "I don't need space, Natalie. Time maybe, but I know exactly where my heart lies. I was confused for a little bit, but tonight I realized two things. How much I love being a pastor, and how much you mean to me. I can only pray you feel the same."

She placed her hands on his chest, felt the rapid beat of his heart under his shirt. "What exactly is required of a pastor's wife, anyway?"

Jared scratched the dark bristles on his chin. "Well, let's see. She'd be expected to go to all the ladies functions and attend every Bible study. Sew and mend all the children's Christmas costumes and make cakes and pies for every bake sale. Oh, and in her spare time, direct the choir and play the organ." He stopped to catch his breath then chuckled.

"I hope you're teasing." She thumped his chest with her fist.

"You want the honest truth?"

Natalie gazed into his eyes and recalled the talk she'd had with Chelsey about falling in love with a man. She'd told her sister that a man and woman should be friends and enjoy being together, and some ridiculous gibberish about clammy hands and racing hearts. But maybe it was the incomprehensible knowledge that by being with him, he would complete her and make her into a better person, which was exactly what Natalie's heart and soul told her about Jared. That she needed him in her life. "Always the truth."

"The truth is I don't have all the answers." Jared traced her bottom lip with his finger, his touch a feather-light caress. "But I know this—I love you, and I want what's best for you, even if that means walking away." No matter what happens though, if we make Jesus our foundation, everything else has a way of fitting together."

Natalie leaned in to his whisper, her eyes drawn to his mouth. "I don't want you to walk away." Her lips parted in anticipation of a kiss. Then a cough sounded from the bottom of the stairs.

"Sorry for interrupting, Nat, but you have a phone call." Chelsey snickered with delight.

NATALIE TOOK THE CALL IN HER DAD'S OFFICE, HER CHEEKS STILL WARM from Jared's attention. The woman greeted her, and Natalie gasped upon learning who it was on the other end of the phone.

"I'm calling about your duties as first runner up to Miss Rodeo America," the MRA Executive Director began. "As you may have heard, we've been worried about Lisa for awhile now. This spring, she began suffering terrible headaches and then at a marketing event in May she had her first seizure. Upon a full medical exam they diagnosed her with a brain tumor."

Natalie's throat tightened at realizing the rumors she'd heard were true. "I'm so sorry. Is she going to be okay?"

"They've begun intensive treatments on her, and the doctors are quite optimistic." Rosemary said. "Unfortunately because of her situation, she needs to step down from her queen position. Of course our thoughts and prayers are with Lisa, but because of these extraordinary circumstances, we are calling on you to finish her reign as the First Lady of Professional Rodeo."

Natalie sank into her dad's leather chair, trying to keep up with the director's words. Though saddened by Lisa's illness, Natalie's heart raced with disbelief. Could it be true?

They want me to be Miss Rodeo America?

"Are you there?" Rosemary asked with concern.

"I'm sorry." Natalie regained her composure. "I'd be honored to stand in for Lisa. It's an incredible opportunity, heartbreaking as it may be. What would I be required to do?"

"Ah, wonderful. We knew we could count on you," the woman said, and Natalie pictured Rosemary's warm smile, having met her in Las Vegas last December. "As you know, we're well into the rodeo season so Lisa's calendar is booked solid. We'll need you to fly out to Colorado next week to fill her position at the Pro Rodeo Hall of Fame inductions."

"Next week?" Natalie's hopes crashed at her feet. What about Dillon and Chelsey? Who would take care of the ranch? Her excitement evaporated as Natalie realized she could never accept the responsibility, her own responsibility too great. She then proceeded to explain her situation to the director.

"Would you like some time to think about it and talk to your family?" Rosemary responded with compassion. "We can give you until Tuesday morning—but if you decide to go through with this, you'll need to be ready to hop on a plane so we can transfer the crown and sash and take some publicity photos before the induction."

Natalie expressed her gratitude and promised to get back to her. What in the world was she going to do now?

FIFTY-ONE

JARED FOLLOWED CHELSEY THROUGH THE LIVING ROOM, WONDERING WHAT the girl must think of him — a pastor — her unofficial guidance counselor — about to secretly kiss her sister on the stairs. He found his predicament incredibly embarrassing.

"I want you to know, Chelsey, that your sister and I, we've come to realize—"

"You don't have to worry, Pastor J. I think it's cool you have the hots for my sister."

Jared swiped his forehead. "You think it's cool?" his voice cracked.

Chelsey glanced back at him with a triumphant grin. "Yeah, we've all been wondering when you'd take the plunge. It's taken you long enough."

"You've been waiting?" His jaw tightened in skepticism.

"Yeah, all of us and Willard too." She giggled with pure pleasure. "Are you hungry? I'm making spice pancakes while Dillon and Willard search for the money. I still can't believe Dad hid all that cash for us. We're going to be rich."

"Chelsey, you're already rich, with wealth of another kind." Jared had watched this family go through the horrible pain of losing a loved one and nearly crumbling as a unit, to embracing each other with a bond as close as any he'd ever seen. God had sent him here to help this family, and in the process Jared had gained the love of a woman so dear to him, his heart quivered just thinking of her.

He joined his male companions as they searched through the cabinets, the aroma of apples and cinnamon causing his stomach to rumble with hunger. When Natalie entered the room, he noticed her troubled expression.

"You'll never guess who was on the phone." She plopped down at the table and rested her head in her hands.

Chelsey turned from the stove with a metal spatula. "More trouble with Dad's estate?" Dillon went to Natalie's side, the ever-protective brother.

"They've offered me the Miss Rodeo America title." She raised her head, her eyes glistening with unshed tears.

"That's awesome," Chelsey said.

Jared watched from the other side of the room, his mind a mixture of emotions. Joy and elation flowed through him for the woman he loved, yet he wondered what this would mean for Natalie's future — for their future.

"It's all I've ever dreamed of." Natalie sniffed, but shook her head as though the news wasn't great and astonishing.

Willard joined her at the table. "Then why is it that you don't sound happy?"

Natalie's sniffles turned to gushing tears. "I can't accept their offer. I have to turn it down."

Dillon placed his arm around her shoulders. "Why? You have to accept, Natalie."

"Yeah, Nat. You've wanted this forever. You can't turn it down," Chelsey added.

"I don't have any other choice." She offered her brother and sister a tender smile, and then her gaze traveled to Jared. "I can't leave you guys. You mean more to me than the crown, and there's Dad's estate, and the ranch to deal with—the cattle drive at the end of summer. I can't just take off for weeks at a time to promote rodeo."

"When do you have to give them an answer?" Willard asked.

She shook her head. "It doesn't matter. I know my answer."

Jared went to her then and sank down on one knee. He captured her hand, his thoughts only on her, wanting to please her. "You're tired, Nat. Take some time to think about this. You don't want to look back some day and regret your decision. Maybe there's a way to make all of this work out." He meant to encourage her, wanting to show his devotion—that he would be there for her—that they could get through this with God's help.

LATE THAT NIGHT AFTER SOME MUCH NEEDED SLEEP, JARED SAT AT HIS office desk, pouring over his sermon for the next day. He took a drink of his coffee, and a knock sounded on his door. "May I come in?"

Jared looked up at the soft female voice.

"I saw the church light on and hoped it'd be okay to stop by," Libby said. "I wondered if I might have a word with you."

From the dark rings under her eyes, it appeared the woman had slept little. "You want to talk about Chelsey?"

"I made a horrible mess of things, didn't I?" She sank onto a chair, all pretenses gone. "What kind of mother am I to endanger my child like that? I can't even tell when my daughter is in trouble."

Jared pulled his chair beside Libby's and allowed her to continue without disruption.

"Even Natalie knew the boy was bad news. Chelsey told me she wasn't supposed to go out with him this summer, but I thought it was ridiculous, and I told her so. I allowed that boy to take advantage of my daughter—I'm such a fool."

Her head collapsed into her hands, and Jared patted the woman's back in an effort to console her. "You've had some hard lessons this week. It's not easy to step into the role of mother overnight. Nor is it necessary."

Libby gazed up at him then. "I just wanted what was best for my kids. When I left all those years ago, I knew Adrian would take care of them. Better than me."

"What made you come back?"

"It's like I told you. I know you didn't believe me, especially Willard, but it's true. When I heard about Adrian's death, an awful longing came over me. It seems selfish now, but I wanted the kids to know me, and I wanted to know them. I had no idea it would be so difficult."

Jared clasped his hands, wishing to have everything out in the open. "Natalie believes you came back for the hidden money—that you knew about it all along."

Her bottom lip wobbled. "I didn't realize there was money until Dillon spilled the news that day in the kitchen. I guess once I knew about that, things started to blur some. But I didn't take any money from them. At least not any I didn't give back. I swear."

Jared gazed out the window at the hazy full moon. "What do you want from life, Libby? If you could have one thing, what would it be?"

She squinted at him, the crinkles at the edge of her eyes even more pronounced than normal. "You probably think I'll say another shot at barrel racing or my youth—all good things." She snickered and then her expression turned sober. "But if I could have just one thing in life, I'd ask for my children's respect. To have their love."

Jared smiled at the earnestness in her voice. "What if I said you could have that now?"

"I know you're in the business of miracles, Pastor J., but I don't think even you could make that happen." Libby cleared her throat and shifted in the chair, clearly uncomfortable with such talk. "I've made too big of a mess. Even if I could gain their love and trust, there's no way Natalie will ever forgive me. Too much water has passed under that bridge."

"Libby, with God all things are possible." He patted her hand, wanting to console her. "But you need to understand that love and trust won't come overnight. It has to be earned over time. Can you give the kids time, without pushing or pressuring them?"

"What do you mean, exactly?"

"In simple terms?" He gazed into her brown eyes, and she nodded.

"For me, the simpler the better."

"Okay, for starters, you could give up the alcohol." He began counting off the directives on his fingers. "You could find a job and get to know the kids. Show them you're not going anywhere, and that you're there for them. And then ... be there for them, without fussing or challenging Natalie's guardianship, because whether you like it or not, Natalie is their mother. That's who she's been ever since you walked out of their lives, and that's who she is today. It doesn't matter that she's their sister by law. In their hearts, she's their mother—their protector and their stability. Can you live with that?"

A flicker of pain crossed the woman's face. "Will she ever forgive me for the load I put on her?"

Jared clutched her shoulder. "Why don't you talk to her and find out?"

FIFTY-TWO

THE NEXT DAY AFTER CHURCH, NATALIE SAT AT HER FATHER'S OAK DESK going through the estate paperwork one more time before signing, when she noticed Libby's yellow sedan drive up to the house.

She met Libby at the front door. The woman's hands were loaded with luggage, her eyes downcast. "I brought back Chelsey's clothes. Figured she'd want them and that I'd save her a trip into town."

Natalie opened the door for her and helped carry the items inside. "That's very thoughtful, but you didn't need to go to the trouble. We were going to come into town this evening to visit you."

"It wasn't any trouble." Libby tugged at her cotton shirt, and Natalie noted her red-rimmed eyes. "I'm real sorry about what happened the other night, and I wanted to apologize to all of you, if you'd allow me that."

The woman's plea spoke to Natalie's heart. "Would you like some tea? I stirred up a fresh pitcher this afternoon."

Libby smiled and followed Natalie into the kitchen where Natalie poured them each a glass of sweet tea. Once she sat down, Libby pulled a slip of paper from her purse. "I wanted to give you this." She held out the folded paper, and Natalie stared down at it with curiosity.

"What's that?"

"I found it in your daddy's bedroom. I should have told you about it, but I convinced myself it was for Chelsey. I know now that your daddy wrote it for you."

Natalie unfolded the piece of paper and read the poem entitled "A Wedding Gown."

A gown of white lace.
Treasure for my little girl.
From my heart to yours.

When Natalie finished, tears stung her eyes. She sniffed them away, never having cried so much as she had this past week. "I thought he wrote one for everyone but me. Where did you find it? I cleaned his room from top to bottom."

"Guess you didn't look under his mattress. Isn't that the first place a person hides his money?" Her stepmom grinned. "When Dillon mentioned you'd found cash in the barn, I figured the old coot must have hidden money in the house so I went on a treasure hunt of my own. I swear I never found any except for what you caught me with in the office. But I did find that poem."

"Thank you for giving this to me." Natalie believed the woman spoke the truth, but she still had questions that needed answered. "Were you and Tom in this together? Did Tom know about the hidden money too?"

Libby shook her head. "We talked about it in the barn that day he came by the ranch. I thought he might know where some of the money had been hidden, but he refused to get involved. Said he had enough trouble to deal with and needed to keep his hands clean."

Her bottom lip wobbled. "I know I have no right to ask, that I gave up my rights a long time ago. But if you could see it in your heart to forgive me for my wrongs, I'd do just about anything to have another chance with you kids."

Natalie leaned back in her chair and sipped her tea, the condensation cold and wet against her fingers. "That's something Dillon and Chelsey will have to answer themselves. But if they're agreeable, I'm willing to give you another chance ... on my terms."

"I understand." Libby held up her hands as though in submission. "I know I have a lot to learn and make up for. But maybe I could come out to visit from time to time, on weekends or something. I want to get to know them. They're good kids."

For probably the first time in her life, Natalie agreed whole-heartedly with Libby. "Yes, they are."

LATER THAT DAY, JARED STOPPED IN AT WILLARD'S PLACE AND FOUND the old man in his shop working on a pair of white boots. "You look mighty busy in here. Don't you know you're supposed to take a nap on Sunday afternoon?"

Willard raised his head and nodded. "Any other day I'd agree with you, but there's no time for a nap today."

Jared neared the workbench and noted the meticulous crafts-manship on the upper vamp, finely detailed with scrolling wings and stars. "Working on a special project?"

The man held up the ostrich hide boot with admiration. "I planned to build them for Natalie when she won the queen title last December, only she didn't win. After that, I didn't have the heart to finish them, afraid I'd hurt her more with the reminder. They've sat here in my shop, half made. I figured it was time to finish the job."

"What if she doesn't accept the title?"

Willard scrunched his mouth. "Won't matter. I should have given them to her long before now. And as for her accepting the title, I reckon you and I should do some talking about that."

Jared nodded. "That's why I'm here." He pulled up a stool, and together the two men discussed possible ways to help Natalie fulfill her journey. An hour later, content with their decision, Jared traced the boot's red stitching with his finger, able to imagine Natalie wearing them along with one of those fine leather gowns she wore for competition.

Now all they had to do was convince Natalie of their plan. In order to do that, everything would need to fall perfectly into place, and the best place to start was in prayer.

JARED DROVE TO NATALIE'S HOUSE, AND JESSIE MET HIM AT HIS CAR, HER tail wagging. Dillon greeted him with a rope in his hand, probably out chasing goats as usual. "Hey buddy. Is Natalie around?"

Dillon pointed to the pasture. "She went for a ride. I think she wanted to be alone."

"Well, that's okay," Jared said, thanking God for his perfect timing. "I needed to talk to you and Chelsey alone anyway."

The boy walked with him to the porch, then went inside to get Chelsey. A few minutes later, Jared sat them down, needing their permission before going any further.

"Of course we approve," Chelsey said after Jared explained the plan to them. "It's the least we can do after everything Nat's done for us. Isn't that right, Dillon?"

Her brother gave an emphatic nod. "Want me to saddle my horse for you, so you can tell Natalie yourself?"

Jared hesitated, wondering if he could handle any other horse besides Jackson. "Sure, why not." He might as well get used to such things, for if his plan went according to schedule, he'd be spending a good deal of time in the saddle.

A short while later, Jared trotted off on a pasture trail in the direction Natalie had gone. The lush green bluestem dipped and swayed over the hills and rocky crags, a veritable ocean of grass. Beneath him, Adrian's saddle creaked as Dillon's horse traveled the familiar cattle path. Jared scanned the mounds and valleys for Natalie and her gray horse. He found them by a shady stream. Natalie waded barefoot in the water, her jeans rolled up, and her socks and boots lying on the rocky ground nearby.

"I was beginning to think I wouldn't find you." Jared reined in Dillon's horse and stepped down from the saddle.

Natalie splashed toward him with an anxious expression. "Is everything all right?"

"Nothing to worry about." He offered a sheepish grin and tied the reins to a hanging bur oak limb.

Her gaze traveled from his boots to his hat, her mouth tilting in satisfaction. "Why are you here then? Out for a Sunday ride?"

Jared took her hand as she stepped from the stream, her feet dripping water onto the rough pebbles. "I came to see you, to talk to you about something."

"If it's about the title, you can save your breath. I'm not going to accept. Even if I figured out a way to deal with the ranch, there's no way I can leave Dillon and Chelsey after everything we've been through this summer. I'm not going to abandon them so I can follow a dream."

He led her to where her boots lay on a sheet of bedrock. "Before you refuse, would you care to hear what Willard and I have come up with?"

Natalie shook her head. "You think I haven't been racking my brain trying to figure out a way to make this work?"

"You know what they say about two heads being better than one." He sat with Natalie on the rock and handed her a boot.

"I'm telling you, I've been through every possible scenario. There are none — it's useless." She tugged the cotton socks onto her damp feet and then shoved on the first boot.

He clutched the other boot to his stomach. "I'm not going to give this to you until you're ready to listen. Are you prepared to hear our proposal?"

Calling his bluff, Natalie lunged and nearly toppled him onto the flat rock, but Jared managed to hold the boot out of her reach.

"No fair, Miss Adams." He chuckled, enjoying her close proximity. Unable to resist, he snatched a kiss from her soft, yielding lips.

Natalie pulled away. "I'd say you're the one not fighting fair, Pastor Logan." She grinned and settled back on the rock, her legs crossed with her bootless foot exposed. "Okay, I'm listening."

"Are you sure?"

Her nostrils flared with mock exasperation. "I'm certain."

"Good, because I've already discussed this with Dillon and Chelsey, and they heartily agree with this plan." Jared handed Natalie her boot, then grazed her cheek with his finger, loving every inch of her, including her stubborn will.

"Willard and I will finish off the grazing season. We'll gather some neighbors for the round-up, and we'll see to it that the ranch is cared for properly while you're gone."

"That's too much responsibility—" Natalie started to protest, but he hushed her with his finger on her mouth.

"As for Chelsey and Dillon, Willard has agreed to stay with them at the ranch and serve as their guardian during your reign. He figured you'd object and told me to remind you of his promise to your daddy, that he'd look out for you and the kids—and that's exactly what Willard intends to do."

Jared slipped his arm around Natalie and hugged her to his side. "As for the two of us ..." He pressed his lips to her forehead. "I love you, Natalie. I know you have questions about being a pastor's wife, whether it's the right decision for you. And that's okay. The last thing I want to do is pressure you into loving me."

Natalie removed his hat and smoothed a hand over his cropped hair. "Don't you know that I love you already?" She reached up to kiss his cheek, and he reveled in her touch. "The wife thing is a bit scary, but I'm not adverse to it."

He smiled at this, his confidence growing. "That's why this separation will be good for us. You can fulfill your duties as queen, and while you're away, I'll play cowboy. And you'll come home every now and then. It's not as though you'll be gone the entire time. We can use this time apart to see if a union between a pastor and a rodeo queen is the right choice for us. Because that's my intent when your reign is over—a full-fledged marriage proposal."

She surprised him by resting her head on his shoulder and murmuring against his neck. "I like the sound of your plan ... and your proposal."

EPILOGUE

NATALIE STARED OUT AT THE AUDIENCE, THE BRIGHT LIGHTS PENETRATING her white leather dress as she made her final parade on the stage at The Orleans Hotel showroom. Her thoughts drifted to when she'd been on this stage the previous year, and how different things were then—watching with the other girls as Lisa received her sash and crown, her dad in the audience cheering her on, despite that she hadn't won. *Dear Lord, what a journey you've given me.*

Above her, the screen displayed a video of her experiences from the last five months—her extensive travels throughout the country as she represented rodeo in public appearances, special events, and for schools and civic groups. As her prerecorded farewell speech played over the speaker, Natalie swallowed back the emotion welling inside—

"My reign as Miss Rodeo America has been one of the most exciting times of my life. What began with a hasty plane ride to Denver to receive my crown and sash before the Pro Rodeo Hall of Fame inductions, has culminated here with friends and family as I pass on my title to the next First Lady of Pro Rodeo.

"As spokesperson for the western industry, I've not only received scholarships and countless gifts from generous sponsors, but I've gained numerous friendships, some that will stay with me for a life-

time. Forever stamped in my memory are the many rodeos where I
carried the American flag in the grand entrance such as the Pikes
Peak or Bust rodeo in Colorado Springs, Cheyenne Frontier Days,
the Snake River Stampede in Idaho, and of course the Dodge City
Roundup in my home state of Kansas.

"My reign as Miss Rodeo America would not have been possible,
were it not for my dear friends and family at home, and for that I
want to thank them. When my father died last May, my future came
to a skidding halt, and the world as I knew it came crumbling down.
Not only did I have the new responsibility of maintaining a fifty-six
hundred acre ranch in the beautiful Flint Hills of Kansas, I became
the guardian for two dear children — my brother Dillon, and my
sister Chelsey.

"The lessons I learned from these obligations helped me in my
understanding of the ranch and rodeo world. They enabled me to
see those around me with new eyes — eyes that could appreciate and
understand the trials and burdens we carry, and that with God's
help are able to overcome."

As the farewell speech concluded, Natalie made one final pass
on the stage, waving to everyone, but especially to those in the front
seats — Willard, Dillon, Chelsey ... and Jared. She gave a special
twirl for Willard to show off the leather boots he'd made for her, and
for that, she received another round of applause.

Though the bright lights made eye contact difficult, she managed to lock gazes with Jared, and her heart fluttered with joy and
anticipation for what waited ahead, as well as the moments they'd
shared these past few months. Those things she hadn't mentioned in
her speech, such as the time they'd spent at home including the one
weekend in August when they'd rounded up the summer cattle, or
the handful of trips they'd accompanied her on. More importantly,
though, was her growing relationship with Jared.

Tears filled Natalie's eyes as she came to the end of this journey, but the road she was about to embark upon held even more

possibilities — promises that left her breathless. After the coronation, she met Jared and her family at the back of the stage and gave
them each a hug, ending in Jared's arms.

"So, what do you think, Natalie? Are you ready to get back to
the real world?"

Natalie gazed up at the ceiling, remembering her dad and praying one day she'd see him again in heaven. She nodded and enclosed
each of her loved ones in a huge embrace. "Oh yes, this time I'm
ready."

ACKNOWLEDGMENTS

THERE IS SO MUCH THAT GOES INTO CREATING A BOOK OF FICTION — endless hours of time, thought, research, and writing. My heartfelt thanks to everyone who helped with *Seeds of Summer*:

To my Lord and Savior, for being with me each day of this journey and for guiding my steps. All praise and glory are yours.

To my devoted husband and daughters, for their love and support, and for their patience while I was on deadline.

To my agent, Rachelle Gardner, at WordServe Literary, thanks for answering all my questions and for being so terrific.

To my editing and marketing teams at Zondervan. Special thanks to Sue Brower, Becky Philpott, Karwyn Bursma, Robin Geelhoed, and Londa Alderink. Thanks for all your hard work and efforts to make the Seasons of the Tallgrass series the best it can be.

To my critique partners and friends, Beth Goddard and Christina Miller. It always helps to have an extra set of eyes. I value and cherish your wise input and your time. Also, I'd like to thank the many friends in ACFW and in my local writers group for their support and prayers — too many to name, but you know who you are! Special thanks to Tamera Alexander and my Kansas friends,

Deborah Raney, Kim Vogel Sawyer, and Judith Miller—I treasure your continued guidance.

To the many professionals who gave their time and help in the research of this story. To the ladies at Miss Rodeo America, for answering my long-winded questions and offering assistance—Raeana Wadhams, DeAnna Power, and especially, Miss Amy Wilson, Miss Rodeo America 2008, for allowing me to tag along on your incredible journey. To Pastor John Stubenrouch, for assisting me with pastoral questions. To attorneys Jeff Feuquay and Daryl Ahlquist for their help in understanding wills and estates. And to Mary and Rich Allen for sharing your knowledge of daily ranch life in the Flint Hills. Your input has been an invaluable resource.

Finally, my sincere thanks to friends and family, and to the many readers who have blessed me with their emails and letters of appreciation. I am amazed and honored that you take the time to write and share your lives with me. Is it a privilege to share my stories with you. May you cherish and fall in love with the Flint Hills of Kansas.

God's blessings to all of you,
Deborah Vogts

CHELSEY'S SPICE
PANCAKES

2 cups flour
3 tablespoons sugar
2 tablespoons baking powder
1 teaspoon salt
1 teaspoon cinnamon
½ teaspoon ground cloves
¼ teaspoon ground nutmeg
¼ teaspoon ground ginger
1 cup milk
¼ cup canola oil
2 eggs, beaten
1 teaspoon vanilla extract
1 cup applesauce

In medium bowl, mix together flour, sugar, baking powder, salt, and spices. Add milk, oil, eggs, and vanilla and mix together with a wooden spoon. Fold in applesauce. Batter will be lumpy. Heat griddle until hot. (To test, sprinkle water on griddle. If it sizzles, it's ready.) Pour pancake mix to desired size and turn when they bubble. Cook until both sides are golden brown. Makes 12–16 pancakes.

Read an excerpt from book 3 in the Seasons of the Tallgrass series: **Blades of Autumn.** *Coming soon!*

AN EARLY MORNING FOG HUNG IN THE DEEP GULLY, THE AIR SO THICK and still he heard every sound — the croak of a nearby bullfrog, the snap of a twig beneath his horse's feet, the beat of his own heart. As caretaker for the Marz Ranch, Ethan Walker took great pains to do a good job, and today that meant getting his count.

He'd searched the entire pasture and had come up short. One steer missing.

Not that his records always showed accuracy, but usually the figures had a way of righting themselves. A calf hidden in the brush one day would be with the rest of the herd the next, or maybe there had been a miscount. Lately, though, Ethan's numbers had been off more than he cared to admit. And that was no way for a pastureman to earn his boss's respect.

Ethan wove his way through the rocks and brambles but found no sign of the missing stray. With a disgruntled sigh, he slapped his gelding on the rump and rode Ben to the top of the next ridge. Up here, the rolling prairie stretched out before him. A dawning orange glow merged with the hazy blue sky and glistened against the dew on the grass. After all these years, it never failed to take his breath away. He and his brother Tom had been cowboying the Flint Hills of Charris County Kansas ever since they were young bucks—and though the work was hard and the pay less than what most men considered decent, he couldn't imagine doing anything else. When the land is in your blood, those things don't matter—at least they didn't to Ethan.

He flicked his reins and headed for the next rise, hoping to discover the whereabouts of the outlaw steer so he could get back to the ranch and enjoy some breakfast. By now, Tom ought to be finished with his chores and cooking up a mess for them on the stove. He hoped so, anyway. His brother had never been one to rouse very easily from sleep unless painfully prodded, something Ethan neglected to do this morning. Listening to his stomach now, he wished he'd taken time for the extra motivation.

His mind on a plate of pancakes piled high, he trotted across the open valley and spooked up a bevy of quail hidden in the tall bluestem, their territory invaded. At the unexpected ruckus, Ben skittered sideways and it took a moment to settle him. In doing so, Ethan caught sight of the old stone cabin left here from the original homestead, a landmark he'd passed by hundreds of times.

This time his gut instinct drew him forward.

Never one to ignore a hunch, he nudged his horse up the hillside. Little more than sixteen by sixteen, the cabin's windows, doors, and roof lay open to the elements, but the structure still stood. For a short moment, Ethan imagined what it must have been like to stand on its threshold and view this scene every morning. Despite its meager beginning, it must have given one lucky man a great deal of satisfaction to have homesteaded this property and called it his own. Ethan dared not even hope for such pleasure, the dream too far from reality.

Then as though called out by the imagination, a Hereford steer appeared at the open doorway, stretching his back like he'd been awakened from a restful night's sleep.

"I'll be darned, will you look at that?" With a pleased grin, Ethan pulled the small notebook from his shirt pocket and tallied the count. Then, clicking his tongue, he urged his horse forward to herd the steer back to the others.

One pasture accounted for. Time for breakfast.

HER LITTLE GIRL WAS GROWING UP.

Clara Lambert knelt beside her daughter on the front sidewalk of the elementary school and stared into her hazel brown eyes — light reflections of her own. She brushed a wispy curl from Sara's cheek. "Do you have everything in your backpack? Your tissues and milk money?"

Sara nodded, the absence of her top front teeth creating a gaping hole in her five-year-old smile — just another sign that time was rushing past. "Can you walk me to class?"

The familiar ache clenched inside Clara's chest — of wanting to please her children, no matter how small or great their request. "I'm sorry, honey, but I need to get to work so I can make my biscuits and pies. It'll be okay, though. Mrs. Alexander knows you're in her class, and Jeremy will make sure you get to the right room."

Her eyes darted to her oldest son. "You heard that, didn't you, Jeremy?"

Jeremy pulled a banana from his backpack and began peeling the thick yellow skin. "Don't worry, sis. I'll take you where you need to go."

"What about me?" Nathan scooted from the back seat of their gray Suburban and tucked his wrinkled shirt into his jeans. "I need help finding my room too."

Jeremy took a bite of the banana and spoke with his mouth full. "You're in second grade. You don't need my help."

"Jeremy …"

At Clara's rebuke, the boy frowned and gave a shrug. "Whatever. But it better not make me late for class."

Clara swallowed her own disappointment, knowing her oldest son was growing up faster than most boys his age due to the load of responsibility she put on him. "Wait for your brother and sister after school too. Then you can all come by the café for a snack." She offered Jeremy a smile, hoping the invitation might appease him as well as his increasing appetite.

"A piece of apple pie?" A broad grin replaced his earlier frown.

"Or maybe just an apple." She caught Nathan by the belt loop as he headed for the playground. "Did you remember to pack your inhaler?"

Her seven-year-old nodded in assurance, but Clara always had to check — especially after last year's attack when Nathan's teacher had barely made it to the office in time for his medicine. After that, the superintendant agreed to let Nathan carry his inhaler with him to class, despite school policy.

Clara released her hold and watched as he raced to the nearby swing set, still amazed that he had an asthma problem. Needing to get on with the good-byes, she snatched a kiss from Sara's round cheek. "You have fun today, you hear?"

"I wish you could go with me, Mommy." Her daughter wrapped her arms around Clara's neck, and Clara breathed in the warm scent of youth and baby shampoo, keenly aware of the fear vibrating in her little girl's chest. Fear of the big, unknown world. Oh, how well Clara knew that fear.

"You're going to have so much fun in kindergarten, and you can tell me all about it when you come by the café later. Every detail." She squeezed Sara with reassurance, then gave her one last going over before Jeremy exchanged his banana peel for his sister's hand.

Clara watched as they rambled toward the front doors of the two-story school building. Seeing that they'd left without him, Nathan hurried to catch up, hitching his bulging backpack onto his shoulder as he ran. Upon reaching them, he glanced behind and waved, his shoelaces flopping along untied and unattended. Clara raised her hand but held her admonishment. He would notice soon enough—and she was already late.

Tears pooled in her eyes as she climbed behind the steering wheel, wanting nothing more than to accompany her kids to class on their first day of school. Why did she always have to be the one to say no? The one who had to be responsible?

With a shake of her head, she turned the ignition and mumbled his name, knowing good and well why.

Because he wasn't.

She pulled out of the parking lot and headed toward Main Street, the tires thumping over the brick covered streets. Three years, and she still remembered the day he left as though it were yesterday. It seemed a lifetime.

Clara pushed her regrets down as far as they would go, where they wouldn't tempt her to worry about the kind of mom she'd become. Certainly not the mom she intended when she and Daniel first married, that was for sure. Oddly enough, the one thing that took her away from her kids was the one thing that consoled her and gave her purpose—and an income. Her work, or more specifically, the operation of a small-town cafe. Her café.

Snow Melts in Spring

Deborah Vogts

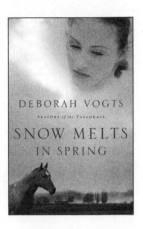

She loves the land.

Mattie Evans grew up in the Flint Hills of Kansas. Although her family has lost their ranch, she still calls this land home. A skilled young veterinarian, she struggles to gain the confidence of the local ranchers. Fortunately, her best friend and staunchest supporter is John McCray, owner of the Lightning M Ranch. They both love the ranch and can't imagine living anywhere but in the Flint Hills.

He's haunted by it.

Gil McCray, John's estranged son, is a pro football player living in California. The ranch is where his mother died and where every aspect of the tallgrass prairie stirs unwanted memories of his older brother's fatal accident. Gil decides leaving the ranch is the best solution for his ailing father and his own ailing heart. But he doesn't count on falling in love.

Falling in love isn't an option. Or is it?

When Mattie is called in to save a horse injured in a terrible accident, she finds herself unwillingly tossed into the middle of a family conflict. Secret pain, secret passions, and secret agendas play out against the beautiful landscapes as love leads to some unexpected conclusions about forgiveness and renewal.

Available in stores and online!

For the latest news and to sign up for a free e-newsletter,
please visit www.deborahvogts.com

Deborah would love to hear from you!
Feel free to write her at debvogts@gmail.com or:

Deborah Vogts
PO Box 232
Erie, KS 66733

Share Your Thoughts

With the Author: Your comments will be forwarded to
the author when you send them to *zauthor@zondervan.com*.

With Zondervan: Submit your review of this book
by writing to *zreview@zondervan.com*.

Free Online Resources at

www.zondervan.com

Zondervan AuthorTracker: Be notified whenever your favorite
authors publish new books, go on tour, or post an update
about what's happening in their lives at www.zondervan.com/
authortracker.

Daily Bible Verses and Devotions: Enrich your life with daily
Bible verses or devotions that help you start every morning
focused on God. Visit www.zondervan.com/newsletters.

Free Email Publications: Sign up for newsletters on Christian
living, academic resources, church ministry, fiction, children's
resources, and more. Visit www.zondervan.com/newsletters.

Zondervan Bible Search: Find and compare Bible passages in
a variety of translations at www.zondervanbiblesearch.com.

Other Benefits: Register yourself to receive online benefits
like coupons and special offers, or to participate in research.

ZONDERVAN®

ZONDERVAN.com/
AUTHORTRACKER
follow your favorite authors